W9-AOJ-091

Praise for
NANCY HOLDER

"Expect the unexpected with Nancy Holder.
She makes readers hang on
breathlessly to the last word."
Matthew Costello, bestselling author (with F. Paul Wilson)
of *The Seventh Guest*

"Nancy Holder consistently provides her readers
with genuine wit, emotion and real people
in stories that always deliver what they promise.
It's as simple as this: there is no one better."
Charles Grant, World Fantasy and Nebula Award winner

"Nancy Holder has an imagination any writer would kill
for . . . With *Gambler's Star*, she brings intrigue,
suspense, humor and a sparkling characterization to
a completely new kind of science fiction universe."
Christopher Golden

"Take an unfettered imagination, add an enviable skill
at characterization, mix with a prose style as
clear and smooth as polished crystal, and you
have the fiction of Nancy Holder."
F. Paul Wilson

"Nancy Holder's stories . . . are invariably
beautifully written and quirky."
Locus

BOOK THREE

INVASIONS

GAMBLERS' STAR

NANCY HOLDER

An Imprint of HarperCollinsPublishers

This is a work of fiction. Names, characters, places, and incidents are products of the author's imagination or are used fictitiously and are not to be construed as real. Any resemblance to actual events, locales, organizations, or persons, living or dead, is entirely coincidental.

EOS
An Imprint of HarperCollins*Publishers*
10 East 53rd Street
New York, New York 10022-5299

Copyright © 2000 by Nancy Holder
Cover art by J.K. Potter
Library of Congress Catalog Card Number: 99-96777
ISBN: 0-380-79314-8

First Eos paperback printing: May 2000
Eos Trademark Reg. U.S. Pat. Off. and in Other Countries,
Marca Registrada, Hecho en U.S.A.
HarperCollins® is a trademark of HarperCollins Publishers Inc.

Printed in the U.S.A.

WCD 10 9 8 7 6 5 4 3 2 1

www.avonbooks.com/eos

In memory of my parents,
Kenneth Paul Jones, III, M.D.,
and Marion Elise Jones

ACKNOWLEDGMENTS

For her hard work in shaping this book, I'd like to thank my wonderful and clever editor, Diana Gill. Thanks, too, to my agent and friend, Howard Morhaim and his assistant, Lindsay Sagnette, who makes my work life bright. To my baby-sitters: Ida Khabazian, April and Lara Koljonen, and Bekah and Julie Simpson, my gratitude. I couldn't have done it without each and every one of you. Jeff and Maryelizabeth, I love you.

PROLOGUE

From the Captain's Log of Gambler's Star*:*

I can tell by the way that space is bending that at last we're approaching !kth-held territory. We're arriving none too soon. Numerous skirmishes with D'inn craft have left the Star *a bit the worse for wear, but nearly all defense systems remain intact. The folks aboard aren't in as great shape. Sparkle, who, I suppose, is legally my daughter-in-law, is not speaking to me. My three grandchildren, Stella, Daniel, and Star, are terrified by the battles.*

We lost a few people in engineering, and I'm sorry for that. I knew there would be sacrifices along the way, and there certainly have been. Perhaps including my own flesh and blood.

My son I left hurtling back to the Moon on a collision course, and I pray on my lucky star, the Gambler, that he is still alive as I write this. I didn't push Deuce harder to abandon the Moon, on the chance that something might happen to me. Deuce can have more children, even though he has no idea that these three are his. I can't have any more at all;

1

I've become sterile, and Deuce is my only living child.

The Castle family will live on in him, if we up here perish.

Cor-!kth, my !kth counterpart, will be waiting to greet me when we arrive. We communicate via holograms; we have never actually been in the same place. If we could do that, we wouldn't need the jumpgate.

I should explain to Sparkle just how strange it is out here. Definitely takes some getting used to.

Together, Cor and I will continue to build the jumpgate. The gate is key. We attempted to create hybrid beings, watered-down versions of !kth, if you will, by using the facilities on their crashed ship, which I found in Earthside Australia. We hoped that in a few generations they might fully adapt to conditions in our space.

That's obviously failed. My former aide, Jimmy Jackson, was initially a willing participant in the experiments, but he turned against us. I'm not sure who he was working for—the D'inn, most likely—but he's dead, killed by Deuce. I'm sure Jackson was planning to hold Stella hostage, probably to get me to turn against the !kth. Deuce knew none of that. He just had "a bad feeling," and I bless him a thousand times for it.

The jumpgate must succeed. If there are enemies aboard this vessel, we must locate them and exterminate them.

Even if one of them is the erstwhile stowaway, Bernardo Chang, whom I promised safe passage. When the fate of your entire species rests on your shoulders, some promises practically beg to be broken.

I've been called ruthless in business, but never dishonorable, and I believe the shedding of my honor would involve some pain. However, I'm willing to do whatever it takes to achieve the dream and to honor my commitment. Still, I'm not so starry-eyed that I don't know the !kth have got me where they want me.

Earth and the Moon are at war now. I got Sparkle out of there just in the nick of time. She kissed Deuce good-bye like someone who's in love, but how could someone who's in love do the things to him that she has done?

On the other hand, I could, even if she was the one I loved. And I'm not sure that I've ever loved Sparkle. Just simply wanted her. Come to think of it, there have been few things in my life I have wanted and not had. All may not be lost there; would I be willing to betray my son with his wife?

Yes.

And so, I pray on the Gambler for the success of the mission. I pray that Sparkle's mind continues to develop, so that we will have no need of computer interfaces. Through her, we will have a direct link to the !kth . . . and I'll have a better idea of where I truly stand with them.

But most of all, I pray for my boy. My moonchild.

Dear God, take care of Deuce McNamara. He's sweating blood all alone in the garden, and there's nothing I can do to help him.

That doesn't make me a Judas, but I'm sure no saint, either.

Hunter Castle
Aboard ship, 2144.11

ONE

So here I am, Deuce thought in the shuttle as the hulking Earth carrier bore down on it, *thinking my last thoughts, which, sad to say, are really nothing to write home about.*

Above him in open space, that is to say neutral territory, a pulse torpedo with the explosive power of a good chunk of meteor flared on course to incinerate not only him, but also Moona Lisa, his currently hysterical dog; Connie Lockheart, his surrogate mother, whom he had just recently met; and Angelo Borgioli, his well-connected Family cousin.

Also, the remote data terminal inside the robot formerly processing data as Mr. Wong, who now turned out to be Deuce's direct comm source to some alien D'inn broad named Iniya.

This broad being the only reason any of them were still alive, because via this remote, she was manufacturing a great deflection shield that shimmered around their pathetic little lifeboat. But she had just announced, in a pleasant, flight-attendant-type voice, that the shield would probably not hold much longer. Too many blasts from Earthside frigates and destroyers had made their mark. Below them, the poor Moon looked like it had a terrible skin disease from all the fresh pockmarks caused by weapons blasts.

"Death probable," Iniya continued. Gone was the sly smile of Mr. Wong. His Asian features were blank, and Deuce was very sorry for the android. Hunter had placed the remote data terminal inside Mr. Wong for safekeeping, and then given him to Deuce so Deuce could use it. Mr. Wong had not been wild about the idea, fearing the loss of his identity. Which, clearly, had occurred.

"About that death. Bet me," Deuce challenged her.

And to his monumental surprise and delight, she blinked, and said, "Odds against survival approximate six million, two hundred fifty-seven thousand, six hundred twelve to one. We bet your fortune?"

"Hey, you made a joke," Deuce said happily. Maybe all was not lost in the Mr. Wong–type department. "You're making book!"

"Book, schmook, *Padrino*. Brace for impact," Angelo said, grabbing the sides of his seat and grimacing.

Deuce knew from impact and bracing, and he reminded himself that they were all strapped in tight. But when you got exploded against, you wanted all the holding on you could get. His terrified surrogate mom had her hands threaded through her seat belts. Even the robot was hunkered down for the big one.

But Deuce didn't want to let go of the dog. Moona Lisa was just about his only living relative, so to speak. If he got through this, he was gonna need someone to buy Christmas presents for, clean up after, that kind of thing. And Moona was a very needy creature, which would be all to the good, him being a giver and abandoned by the woman he loved, and discovering he had no children after all—

BLAM!

The craft seesawed and shook, and began to tumble. Moona Lisa yipped like crazy, toenails raking any part of Deuce she could latch on to. So much for his enviro-suit being useful if they crash-landed on the surface. Deuce hooked his boots under his seat and stubbornly held on.

Speaking was a waste of time for about the next two minutes, so Deuce had no idea what Mr. Wong/Iniya was going on about until his ears stopped ringing. At which point Iniya pointed upward, and said, "Adversary has been defeated."

"What?"

Deuce and the other human beings looked through the front window. Not a lot between them and open space. Deuce reminded himself over and over that it was made of Kevlite, the hardest material known to personkind. It was an alloy of Kevlar and titanium, and it was good stuff. Still, when you're used to living underground and you have a panoramic view of outer space, it makes you hinky.

But now what he was, was dumbfounded. What he saw through said window was that the carrier was gone. Sure, lots of other Earthside craft were still there, firing like crazy, but *il gran fusto*—Mr. Big Shot—was nowhere to be seen.

"*O, Mamma mia*," Angelo murmured, crossing himself. "Where'd she go?"

"Enemy vessel has been vaporized," Iniya bragged.

"The whole thing? Just like that?" Angelo's soulful Mediterranean eyes practically spun like roulette balls.

"You were playing us for suckers all along," Deuce accused her. "About us blowing up and all that *schiamazzo*. What a little drama queen."

"No, Deuce of Moon. Destruction of Deuce vessel was anticipated."

"Listen." He leaned toward her. "You gotta spend some processing power on parsing our language, okay? Or people are going to wonder. Mr. Wong could talk totally normal, and we don't exactly want to broadcast you're not him, *capisce?*"

"You can always just say he sustained some brain damage in battle," Deuce's birth mother suggested. She looked a little green; otherwise, she was a beautiful, if slightly older, woman with a shock of ebony hair and flashing, dark eyes. Everything about her was the opposite of Deuce, who was white-blond, and green-eyed; also, muscular, young, and a guy. She was an Earthsider; she was probably trying to handle the shift in gravity as well as the tension of nearly getting killed. Deuce and Angelo were kind of used to nearly getting killed most of their waking hours, so it didn't affect them as much. Or anyway, that was what Deuce told himself.

"Forget about it," Deuce said, with a dismissing wave of his hand. He handed her the dog.

Then he cracked the knuckle on the ring finger of his left hand for luck, a habit he had picked up somewhere in the twenty-seven years of his life. He glanced down—huh, what to do with the wedding ring, leave it on, take it off? Since no one got tan living inside the Moon, guys didn't have to worry about telltale pale areas the way those Earthsider mooks did when they took off their wedding rings for purposes of cheating or breaking up. Presto-change-o, you went from looking married to looking single in two seconds.

But what about how you felt?

"You know, for someone whose ship's about to blow, you seem awfully preoccupied," Angelo said to Deuce, as they were pummeled by a barrage of snap-crackle-pops.

"My life's passing before my eyes," Deuce grunted. "Lots to see."

"Yeah, well, that's nice, but meanwhile, we need to figure out a way to save our butts." Angelo pointed to the large enviro-dome that covered the main shaft of Moonbase Vegas. It looked to be intact, which was good news. Also, surrounded by Earthside attack vessels, which was not so good.

"We slam into the dome," Deuce's Borgioli cousin continued, "we're squashed like bugs." Many species of which both Angelo and Deuce had seen. But not all. For example, fleas. Never seen 'em. Never would. Quarantine took care of that.

"We get those guys' attention, they'll probably blow us up. No offense to your weaponry, *Signorina* Iniya," Angelo added, with a bob of his head. "I give you my greatest respect. But I figure sooner or later, the jig is up."

"Shuttle, hon, how are your manual controls?" Deuce queried their vehicle.

"Seventy-five percent, Mr. Unidentified Castle Employee," the shuttle replied. "Turbos are not in good shape."

"But could I pull you up and land you?"

"Depends on how good you are," the shuttle retorted. Deuce chuckled as he petted poor Moona on Connie's lap. Hunter's sense of humor showed up in most of the programming of his goods and services. Deuce had never had such witty transportation until he started working for Hunter.

"And now he's laughing," Angelo said deadpan to Connie Lockheart.

"Okay," Deuce said. "Give me control."

"At once, Mr. Unidentified Castle Employee."

Deuce grunted. "Call me Deuce."

Mr. Wong's head swiveled toward Deuce. "Deuce of Moon, son of Castle."

Angelo stared agog at Deuce. So did Connie Lockheart. Obviously, she had not known.

Deuce turned to Iniya. "You got proof of that, that I'm his kid?"

"Known fact on other side of universe."

"*Va bene.*" The hair on the back of Deuce's neck stood on end. It was a real new known fact to Deuce himself that he was Hunter's son and that he, Pop, and the billions of other human beings, Moonsiders and Earthsiders alike, were not alone in the universe. He had assumed that few, if any, living people knew about it. Hunter was that rich.

But there were whole alien species who were practically gossips about the whole deal. What a shocker.

"Known fact that we are about to crash, Deuce of Moon," Iniya continued.

"Deuce, watch it!" Angelo shouted, crossing himself.

Deuce grunted. And then he tried to keep the shuttle from careening into the lunar surface, at the same time dodging about a million, schmillion Earthside vessels.

The dog went berserk.

She was allowed.

Sparkle lay on the bed in her luxurious stateroom aboard *Gambler's Star*. She had been moved from Cabin C to the master suite, which had been redone after the explosion took it out.

The lights were down, casting a soft sheen across the gleaming appointments in the cabin. Gold and bronze and real mahogany furniture—such luxury was practically unknown on Earth or in the Moon, much less aboard a ship. But Hunter Castle insisted upon the best. And he did whatever it took to get it.

Sparkle's platinum hair spilled across satin sheets as she stared at the two cribs where her newborn twins lay sleeping. She had not cried for Deuce—Sparkle never cried—but she knew that the big chunk of ice inside her chest housed a heart. At least, that was what she told herself. Sometimes she wondered.

Some part of her had hoped that the sight of the babies would warm her, or at least make her feel human again. But as she stared at them, all she could think of was the look of betrayal and pain on Deuce's face when she had told him bluntly that they were not his babies, but Hunter's. She had joined the Generational Protection League program long before she had met Deuce, and had, in fact, tried to resign.

But Hunter had made the pot too sweet. He had promised her that Deuce need never know they weren't his children. And he had assured her that they would be provided for—the babies, Deuce, and her—for the rest of their lives. It had seemed reasonable to believe him. The purpose of the Connie Lockheart program was to perpetuate the line of very rich and powerful people. Not necessarily so that their progeny could inherit, or take over. Simply so that they would survive.

Ever since the Quantum Instability Wars of the 2030s, life had become very rough. No one had realized when the group of scientists who discovered the Quantum Instability Principle—how to make matter and nonmatter collide—that the most dangerous bombs ever created would be the result. At the same time, organized crime had been getting restless because there was no more territory to conquer, as well as nervous, because the League of Decency was gaining power. The LOD wanted to outlaw "sin"—just about any kind of entertainment which existed, including, but not limited to, gambling.

When the Caputo crime family decided to build a casino on the Moon, the other families watched in dismay as the Caputos raked in the dough. Soon, there were almost two dozen families on the Moon, each vying for control. Their turf wars were brutal and inconclusive. So Earthside intervened, and with some collusion from various powerful families, six families were given permission to run their rackets on the Moon. They became known as the Casino Families, and they came to regard themselves as Moonsiders. As did the hundreds of thousands of workers who had built their gambling mecca, which was called Moonbase Vegas.

Eight other families had survived the vicious bloodbath, and they returned to Earth disgruntled but consoled by the realization that they would have less competition from the Casino Families for Earthside action.

However, the League of Decency managed, in one fell swoop, to get any and all forms of gambling declared illegal on Earth. The eight families—now called the Eight Disenfranchised Families—cried holy hell for a long time, but eventually they capitulated. Of course, gambling didn't disappear

Earthside; it simply went underground, as had all the Moonsiders, who preferred to burrow inside the satellite to stay away from the solar radiation. But the power of the Eight was terribly weakened, and they vowed revenge.

In over a hundred years, no apparent revenge had been detected. So the Six Casino Families continued to control the Moon, paying protection money—"ice"—in the form of exorbitant taxes to the Earthside government. Everything had gone along fairly smoothly, with the Six running business pretty much the way it had been run Earthside—by declaring Vendettas on each other, putting hits out for various reasons, and generally battling continuously for supremacy.

Sparkle had met Hunter at a party for the rich, the wealthy, and the beautiful. She was the latter. But somehow a stock tip had come into her mind, full-blown, and she had shared it with him during their cocktail chitchat.

To her shock and surprise, both of them made money on the stock purchase. He sent her a diamond necklace and real red roses—in the days of fallout and deforestation, flowers were far more precious than diamonds.

Then he had mentioned the Connie Lockheart program—surrogate mothers were called "Connie Lockhearts," although Sparkle had never figured out why—and she had signed up. She couldn't pretend that it hadn't crossed her mind that he was actually asking her to be his Connie Lockheart, nor that the assurances that she would not know whose child she was carrying were true.

Declaring his wish to open a new casino, Hunter, Earthside's arguably richest and most powerful man, had arrived on the Moon and made everyone crazy with his audacity and his moxie.

By then, time had passed, and Sparkle had moved to the Moon herself, and liaised with Moonsider Deuce McNamara, a charming bagman who was rising fast in the Borgioli Family. Not that that was much cause for pride. Of the Six Families, the Borgiolis were the worst regarded—ill-mannered, uneducated thugs burdened with a dimwitted Godfather named Don Alberto. It was a sad comment on the Borgiolis that the only way Deuce could stand to remain one was to constantly remind himself and everybody else that he had been adopted. The Godfather's own sister had been the best friend of

Deuce's adopted mother, Maria della Caldera di Borgioli. Through her influence, Deuce had been accepted as a full-fledged Family Member.

On the Moon, the only way to get anywhere was by being in a Family. If you weren't a Member—which was generally by way of being born into the Family—then you could try to become Affiliated. It was very, very difficult—most who tried never made it—but it secured a lot of rights and privileges that the rest of Moonside society would never obtain. Those unfortunates—the majority—were called Non-Affiliateds, or N.A.'s, for short. The nicer term was "Independents," but no one used it.

Sparkle had been an N.A. A kickboxing showgirl, the toast of the Casino Strip. Then she had fallen for Deuce.

As soon as they started living together—in secret—Sparkle had tried to pull out of the Connie Lockheart program. She was never contacted, but that didn't surprise her. It was a very secretive organization, and unnecessary communication was forbidden.

But then Hunter came to the Moon. He contacted her and told her she was still obligated to him. She must carry his children—in a frozen embryonic state—when and if he asked her to.

He achieved his goal of gaining permission to build a new casino, and shocked everyone by moving his base of operations to the Darkside. He wasn't just going to build a casino; he was going to build an entire new city: Darkside City, which would surpass Moonbase Vegas in size, scope, and beauty.

He co-opted the bored, restless Young Turks of the other Families, who had no way to secure any significant action for themselves. With rejuvenation a commonplace, their Godfathers and *capos* hardly ever died, unless it was through a hit. There was nothing to do but run errands and sleep with showgirls. They were delighted at the opportunities for growth Hunter offered them.

The Moonsider Liberation Front had also flirted with Hunter Castle. They had hoped that his new city would provide the upward mobility the Non-Affiliated Moonsiders yearned for. But Hunter imported his professional-level employees from Earth and the crappy, low-wage jobs went to the N.A.'s as usual. The few unions the N.A.'s had did achieve a few goals for their people, but the dream of equality was still denied the locals—the ones whose fathers and mothers had had done all the scut work in the Moon in the first place.

Then Hunter's ship—*this* ship—had exploded, killing most of the old regime. During the ensuing crisis, Hunter insisted Sparkle allow herself to be implanted with his frozen embryos. She finally acquiesced. His wife, Beatrice Castle di Borgioli, who apparently had put some of the picture together, pushed Sparkle down a flight of stairs, sending her into premature labor, and then shot and killed herself.

Sparkle gave birth to the twins, Star and Daniel. Then Deuce had learned the truth about the children: They were not his.

Learned the truth? She, Sparkle, had flung the truth in his face. She had pummeled him with it, earning the disdain of her Connie Lockheart superior with it—who turned out to be Deuce's birth mother herself.

And now, here she was with Hunter and his children, speeding away from her husband as he faced a war and a satellite filled with people crying for his blood.

So she stared at the babies and tried to warm her heart.

There was a soft rap on the door. She murmured, "Come in."

Hunter stood on the threshold, in a black-satin smoking jacket and a pair of elegant dark trousers. He held two glasses of what looked to be brandy. His makeover had been redone; he no longer resembled his erstwhile android, Mr. Wong. He was back to his salt-and-pepper hair, dark eyes, and black moustache. To look at Hunter Castle, you would never dream of the power and vast wealth he commanded.

To hear him, you would.

"Good evenin'," he said softly, waiting to be invited. He was a Southern gentleman at the core. A ruthless one, but a gentleman nonetheless.

"Come in," she said tiredly. "I suppose you want to see your babies."

"Hmm. About that." He took one step into the room and looked at her questioningly, as if seeking assurance that it was, indeed, all right with her if he came in. Irritated, she nodded again.

He handed her one of the brandies. She hesitated. "I'm nursing them."

"You can take a washaway," he reminded her. "Besides, it's just a little bit." He held out the snifter. Reluctantly, she took it.

They clinked glasses. He smiled warmly at her over the rim, and she felt herself flush. With Deuce, Sparkle had been an ice goddess. He was sweet and friendly and street-smart, but not too sophisticated. Her normal reserve had been underscored by her contract with Hunter: She hadn't ever wanted Deuce to know about the true paternity of the twins. That they weren't his. And she was afraid to fall in love with him, in case he did find out.

Which he had.

She inhaled the brandy. Her head was spinning already, and she was tired to her bones. Still, the heat seeped through her, perhaps one spindly thread making it to her heart.

"They're beautiful," Hunter said, crossing to the babies. He leaned over them. "Which one is Star?"

"On the right. Daniel's on the left."

He smiled. "Just beautiful."

She took another sip. She felt his eyes on her and knew he wanted her. Before Deuce, she would have counted herself in paradise to be in Hunter Castle's bed.

"Sparkle, honey, I have to talk to you about something," he ventured. "Something very important."

Without her invitation, he came and sat down on the bed. She pulled the sheets protectively around herself and waited.

Hunter set his brandy down on the nightstand. He took her free hand with both of his. She was wearing her wedding ring.

"Sparkle, I have deceived you," he began. "About the little ones."

The hair on the back of her neck rose on end. What was he up to? "How? They're not yours?" she asked sharply.

He cocked his head. The subdued light cast blue highlights in his hair. "Not . . . directly. They're my son's little babies." He took a deep breath. "And Stella? She's his baby, too."

She stared at him. Blinked slowly. "What . . . what are you saying?"

"You have a very agile mind. A kind of intuition. A very

special mind. I thought you might already know what I'm trying to tell you."

She simply looked at him. Waited.

"Deuce is my son." He gave her hand a strengthening squeeze. "That dark-haired gal who's calling herself Connie Lockheart carried him for me." He gazed at her levelly, and even at a moment like this, she saw his desire for her.

"I've become sterile, Sparkle. I don't know why. Deuce is the only child I've ever had. But I got his DNA from hair, nail clippings, and I had it reproduced, and did the same with you. The result is not only those twins, but the baby my wife had. Little Stella." The two-year-old who was asleep in the nursery, one cabin over.

Sparkle took all this in. She had carried Deuce McNamara's babies without even knowing it. And Hunter had had Beatrice implanted with the child Beatrice had always longed to have with Deuce. Beatrice had always loved Deuce. She had died loving him.

"Why didn't you tell us?" she asked softly. "Why did you let him go back down there thinking I had . . . that they . . ." She stared at him. "You didn't want him to come with us. You *bastard*."

He shrugged. "I wanted my line to continue somewhere, somehow. I freely admit that. If something happened to us, I wanted Deuce to have more children. Surely your background in the Generational Protection League makes this make sense. to you. It should certainly not be a surprise, at any rate, that I have this attitude."

Her expression once more became a blank as she sipped the brandy. Slowly, she let the heat move through her body. The ice around her heart cracked and sluiced down her ribs, bruising them. Her heart began to beat sluggishly, like that of a half-frozen animal.

"Penny for your thoughts?" he asked, giving her a small smile.

"That you're even more cold-hearted than I am," she said. "You let him go back there, probably to his death, without knowing that you're his father, and that these are his children."

He shook his head. "Deuce is my kin. He'll survive. I wouldn't have let him go back down there if I didn't believe that."

She shook her head. "You were just doubling down. If this hand goes bad, you'll have another hand to play."

Hunter Castle couldn't help his guilty smile. "You know me too well, darlin,' " he drawled.

She glared at him. "I don't know you at all," she replied. "And I don't think I want to."

"Well, you're going to have to, Sparkle," he said frankly. "Because we're going to be in a whole new ball game, and I'm the only batter on your team."

TWO

"**N**ot for nothing am I a legend in my own time," Deuce informed his mother, his cousin, his data terminal, and his dog, as he yanked the shuttle out of its death-inducing nosedive and chittered back and forth above the cratered lunar surface to avoid the thundering hordes of Earthsider ships.

"Or in your own mind, *cretino*," Angelo said, teasingly.

Deuce was not sure which way the wind was blowing with his Borgioli cousin. Angelo had kissed his ring, Godfather-style, declaring his loyalty and calling Deuce *il Padrino della Luna*—the Godfather of the Moon. But Angelo had also flatly stated that he was not sure he wanted to fight a war with Earth.

Oh, yeah, like Deuce *did*.

But Angelo had also made it clear that he blamed Deuce for starting the war, which was nonsense. Not even Hunter Castle could start a war just by saying, "Tag, you're it" and blowing one ship out of the sky. There was a progression to these things. A protocol.

And speaking of protocol, Deuce sure didn't know who was commanding the Lunar Defense Forces. Because such friendly fire as existed was peeking out of the main shaft and spreading out beneath the dome, such strategy obviously not a good idea because the Moonside offensive vehicles couldn't—or had better not—shoot through the dome. If anybody—black hats or white—blew the enviro-dome, that was pretty much the ball game. There were redundant systems and safeties and all like that in the shaft and all the major tunnels, but the dome was the biggest deal in terms of long-term survival for Moonbase Vegas.

Of course, there were other, smaller domes that covered the underground miles of tunnels, warrens, and caverns, and the quarter of a million inhabitants or so, but you lose atmosphere in the big guy, you'd pretty much have to pick up your deck and start playing another game.

Which could make for interesting power plays later on, he realized. The majority of Hunter's new gambling paradise was domed and pumped with oxygen-rich atmosphere. There were not so many buildings yet, but there were lots of finished or almost-finished tunnels. The superconducting mesh was in place.

It would be a heck of a place for refugees.

Deuce shook his head in amazement at the cards Lady Luck kept handing him. On a personal level, he had the luck of the Irish, a member of which Earthsider nation he was said to have been. He'd pretty much clung to that notion during his tenure as a full-fledged Member of the Borgioli Family. It made it easier to be a Borgioli, who were considered the lowest class of the Casino Families.

"Why are the lunar forces inside the dome?" his mother asked, struggling with the dog, who was out of her mind by now. "They can't shoot in there."

"It's the fastest route to the surface," Angelo filled in. "There are emergency airlocks on either side. They're supposed to be used for evacuation only, but I guess this counts as a major industrial accident." He glared at Deuce as if to say, *For which the entire population of the Moon thanks you.*

Deuce pretended not to feel the hostility in the glare, nor accept the blame. Less than a day ago, he had jokingly told the remote data terminal to declare war on Earth, and it had done so. That was when it had been a remote data terminal for the !kth, the species Hunter was parleying with. Only after it had been damaged saving Hunter's life had the data terminal been accessed by Iniya, who claimed that the !kth were the bad guys. And, putting two and two together, that the !kth had pretty much wanted war to happen so they could do something like conquer the known universe.

He'd have to sort all that out later. Right now, they had to save themselves or there would be no sense in worrying about whose deck was marked.

"Is the Borgioli airlock still where it was when I was in the Family?" Deuce asked Angelo.

Angelo actually hesitated, and Deuce mentally rolled his eyes. It was an offense punishable by death to talk about your Family's airlock—such as where it was and how to access it—but with all the Family Godfathers and the Aadams Family C.E.O. recently blown to smithereens, it wasn't exactly time to follow protocol.

"*Mio fratello,*" Deuce reproved. "Now is not the moment for pretending there are any rules in place. For all we know, there are no Borgioli *capos* left, except for you. I sincerely doubt anyone is going to mess with you under the circumstances."

Angelo glared *un gran glarissimo.* "Do you actually think I'm such a craterhead that I'm worried about such a thing?" He gestured appropriately. "*Eh, fatti sparare!*" Which in the language meant, "Go shoot yourself."

"I won't need to shoot myself if we don't get the hell out of firing range," Deuce retorted.

"Boys, boys," Connie Lockheart said. The dog barked hysterically.

"Our airlock's wired six ways to Sunday," Angelo cut in. "As you know. I was just thinking through the codes, all right, *mio Padrino?*"

Deuce took the hostility and the mocking use of the language for "my Godfather" and filed them away. Not important now, but important later, if they lived through this.

Deuce made a show of touching his chest. "Angelinino, forgive me if you thought I was questioning your loyalty. Of course I'm not. I'm just worried for my mother." He gestured to the beautiful raven-haired woman. "And for the future of all the Families, and the Moon, especially if this Iniya is telling us the truth."

Angelo made a noise Deuce could not translate; but by then Iniya was busily deflecting fire, and Deuce was more interested in convincing Angelo that time was of the essence. He spoke in rapid-fire Italian, using the dialect, and crossing his fingers that his mother did not speak it. Even for a mother you didn't know you had, you showed respect.

Angelo turned to Mr. Wong—that is to say, Iniya—and said, "I'm going to give you coordinates for the disarming of the Borgioli Family airlock. Code word AlPacino. Can you verify and disarm?"

There was, like, nanosecond of time before Iniya replied, "Accomplished."

"Good." Angelo smiled at her. *"Grazie mille, signorina."*

"Prego," she responded, with a smile.

Humph, Deuce thought. *To me, she talks like a cheap slot machine. To him, she's a Family woman.* He actually felt a little jealous.

Then they reached the airlock, which, if you could hear it, was going *pffft* with all the vacuum and pressure and all that *schiamazzo.* Dealing with airlocks was one of the inconveniences of living in the Moon, of which there were many; and Deuce had time to drum his fingers on the armrest of his chair and take the dog off his mother's hands for a few seconds.

The dog sat back on his lap, panted, and urinated.

"Oh, fabulous," he grumbled. His mother and Angelo chuckled. Iniya pointed at the wetness and *pffft!* it was gone.

"Hey," Deuce said, impressed.

And then they were inside the airlock and on their way to the Borgioli compound.

Such spires, such swirls of gold and ornate piles of cupids and gondolas, festooned the Borgioli HQ. Even in his ignorant youth, Deuce had known that the Family sense of taste and style was unlike that of other people. Now, having completed both an art appreciation and a wine class, he knew that all these extra bits of *sciochezza* truly denoted a lack of class.

The thing was, as he explained to his unlearned birth mother, Connie, on their way here, there were the Six Casino Families in the Moon, which had complete control of Moonbase Vegas and were jostling for turf of Darkside City (at least, before the war that had broken out today, and now it looked like absolutely no one had control of much of anything) and this was how they broke down:

The Van Aadamses were—had been?—the classiest. They were old school, old boy, tut-tut Australians who cultivated an image of fitting right in with genteel society. Their dames dressed nice and they gave lots of money (most of which they got back later, after the charity gave them a bunch of publicity in return for whatever percentage got left behind) to all sorts of Moonsider charities. They made nice with the Mayor of Moonbase Vegas, the Chief of Lunar Security Forces (who had almost married into the Family), and all the figureheads who got elected or appointed into prominent non-Family positions of lunar authority. The only people who were fooled were some of the stupider rank and file of Non-Affiliateds and the tourists.

Keeping the tourists fooled was a high priority among all the Families, so the other five Casino Families let the Van Aadamses have their fun. They were the only Family run like a business corporation; i.e., they had a C.E.O. and a board instead of a Godfather and his *capos*. But trouble was, their C.E.O.'s Designated Successors (or in Family parlance, Heirs,) kept dying. Deuce himself had assassinated Wayne Van Aadams, who had tried to kill him first, mostly over a misunderstanding about Wayne's girlfriend and which Borgioli brother she was cheating on Wayne with: She fingered Deuce in order to protect Deuce's brother, Joey.

Plus Wayne had tried to kill Sparkle and steal the ultimate weapon from the Smiths, only it now appeared that the Smiths did not have an ultimate weapon.

But he digressed.

Joey was dead now, killed in the bombing of the Stellaluna restaurant, where the last sit-down of all the Families had been held—*Dio mio,* was it less than forty-eight hours ago?

So, the cast of characters: Van Aadamses: Wayne was dead, and then a couple more Van Aadamses had come and gone, and now, who knew who was in charge?

Then there were the Scarlattis, who had always frightened Deuce the most. This was the techno-fringe Family, on the cutting edge of anything that was *molto* weird: circuitry that made you think you were flying, and hallucination modules, implant tattoos, and all the very, very out-there stuff. To be in the Scarlattis, you had to get branded, and that was how Deuce had figured out that Sparkle's old roommate, Selene, had been an undercover Scarlatti widow bent on revenge, rather than the innocent showgirl she had made herself out to be.

After the Scarlattis in the scariness department came the Smiths. The Smiths had assimilated a number of other Families during the turf wars when the Moon was up for grabs—

the Mitchells and some of the Goldbergs. The Smiths were union-busting thugs who provided most of the weaponry everybody employed, versus all the spy and eavesdropping equipment they bought from the Scarlattis.

But there was no getting around the fact that the Smiths were the most physically beautiful Family in the Moon: the majority were dark-hued, and on a satellite where no one got a tan except through artificial means (which were generally disdained as way too vain, even for Moonsiders, who were far vainer than Earthsiders,) it was something to be other than very, very pale. The Smiths made it extremely difficult to Affiliate (much less join) their Family, and the fact that Deuce had Honorary Papers of Affiliation with them had gotten him through a number of doors that might have otherwise been closed.

Likewise, he had Scarlatti Papers. And Caputo Papers. The Caputos, he understood the best: old-style Mafia. Old Earthside Sicily. The Caputos had kept the romance of what the Families had originally been about. In Hunter's private log, part of which Deuce had read when he thought Hunter had been killed, he had likened the Six Casino Families to "gunslinging accountants." Not the Caputos, however, who had never lost their touch for the old-fashioned ways: stilettos, poisons, that sort of thing. They had been instrumental in codifying the Moonside notion of Vendetta, one of the most sacred bonds among the Families, as well as Registering hits.

The thing was, back before the Families had moved into the Moon, Don Giovanni Caputo had wanted very badly for his own Family to go there. He was tired of all the *sciochezza* organized crime put up with. The League of Decency was perpetually trying to get rid of the Families and all they stood for, which was merely making a profit on pleasure of various sorts: gambling, drugs, dames and boys, that kind of thing. When the Quantum Instability Wars took place, the League claimed it was on account of God's wrath regarding all the sinning that was going on.

So then Earthside Las Vegas blew up, and while the League was too smart to claim responsibility, they did manage to blame it on God—remember Sodom, remember Gomorrah? Don Giovanni was martyred at the big wrestling match between Doom Lord and Archangel, and the Caputos put the pedal to the metal and went to the Moon.

The Caputos had the first casino, and the first brothel, and they were royally ticked when everybody, having seen that money could be made after all, scuttled on up and horned in. So they were very happy when, during a major power play, Yuet Chan, the Godmother of the Chan Family, was fingered for Wayne Van Aadams's assassination—a murder Deuce actually committed—and sent to jail Earthside. Control of the Chan casino, the Pearl of Heaven, had been given to the Caputos.

The thing about the Chan Family was that they were the mandarins of the drug trade. They made an intensely addictive concoction called Chantilly Lace (hard ch) and almost one-quarter of the Moonside population was hooked on it.

Deuce's own brother, Joey, had been so pulled into Chantilly Lace that he had had to have almost every single organ in his body cloned (thank God Wayne Van Aadams had tried to fatally poison him, or the doctors would never have known what bad shape Joey Borgioli was in.) Joey had lived through it and had become, like Hunter Castle, seriously anti-drug.

Deuce had taken Chantilly Lace exactly once. It had been the highest high of his life, except for falling in love with Sparkle de Lune. She had been with him when he tried it, and she had saved him from it. Seeing how amazingly good it was, she had given him an ultimatum: her, or Chantilly Lace.

Only in terms of physical longevity had Deuce chosen wisely.

Which was why, Deuce suspected, it had proved easy for whoever—the Eight Disenfranchised?—to execute the coup that had restored antidruggie Yuet Chan to power as the Godmother of the Chan Family. The Earthsiders who backed her felt like they were picking a much lesser evil as their route to Moonside action.

The overly overcompensating, ornate spires of the Borgioli HQ loomed large as the shuttle approached the parking structure. Here he was again; it had been less than two years ago that he had been a mere Casino Liaison, positive that he had been called to this very building by his Borgioli Godfather, Don Alberto, for purposes of being executed. But he had had hope, in the form of a business card passed surreptitiously to him by two men who had subsequently gone on to meet their Maker: two Van Aadams security men, who had slipped him Hunter Castle's business card.

Deuce was still alive, and just about everyone who had tried to kill him—on purpose, anyway—was dead. Correction: Now that Earth was at war with the Moon, there were more than a handful of folks who would like to rub out permanently the guy who had been christened "the Godfather of the Moon."

Deuce cracked his left ring finger and turned to his brand-new mother. "So," he said with mock casualness, "is this the way life goes on Earth?"

"It's . . . not like this at all," she said, after a moment's deliberation. The dog was resting on her lap, enjoying her attention. Little brat was certain not to pee on *her*.

"Actually, it's incredibly boring. Stifling." She smoothed his white-blond hair away from his forehead. "But here's something I'm wondering, my son. As you can see, you and I are very different. It's not impossible, of course, that I am your biological mother. I also don't discount that your adoptive mother, Maria Caldera, is your biological mother."

"Right now, I got more important things on my mind," Deuce said gently, trying very hard not to sound impolite. The fact was, he was interested in all this kind of stuff. But he was more interested in keeping everyone alive.

Angelo spoke to the shuttle and told it what kind of coordinates to give so that the surviving Borgiolis wouldn't blast the hell out of it. As it was unmarked, no one would know Angelo Borgioli was inside it.

Better that they not know Deuce McNamara di Borgioli was there, too. If other people believed that Deuce was responsible for the declaration of war against Earthside—

—But that was *schiamazzo*; no one could actually blame an individual for such a thing; if Earthside was ready to attack, one single person could not say yay or nay.

Angelo spoke into the comm link, giving all the passwords—the code of which Deuce could break in half a minute. Instead, completely counter to his upbringing, he let Angelo do all his secret handshakes in private and passed the time reassuring Moona Lisa that she was still alive and likely to be so for the next few minutes or so.

They landed on the Borgioli parking structure without in-

cident, except for the fact that about two dozen men stood
around the landing pad packing major hardware. They were
dressed in Borgioli colors—red, green, and white—and, for a
moment, Deuce was extremely nostalgic for the old days. He
used to hide his Borgioli colors whenever possible, preferring
press-on badges to more permanent affixations. Most men and
women who were Members of a Family were proud that they
held some aces in their hand. Problem with Borgioli colors
was that you pretty much held a joker.

But anyway, that was neither here nor there as Deuce and
the others got out of the shuttle and the guys with guns
snapped to. Angelo was out of the cockpit first, and the Borgiolis were really rolling out the red carpet for him, if the
Borgiolis could be said to have a red carpet. Deuce trailed
along behind him, taking notes, and wondered if he had mis-
judged Angelo. Sure, he'd known Angelo was in the winner's
circle, and highly favored, but just what kind of face card his
cousin was, Deuce was now not so sure.

His *mamma* carried the dog.

"*Buon giorno, Padrino*," one of the official welcoming committee said. To Angelo, not Deuce.

Angelo made no reaction. He simply swept along, not strutting, not being overly obsequious—a word Deuce had learned
during a vocabulary-building seminar, in an effort to class
himself up—simply giving notice that he was very comfortable with the status quo. The problem was, Deuce had no clue
what the Borgiolis thought the status quo was.

He actually smiled, because this so reminded him of the
days when he was a Casino Liaison. Dropping off the night's
chits, making nice while his counterpart at each casino totted
up the percentages on debits, credits, dishonors, Vendettas—
it had been a very dangerous and exciting life. Liaisons either
traveled up the food chain very quickly or got eaten.

Deuce had become the most important Moonsider on the
satellite. And that was not bragging. It was just a fact. When
people called him the Godfather of the Moon, he demurred
and told them not to. But the truth was, he pretty much was
the Godfather of the Moon. Or had been, until that stupid
remote data terminal had declared war on Earth.

But that only proved his point—after all, if some poor N.A.
bag-lady type stood up from the sidewalk, and said, "Let's

pound Earthside into the Stone Age!", chances were she'd get free food and lodging for a couple days at a local mental-health institute. Or at the least, a stern talking-to.

But when Deuce McNamara said something like that, it carried weight. Things happened, in a big way. And he couldn't deny that that was exciting. Not that he had wanted to start a war, but deep inside a guy's psyche, it was pretty darn exciting to know that he *could.*

If you were the kind of guy that Deuce was, anyway.

They stepped onto the escalator that would lead them down to the bunker of Borgioli HQ. Deuce felt a bit nostalgic. He couldn't even count the times he had been down this escalator. The belt still squeaked and the carpet, though newer and nicer than the old threadbare one, exhibited uncommonly bad taste: a very subtle red and green silhouette of the Madonna, smiling down on a craps table.

Deuce said to Angelo, "I can almost hear Big Al laughing behind the bunker door." He was made uneasy by the fact that Angelo didn't so much as crack a smile. *Maybe he's still in mourning,* Deuce told himself, which would not surprise him at all. As ham-fisted and overbearing and—may the Blessed Virgin forgive him, but the Godfather was pretty stupid, after all—less than genius Don Alberto had been, still he had been the head of their Family. You automatically got respect when you were in a position of authority. The best was when man (or woman) matched status, but still, you gave respect to the office.

Don Alberto had been a terrible Godfather. Some Borgiolis claimed that before he had assumed leadership, the Borgiolis had finally started rising from the depths of uncouthness. Deuce had no idea if this was true. He did know that in his time as a Borgioli Family man, if they were less uncouth than they had been before the reign of Big Al, then they were fairly unredeemable, if he did say so.

However, all musing aside, they were being ushered into the conference room. Back-Line Tony, who had hated Deuce all both of their lives, looked mighty unhappy to see that his nemesis had landed on both feet again. Deuce couldn't re-member precisely why Tony hated him so much, but the over-ly enhanced bodyguard appeared to have a much better memory.

Angelo, Deuce, Mamma Connie, the dog, and Iniya of the D'inn—*has a nice ring*—filed into the room. Of the twenty-aught *capos* who had been Don Alberto's to command, there were seven, and one of them was in a medical capsule. Which indicated that his days in the world—God rest his soul—were numbered.

The six who were ambulatory rose and kissed first Deuce on the lips, and then Angelo. It was the total Godfather package, but Deuce didn't buy it for a minute. In the Moon, everyone was always playing side wagers; no one with an ounce of brains played the house odds. The thing was, you played the way the guys with power wanted you to play, sooner or later you lost everything. The way the odds were built, you could win for a while. A tiny little bit, could you win.

But sooner or later, bad luck would activate, and you wouldn't lose a tiny little bit: You would lose your shirt, and your mother's shirt, and your little daughter's lunch money. And you would be so close to going outside the dome and suffocating yourself in a crater, that when some Family guy said to you, "I can make it right for you," you ended up owing your soul to the company store.

That was, in large part, why Deuce had opted out of the Family system. It was a revolutionary move. No one had done it before. Membership in a Family was so coveted that even if you wound up in the Borgiolis, you accepted Membership status with humility and gratitude. To refuse not only Membership in the Borgiolis, with which he had been born, but also the offer of full Membership in the Smiths and Scarlattis, and in the Chans and Caputos, too, if he had made the slightest indication that that was his wish—made N.A.'s reel. It made them question the notion that they had no value.

It made the Moonsider Liberation Front claim Deuce as one of their own, although he consistently insisted that he was not one of them, and never would be.

Deuce considered himself a man without a loyalty . . . except to the Moon as a whole. Inadvertently, that was how his legend had grown. Deuce, of the Moon. Owned by no one, except the dry lunar surface with its craters, rilles, and seas.

It made the people who scrabbled in the helium dust and lived in depressing cinder-block apartments and cheesy, low-rent trailers proud to be who they were. They clung to their poverty like it was a badge of honor.

This, Deuce was not proud of. It was not anywhere in his agenda to make Independent Moonsiders glory in misery. The phrase, "We may be poor, but at least we're honest," turned his stomach, frankly. Because the poor had no power. And without power, you were a victim.

But the time for such profound thoughts was over. Deuce and the others had reached the heavily guarded and fortified doors of the bunker. And there was good old Back-Line Tony, a little grayer, maybe a little hunched, supremely pissed that yet again, he had to let Deuce through these doors without whacking him.

There being so little joy in Mudville that day, Deuce made a point of smirking at Tony. Okay, it was immature, and it might get him killed one of these days, but Deuce had this self-destructive streak wherein he talked too much when he was nervous and he tried to piss people off when he was afraid. It used to drive his *mamma*, Maria, completely off her nut.

"Duchino, whattsa matter with you?" she used to demand, stirring her famous tomato sauce and waving her hand at him. "You need to be more like your brother."

Which, seeing as how Joey had aggressively managed to get Deuce disinherited from Mamma's will because he was adopted, he was not so sure she would have wanted. Plus there were Joey's dames and his drugs. Deuce, okay, he was not the best guy in the Moon. But he was not so careless of Mamma's memory as Joey had been.

"*Ah, mio fratello*," he murmured, and crossed himself. Lots of guys crossed themselves, they came into the main meeting room of any Family, even the Borgiolis. A lot of the discussion in the room centered around whether or not some guy— usually the guy knock-kneed in front of everybody—should be disposed of; and if so, in a humane manner. Or not. Deuce himself had faced such a tribunal.

To this day, he figured he had been spared because Big Al had loved him like a son. And Beatrice Borgioli had loved him like a . . . lover.

But they were both dead, and Deuce was still here.

"Okay," Angelo said, to the handful of upper-crust Borgioli.

An oxymoron if there ever was one, but there it was.

"We need to make some hard decisions," Angelo said. "There are very few of us left. Do we band with Don Mc-Namara, or do we stay separate, claiming all our rights as the Borgioli Family?"

Silver Tongue Tommy, the Family *consigliere*, glanced cautiously at Deuce.

"I mean no disrespect," he began, inclining his head. "You have done great things for the Moon, Don McNamara. But also, some destructive things. This war, for instance."

Deuce waited, although he already knew which way the wind was blowing. Not that he had ever seen wind. You didn't have wind in an airless vacuum, and that was what the Moon's atmosphere could boast.

Silver Tongue Tommy continued. "Again, Don McNamara, I am not trying to say you should not have a say in things. A place in our structure. But I am saying that it's not yet time for the Borgiolis to disband. I know you promised this to the Smiths when you joined their Family in an honorable Affili-ation—"

—*They always know everything,* Deuce marveled, half-forgetting that he was still someone like that.

"But we are still a strong, united Family, and we need a leader." Silver Tongue Tommy took a breath. "And we feel Angelo is the best choice for that position of honor and re-sponsibility."

Deuce applauded. "I couldn't agree with you more, Silver Tongue Tommy. And so." He turned and faced Angelo dead on. "Seeing as how I and my handful of followers are perse-cuted all over the satellite, I request political asylum for me and mine."

He truly couldn't tell if Angelo was amused, angry, a com-bination, or what. But his former right-hand man said, "Done. Get the *don* and his people sleeping quarters, surveillance equipment, minipads, whatever they need."

He smiled grimly at Deuce. "You started this war," he said under his breath. "I expect you to stop it."

THREE

Alas, it was not to be that Deuce could stop the war. At least not in one measly week. He tried his best, though. Using massive amounts of Chan up-drugs to stay awake, he logged thousands of calls Moonside and Earthside; got interviewed on the viso scan and the zipper; and conducted more secret sit-downs with more mucky-mucks than all the Godfathers in the Moon in the century-plus since it had been founded.

But the Earthside troops landed faster than moths in flames—not that Deuce had ever seen a moth—and it was clearly time to move either to Plan B or Plan C: B being conducting the war by beating the crap out of Earthside and all her sympathizers, which clearly wasn't an option for an undergunned, unorganized Moon; and C being concluding it via surrender.

Because people were dying, as Earthside pummeled the surface; and more could die, as Earthside made noises about blowing the domes. Earthside public opinion was very against that . . . but now and then, some Earthside troops got killed, so the tide could turn. When some Moonie killed your soldier boy or girl, you wanted them all sent to hell.

The Families had massed at each of the Family airlocks and were holding them pretty much okay. That the Moonsiders had held the airlocks for this long was a miracle, and the three Italian Catholic Families were doing all kinds of religious observations in gratitude to God, His Mother, and all the Saints and Apostles. That was only right.

However, the war raged on. Various persons wanted to surrender, but nothing happened. Part of the supposed problem was that Earthside claimed to have no idea who they were supposed to be dealing with. There was no official vested with the power to negotiate terms. The official mayor of Moonbase Vegas, Jeanine della Fortuna, was being ignored, which was fine with Deuce, because she was an idiot. There had been discussion about a sit-down with the heads of all the Families, but most of them were dead, and the internal squabbling to promote new ones was substantial. Add to that the MLF's insistence that they be included in peace talks, and you had a mess. One Earthside was doing absolutely nothing to clear up.

"It's obvious," Deuce said to his mom. They sipped *grappa* together in Angelo's bunker while Iniya sat looking detached. Actually, she was shut down. That happened when the real Iniya needed a break.

Deuce was helping Angelo with battle strategy. He had a mini open with diagrams of various tunnels and a list of the weapons still left in the Borgioli inventory.

"They want to destroy us," he continued. "Earthside's been itching for a reason to come in here and take over ever since us Moonsiders turned our first onechip of profit. So they'll just bump us all off."

His mother nodded. "That's the aim of some factions, certainly. The Eight Disenfranchised, for sure."

"I'm not so simple I think it's on the official party platform. 'Item number six: Kill all the craterheads and take over the Moon,' " he retorted. "But Ma, you have to—" He stopped at the look of radiant joy on her face. He smiled. "Ma," he said again.

"I'm not your biological mother," she reminded him. "I only carried you." She preened a little. "And gave birth to you. You were a large baby. Nine pounds plus."

"*Mi dispiace,*" he said feelingly.

"It was a joy to bring a new life into the world. I loved every minute of it." She touched his hand. "But I'm still not your biological mother."

"You're the closest to an official mother I've got."

Actually, he felt a little guilty saying that. Connie had told him that she thought Maria della Caldera was his genetic mother. Why Hunter would have mixed his gametes up with Mamma's was something Deuce couldn't fathom. On the other hand, how he, Deuce, had ended up on the Moon, adopted into the Borgioli Family, was also something he—and many dozens of others—couldn't fathom.

Howsoever he had gotten to her door, Maria had loved him like a son, no matter what Joey—God rest his soul—had said she had said, in order to get the inheritance.

Now he pretty much had to laugh that Iniya had bet him "his fortune" that their little shuttle would be destroyed. Hunter could have, and should have, shuffled a bunch of credits in and around various accounts before he left, and dumped a truly astronomical amount into Deuce's account.

But the truth was, he hadn't paid Deuce in forever. Plus Deuce's lux penthouse apartment had burned down. Meanwhile, all the assets of all the Families, their Members, and Affiliates, had been frozen by the Earthside government, through the Department of Fairness. So now everybody was scrabbling to borrow money on the brand-new black market that had sprung up, and the N.A.'s were the ones loaning money to people at exorbitant rates, and promising broken kneecaps if it was not paid in full when due.

The only thing kept the Families going was that they instantly switched to using casino chips for currency. It was kind of exciting to carry around a load of actual objects which stood for credits. The human race had not used paper money or coins as legal tender in over a hundred years, although Deuce collected it because he thought it was fascinating. He had this paper fetish. Sparkle used to think it was "cute." Especially in the Moon, you did not go around wasting valuable resources—like newsprint, which he also collected—when reading the morning news off your mini was just as good and didn't make any muss or fuss.

Iniya—who was still dressed in Mr. Wong—blinked, and said to Deuce, "You must relocate. Cousin Angelo no longer supports your position."

Deuce blinked and glanced at his mother. She sighed. The thing was, having Iniya around was both scary and very nifty. The real Iniya, wherever and whatever she was, reminded him of himself—cagey and well webbed with a network of spies or informants or whatever. She was still manufacturing some pretty wicked firepower and extremely sophisticated reconnaissance technology. Otherwise, the war would have already been over.

By the end of the first week, there were practically more Earthside troops landing on the Moon than there were Moonsiders living in the Moon. The Moon had never had anything like an official military, just a police force, the Lunar Security Forces. Each Casino Charter, granted to the Six Families by the Department of Fairness, expressly forbade the creation of private armies. Never mind the fact that each of the Families armed their soldiers with more of the good stuff than Earthside supplied their fairly well paid and legally trained infantry persons.

However, there *was* a real Moonside army, the completely illegal terrorist group called the Moonsider Liberation Front. Ever since Deuce declared himself outside the influential sphere of any particular Family, the MLF had been after him to ally himself with them.

The frustrated N.A.'s, denied the good life—or so they believed—by the Families, had wanted them off the Moon, or at least so weakened that they lost control of the economy. The MLF promised to help with that, usually via bombings and assassinations, none of which was ever registered with the Charter Board.

This did not seem to bother the majority of the N.A.'s whatsoever, but it bothered Deuce plenty. The MLF wanted to play, but they didn't want to name the game or pay the ante. Plus, nobody but him seemed to understand that the MLF was a bunch of religious fanatics. When they had first contacted him—by kidnapping him and the Missus—they had so much as told him they believed he was the Messiah, which to him, a good Catholic, was pretty darn impolite to God and His Designated Heir. Like other Family Members, he assumed the MLF were a branch of the League of Decency, which was officially banned from the Moon.

And then, of course, there were the Mormons, officially allied with the Van Aadams Family, mainly because the Van Aadamses were the most genteel of the crime families, but also, because the Mormons had been getting tired of being conned. They were a kind and trusting people, organized just like a normal crime family, very top-down. So once the big guns bought into some scam, they passed it on down the org chart like an infection. The Van Aadamses put a stop to all that.

But the most recent official head of the MLF had been a Mormon. An old friend of Deuce's, in fact, whom he had known back when Sparkle was a showgirl at the Van Aadams casino, the Down Under. His name was Brigham, not such an unusual name for a Mormon, but what had been unusual was that Brigham had been totally on board with whacking Deuce. To put it plainly, that had been a shocker. He and Deuce had not exactly been drinking buddies—since Mormons didn't drink—but they had been pretty good friends.

Deuce had felt very bad when the remote data terminal had blown Brigham up.

He turned to Iniya and gave her a wave. She blinked, coming back in. Weird, how he could stare at the chassis of Mr. Wong and imagine a broad. It worried him a little about his masculinity, if truth be told. Not that he was telling anybody.

"So, let's go through this one more time, on account of how important it is," he said, picking up his wineglass.

She squinted at it. "It's a very nice Merlot."

"Oh." He was impressed. Months, he had taken a wine class, and still he had no nose. And here she was, off in some kind of topsy-turvy quadrant of space where maybe they had no noses, and she could tell a burgundy from a cabernet like *that*.

He put down his glass. "As impressive as your wine-tasting abilities are, and I mean no disrespect, I am referring to the notion that you are running a simulation to fool the !kth into thinking I'm still connected to them."

She had these cute habits. Nodding she had not yet fully gotten. How you could assimilate an incredible amount of facts on wine, and yet only lower your head, not raising it back up?

Also, she was intrigued by smoking. Thus, she had mastered lighting cigarettes, comming to pay the pollution levy (thank you, MLF, which had concocted some bogus scientific research about secondhand smoke to get decent people to pay a sin tax), and inhaling.

But she often forgot to exhale. Since she was wearing Mr. Wong, and therefore obviously a mechanical to the public, no one got too frantic or patted her on the back to help her stop choking. It was amusing, at the most. Deuce figured she should get a rebate on part of the levy. He also wondered where all the smoke went. If Mr. Wong had some kind of filtration system going on in there, or what.

Deuce's surrogate mother straightened a little and looked intently at Iniya. It was amazing to him how she had taken on all his battles, badda bing, badda bong, just like that, and made them all her own. It made him lonesome for Mamma Maria.

More lonesome for Sparkle.

What kind of mother would she prove to be? He had no notion.

What kind of wife had she been?

Let's don't go there, he told himself. *It don't matter anyway. She made her choice.*

He sighed and looked at Iniya, who said, "Only moment of uncertainty in execution was the first time you accessed Iniya instead of !kth correspondent. Suspicions may have been aroused at that point. Traceability is possible."

"Is it probable?" Connie asked, leaning forward.

Deuce moved his shoulders. "Meaning no disrespect, Ma, as well you know, but we cannot deal in the odds of the probable. Those are the house odds. And we are playing against them."

His mother, who clearly knew next to nothing from gambling, nodded like she did know. He liked that; she had a BS factor, same as him. Okay, not genetically linked; but after you've spent some time in close quarters—say, for nine months—surely some of your habits and eccentricities wore off on the other guy.

"Program is running," Iniya said. "You are asking questions, they are answering. I am storing all the data and you may access it whenever you wish." She blinked and dropped her head, which was that nodding thing again, and said, "I recommend you execute a brain dump every evening."

He was a little shocked. "A dump? *Mi scusi?*" he blurted, but at a grin from Connie, he regained his composure and said, "Oh. Sure."

"Translation: that you access the simulation, requesting highlights, in the event that you meet, or are captured by, !kth."

"Captured by." Deuce looked at his remote data terminal and his surrogate mother, and thought, *It is very likely that my world is going to end in fire.*

* * *

"Okay," Hunter said, seated once more on Sparkle's bed. She had not moved from it. Nurses had brought the children to her for breast feeding. Additionally, she had requested the presence of Stella, who was almost two, and who had no idea that Sparkle was her mother. All she knew was that she had a grandpa, and his ship could make wonderful toys. She also vaguely remembered another woman, much fatter and with dark, curly hair, who wore a lot of different colors on her face and who yelled and cried a lot.

Stella regarded her seriously, and said, "Stella gots dinky-pookuns," which Sparkle could not decipher. Her icy heart longed to feel guilty or sad that she could not decipher her own daughter's verbal code, but her rational, reasonable mind explained the lack away by reminding her that until a few hours ago, she had not realized Stella was remotely related to her, much less her daughter.

But many mothers would have embraced their daughters and cried tears of overwhelmed emotion—joy, terror, reunion, remorse. Sparkle did not cry. Yet at some base level, some Jungian sort of subconscious level, she connected with this little girl. In fact, of the three children who were allegedly her flesh and blood, it was Stella to whom she was drawn the most.

Stella looked at her grandfather, whom she believed to be her father, and said again, "Stella gots dinky-pookuns."

"I believe it means her diapers are messy," Hunter drawled. "I'll call for the nurse."

"No," Sparkle said. "You change her."

Hunter looked startled. He smiled at Sparkle, who did not smile back. But in that smile of his, she felt so many things shatter; youth and trust—not that she had ever really trusted anyone, not even Deuce; or rather, most of all, Deuce—and gentleness.

She had to be on such guard, such alert. She felt surrounded by enemies and unknowns, no one who loved her. She was truly alone; she had always *felt* herself to be alone, but when she was with Deuce, she had also known that she was loved. She realized now, with the clarity of despair, that she didn't know that anymore.

For all she knew, he hated her. For which, she could not blame him.

Hunter changed his granddaughter, murmuring softly to her while she wriggled and chuckled at him. Stella was happy, incredibly at ease and joyous; had she, Sparkle, ever been like that? She couldn't imagine it. She'd always been so somber and guarded.

Why?

If you grew up in the Moon, you assumed life was out to get you. But she was not a native Moonsider.

Back Earthside, Satan was out to get you, if you believed the League of Decency. The LOD would have everyone believe that evil surrounded you like a Feynman Field, and it was something to be kept out of society and protected against constantly.

Sparkle's father had been LOD. She didn't know if Hunter knew it. Her mother had not been. A beautiful woman, her mother. Very happy and lighthearted. Pleasure-seeking, pleasure-loving. She would never have a simple cup of tea; there was a lamp on the table, and a pretty cloth. Maybe a simulated floral.

Her father distrusted all these niceties. Sparkle had no idea why he had married such a "carnal" woman, as he used to put it. He had lofty ideals, notions of platonic love that transcended "ordinary" marriages. He would have made a hell of a LOD preacher, but he was actually very low in the ranks of the League. That embarrassed him, but Sparkle was relieved about it. She had a feeling her mother was, too: the higher up you were, the more was expected of your family.

Sparkle was already tired of expectations. She was extremely beautiful—that was not any kind of vain judgment; just a fact. Everyone noticed it. Everyone commented on it.

Her father was terrified of it. So he tried to beat it out of her.

It was then that Sparkle's mother left him. She went kind of crazy. She couldn't stop buying things, and she couldn't stop smiling at men. Pretty soon, the social-care workers noticed that Sparkle wasn't attending school on a regular basis, and that her grades were slipping.

So there was a committee meeting, and she was taken from her mother and ordered to live with her father.

Sparkle couldn't do it. She knew he was hell-bent—so to speak—on keeping her safe by making her ugly, and making her ugly by hitting her over and over—and so she ran.

When you're as beautiful as Sparkle, you don't have to run far. Protectors come out of the woodwork. And of course, one did. Her name was Yuet Chan.

At that time, both girls were very young, perhaps fifteen and sixteen. Yuet was a Member of the Chan Casino Family, headquartered in the Moon. She had been sent Earthside for her education, which was common among Casino Families, and also to give her a chance to grow up before Family life took her over and made her old before her years.

That was also common among Casino Families.

Later, in the future, Sparkle would know that Deuce wondered about the two of them. She and the beautiful young Chinese woman were affectionate with each other, and Sparkle was rarely affectionate with anyone. Sparkle risked her life to help Yuet when she tried to take over her Family. Later, when Yuet was successful, Sparkle had been there, again, to lend her support, having led Deuce into the fold as well, although his Godfather had ordered him to back Yuet's stepbrother.

Sparkle had never explained her relationship to Yuet. Deuce had not asked, and she had not offered.

But there were many times she wanted him to ask.

About many things.

It was easy to remain cool and collected if nothing was demanded of you. That was the flaw in Deuce's relationship with her. She didn't have to give because he didn't take. She knew he thought he was being a good man, a kind man.

But it wasn't what she needed.

It was very much what she wanted to want. But she did not believe she was the kind of woman who ever would.

Angelo commed Deuce and asked to meet him in the Family meeting room. That was the kind of message you got when someone was thinking very seriously about whacking you. It was not the kind of place cousins on good terms met to play some cards and smoke some cigarettes.

Deuce was alarmed, but he kept his voice calm and told him, Sure, after vespers, if that was all right with him. Angelo had agreed.

To Deuce's surprised delight, his very un-Italian surrogate mother was a devout Catholic. So they had that in common, too. Not bad, for a world filled with faulty wiring and worse connections.

And potential hits in the Family meeting room.

It used to happen all the time when Deuce was in the Borgioli Family. In fact, Deuce had once been summoned to that very room specifically to be hit. He had fast-talked his way out of that one.

He only hoped he could talk his way out of this one, too.

Deuce and Connie went to the Borgioli chapel together. It was an ornate place, very operatic, very swirly, with gold and gemstones on the robes of the saints, which were carved from real wood, not crater. But way too much of everything, too many curlicues.

It reminded him, mournfully, of Beatrice, who had never learned how to dress. With Bea, if one gold bow was good, sixteen were even better. Frowzy and blowsy, even after Hunter married her and she could spend, literally, millions on her clothes. No matter; she still looked like a cheap Mafioso's daughter.

Hunter had married her for purely political reasons. Deuce wasn't sure she ever realized that. She did freely admit that she had never stopped loving Deuce, and had thrown herself at him at every opportunity. Sparkle had taken it all in stride ... or had she simply not cared?

So, back to basking in the warm glow of the cheesy chapel, decorated with very bad art. The stained-glass windows of the Last Supper and Christ in the Garden were atrocious.

There was a priest in the chapel, not the big-shot Monsignor who had stood in shock as Angelo gunned down one of his own men, who had seemed hell-bent—ha-ha—on taking Beatrice hostage when Hunter had been declared dead.

Thinking of those past times, Deuce bristled. Bea had not even had the backbone to rush to her sick daughter's side when Stella had nearly died in a fire. Overwhelmed by the deaths of her father and husband (a ruse, it turned out, but she didn't know that, no one did), she had medicated herself and holed up in there, in the chapel.

The Monsignor had appealed to Deuce: With Hunter gone, whoever was married to his widow was the most powerful man on Earth and in the Moon. A whole lotta people had wanted it to be Deuce. In fact, it was around that time that people had started to call him the Godfather of the Moon.

His *mamma* knelt in the pew while Deuce stared at the hundreds of little drawers neatly labeled with brass plates in the semicircular rooms behind the altar. Beatrice was buried there. Big Al, too, and Deuce's brother, Joey. Most of the upper echelon of the Family was gone, blown to bits.

Angelo had been picked to be the Borgioli Godfather by popular consensus of the survivors. That he was so resentful toward Deuce over the current state of affairs was not good news.

And that was putting it mildly.

His mother tugged on his wrist, indicating that he should kneel beside her. He did so, lowering his head and closing his eyes.

Then he opened one in surprise as she whispered, "We may have to take Angelo out."

"Ma," he murmured, shocked.

She crossed herself. "I gather that you two were quite close. But he's still carrying a torch for Beatrice Castle. And she was still in love with you until the second she blew her brains all over the walls of your guest bedroom."

"That is true, *Mamma*. But I did nothing to encourage her." He shrugged. "Okay. I didn't tell her about Sparkle and me until she was engaged to Hunter. Then I let her think it was a rebound thing. She took it okay for a while. But I guess the truth is that I let her think I loved her."

"Which was the wisest thing to do, under the circumstances," she said firmly. "Big Al was not the kind of man who forgave slights to his loved ones. And he loved no one more than Beatrice."

"How do you know all this?" he asked, amazed.

She smiled. "I network."

He sighed. "You would have made a great Casino Liaison."

"Like son, like mother." She put her hand over his. "I've heard you were a wonderful Casino Liaison. One of the best. You have Honorary Papers of Affiliation from almost all the Families."

"Yeah, I wear 'em on a sash like merit badges," he said, embarrassed. He wanted to say to her, Listen, I'm not that good a person, but she was enjoying being proud of him.

"We need to be serious," she admonished him. "Is there another Borgioli who could head the Family? Someone who likes you better?" She crossed herself as the priest glanced their way.

Deuce considered. "I'll make a list."

"Good." She got off her knees and sat back in the pew.

"My son?" the Borgioli priest said softly, walking toward Deuce and his mother. He wore a clerical collar and a dark suit. There was a black armband around his biceps. "Is there something I can do for you, Don McNamara?"

Deuce licked his lips. "Better you call me Signor Borgioli," he said. "It's on my birth certificate."

The priest had that goony smile the MLFers got when they talked about Deuce being the Messiah.

"What," Deuce said tiredly.

The priest glanced at Connie. "She's fine," Deuce said. "She's my mother."

"Ah, *Donna* Borgioli, so pleased to make your acquaintance."

"Mamma's been living Earthside. Overseeing some Family business down there."

The priest nodded. He paused, and said, "There is Family business here also, Don McNamara, which many of us wish you would . . . execute."

Deuce kept his voice very calm and extremely neutral. "I am not in the Borgioli Family anymore."

The priest smiled tiredly. He looked world-weary beyond belief. Deuce wondered why he was embroiled in this Family matter. Not that Family priests weren't expected to have their own agendas. Far from it. But this talk was on a very big agenda.

"Okay, and what is it you wish I would do?" Deuce queried.

The priest's large brown eyes got very much larger. He glanced around as if he was terrified someone was listening—which could very well be the case; there was truly nothing sacred anymore—and whispered, "Whack Angelo."

"Mmm." Deuce looked down, then back up.

"Why? Don't ah, prevaricate." He had one of those word-a-day calendars. He was still learning the big words, even after all those years of living with Sparkle, who had the brain of a college professor, at least.

"He wants to kill you first," the priest explained, glancing over his shoulder again. *Jeez, don't look guilty or nothin'.*

"Because I started the war?"

The priest gestured. *"Va bene.* A little of that, to be sure. But frankly, *Padrino,* he thinks you're too dangerous to be left alive. You wield too much influence, and he doesn't feel he can control you. He's afraid of you."

"He's my cousin. He's saved my life a million times. And I've saved his." He felt stupid saying these things. Business was business. It was nothing personal. No matter how much you liked somebody, if they were bad for you and yours, they had to go.

"Is there a plan?" Deuce asked. Then he glanced at his mother. "Mamma, why don't you go stripe your account card against the poor box? Give the orphans some folding money."

The priest crossed himself. "The poor little children. So many of their parents are dead."

"But they're in a Family," Deuce reminded him. And debased as the Borgiolis were, they always took good care of their children. The Borgiolis adored children.

"That is true. But there are so many of them. We fear that the system will break down, Godfather." His eyes filled with tears. "These children are only the first wave, if this war continues."

Deuce got it: The priest represented people who figured Angelo for a weakling. He was letting those *cretini bastardi* Earthsider forces make orphans of the next generation of Borgioli. Without strong Family structure and good role models, the current crop of young women and men could not hope to keep their Families going. They would collapse under the weight of their own confusion and lack of guidance.

"Nicky Borgioli is extremely popular with the young people," the priest continued. "I'm sure that in time, he could be groomed to head the Family. If only he can survive for a few years and get some seasoning."

Deuce hung his head. He felt very sad. There was nothing in him that wanted to move forward with this plan.

Then suddenly Iniya appeared in the back doorway. Though the chapel, like every single square inch of the Borgioli compound, was underground, a nimbus of light surrounded her silhouette, like a heavenly visitor had come to talk things over with a few select sinners.

She saw Deuce and headed straight for him. Deuce gave her a wave, and she slid into the pew behind him. She raised her lips to his ear—a pleasant tingle of warmth which stirred him—and she murmured, "We have to get out of here, right now. No questions. It may already be too late."

Without another word, Deuce rose, pulled his mother to her feet, and dragged her for all he was worth out the back door, around a corner, and into a service tunnel.

"What's going on?" Connie asked querulously, as he pushed her to the ground and covered her as completely as he could with his own body.

"Not sure," Deuce replied.

Then the chapel blew. The tunnel shook. Something broke loose and smacked Deuce in the middle of his back. He grunted and was very glad it had hit him and not his mother.

Crouching beside him, Iniya smiled with Mr. Wong's mouth and said, "Thank you for listening to Iniya, Deuce of Moon. You are alive."

"That's a fact," he said gratefully to the remote data terminal. "And, gee, this day is certainly shaping up, isn't it?"

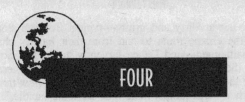

FOUR

When I look at thy heavens, the work of thy fingers,
the moon and the stars which thou hast established;
what is man that thou art mindful of him,
and the son of man that thou dost care for him?

PSALMS 8:3–4

The back door to the chapel blew out when the rest of the chapel blew up. Deuce kept himself still over his mother, whispering, "It's okay, *Mamma,* it's okay," to keep her calm. She didn't make a sound, but she did pat his wrist.

As soon as he was certain the explosion was over, Deuce jumped up, and said to Iniya, "Can you make us some kind of shield?"

"Yes. Of short duration." She got that faraway look she got when she was processing information and making things—he still had not figured out how she manufactured weapons and like that seemingly out of air, but now was not the time to film a documentary—so while she was working on the problem, he turned to his mom, and said, "Can you run a lot? Can you run fast?"

"Absolutely." She took his hand. "Just so you know, I took an oath to protect you with my life."

He was alarmed. "Humph. Just so you know, Italian males don't put up with that kind of *schiamazzo.*"

She actually smiled. "What a quaint society."

"Iniya, we're running," he said, charging into the depths of

43

the tunnel. It was dirty and grimy—typical Borgioli sloppi-
ness, that the escape route to and from their Family chapel
was not maintained—and Deuce fervently hoped his mother
would not die in it. It would be such a disrespect to her. Of
course, the thought of her ever dying—especially now that he
had found her—was almost more than he could handle.

When you were raised in a Family, death was something
that was on your mind most of the time. Not in a grim way,
not in a scary way. It was the sort of thing you kept track of,
same as if you checked to make sure your blaster was charged
before you went out of your apartment.

That was why he was now dragging her relentlessly as she
slowed, trying not to worry if he was making her go too fast,
because better that she was winded than dead.

Then the blasting started. Deuce was crushed. He had no
doubt it was Angelo.

"How's the shield?" he yelled to Iniya.

"Current status good, but too many variables," she replied.
"Will not hold."

Variables as in, blaster pulses? The chance that the bad guys
would blow up the tunnel? Deuce didn't know, but he didn't
have time for the details.

"We've got to get out of here," Deuce said to his mother.
In his day, there had been a secret exit about twenty feet up
and to the right. It looked to be maybe their only escape route,
if the damn thing was still there.

No doubt he had the current, general state of chaos to thank
for the fact that no one was bulleting toward them from the
other end of the tunnel, which was just your basic SOP when
you were trying to take someone out . . .

*Whoops. Careful what you pray for, Deuce. Because baby,
you just got it.*

In the form of a fully loaded aichy bearing down on them
at high noon.

He yanked Connie behind himself and threw both of them
to the right side of the tunnel.

"Crawl," he shouted at her. "Don't stand up."

To his surprise, she crawled the correct street way, fists
clenched, forearm over forearm, and she hustled right along.
What do they teach these surrogates, anyway? Despite the

tumult, he had a fleeting image of some seriously enhanced mercenary bellowing, "Go, go!" to a bunch of very pregnant women.

The aichy started blasting, missing them wildly. As in not trying to hit them at all.

Friends, he thought. *Thank God I've got some.*

"Can you identify approaching vehicle?" Deuce shouted at Iniya.

"No," she yelled back, although it sounded more like an increase of Mr. Wong's normal voice than a yell.

"Don't matter," he yelled. "I think it's friendly." To his mom and the robot both, he added, "If they stop, jump in. Iniya, help my mom if you have to make a choice."

They both stared at him blankly.

"Do it," he insisted.

"Deuce of Moon, you are key," Iniya said.

"Baby, I'm just a guy. Guys, there are lots of." He jerked as a blaster pulse slammed into a crate beside his right hand. "You're a remote data terminal to an alien race, for God's sake." He looked at Connie. "And you're my mother."

"You are Godfather of Moon," Iniya insisted.

Then the barrage really heated up, with pulse after pulse homing in on them. The aichy returned fire; it moved slowly, almost hovering, and Deuce was slightly more inclined to think it might contain a friend. Or else someone who wanted him dead even more than Angelo did.

But it kinda didn't matter at this point, because they clearly were not going to make it to the exit. The boxes and crates round them were just about gone, and Deuce figured the only reason none of the three of them had been hit was because he and his mother had prayed in church.

There was no more time to dither. The aichy pulled up and a gull-wing door opened up.

"Go! Go!" Deuce shouted.

Iniya grabbed him around the biceps of his left arm and did the same with his mom's right arm. Then she practically threw them both at the opened aichy door.

A blaster pulse sliced Deuce's arm.

"Damn it!" he shrieked, and passed out.

* * *

He woke up because Iniya gave him something to wake up. He stared into Mr. Wong's robot eyes, then turned his head and looked at his mother.

"It's the left one," she said wryly.

It was the same arm that the main data terminal aboard *Gambler's Star* had regrown. He had originally lost the limb during the attack on the Moonsider Liberation Front canteen. It hurt like hell—not that he would ever say hell in front of his mother—and he grunted in almost-silent pain as he tried to ascertain their current situation.

The interior of the van was dark, and Deuce detected no other passengers. No clue as to whether they had been picked up by friend or foe.

"Deuce of Moon, all instrumentalities available to this remote terminal have been exhausted," Iniya said.

"In English," he groaned. "Or Italian."

"More weapons and shields impossible without access to manufacturing facilities."

" 'Kay."

He thought about all the gas movies and flatfilms he had seen about mobsters. Copsnrobbers, they were called. Family men often showed them at get-togethers—bachelor parties, war meetings, wakes. Most of them were a real hoot, especially how everybody could get shot a hundred million times and still run around like maybe they had chipped a tooth.

In the real world, pain hurt, and Deuce was definitely not feeling so good. He tried to turn his head to look at his wound, but not surprisingly, he couldn't move. He knew he was going into shock. The first time he been shot in his real arm, Mr. Wong had been able to stabilize him long enough to conduct a sit-down. Also, to be interrogated by that moronic policeman, O'Connor, who, he sincerely hoped, had died in the explosion the MLF had perped on the the last Family sit-down held before the Moon got invaded.

Then the docs replaced his arm, and it was better than new. He had a slightly increased respect for cyborgs, who, as a rule, he did not feel all that comfortable around. It was not so bad having a mechanical part or two.

The faces of his mother and his remote data terminal swirled and blurred. He was going, and going fast. He said, "Ma, you do what they say if they got ultimatums."

"Deuce," she said urgently.

Then he was dreaming that he and Castle were on a yacht in a real ocean—which he had never seen, only holos—and Hunter had his arm around him. Hunter was spouting the Bible verse he had laid on him when they both thought Hunter might be dying:

There were giants in the earth in those days; and also after that, when the sons of God came in unto the daughters of men, and they bare children to them, the same became mighty men which were of renown.

We ain't people, Deuce thought muzzily.

"That's right, son," Hunter drawled in his syrupy Southern accent. "Especially you, son. You're beyond all that. You just don't know it yet."

Then Deuce's eyes opened. He was looked straight into the eyes of a woman who looked vaguely familiar. Pretty but care-worn.

I gave her food, he thought, searching through his mind. *And a job.*

"Leslie," he whispered. Bonnanio, yeah, that was her last name.

She smiled. "Don McNamara."

"Annie?" he asked, dread washing through him as he struggled to sit up. If the little mite had been hurt . . . or worse . . .

"She's fine."

Images flooded through his mind: picking up Annie Bannany as she was running away from home to spare her mother the added burden of feeding her as well as her four other brothers and sisters; learning of the trouble there—her father had run off with some whore—and they were starving. He had commed his employees for supplies to be sent over.

And then the world had pretty much ended.

"Lie back," she said. "There's a medical team on the way."

"How?" he asked. He hurt. Bad.

"When you ordered the food for me, your people had my name on file. They needed a safe house to bring you to."

"*O, maledetta,*" he said fiercely. "That was wrong of them. A woman alone, N.A., you got kids—"

"No. I'm honored. And proud." She reached out to touch him, and hesitated. He wanted to tell her to go ahead. Because he needed someone solid to hold on to. His mom was good. Iniya, in her strange form, was good. But a young, pretty woman, a Moonsider, like him . . . that would be the best.

But he kept his mouth shut. Mostly because he hurt so much he couldn't talk.

Then he was swimming along in his sea of pain, he didn't know how long later, and Annie Bannany herself came to visit him.

She whispered, "Mr. McNamara, I've got a doll."

He grunted.

"Her name is Sunshine. Here she is."

It was very difficult to open his eyes, but he did it. Her face pitched and rolled, but he saw the serious little face, the big, brown eyes, the masses of black, curly hair. He managed a smile.

She raised the doll to his lips and made a kissing sound. Then she nestled the doll at his side.

"I'm not supposed to bother you." She turned and tiptoed away.

Don't go, Deuce wanted to tell her. But she was gone, and he was swimming along, just barely treading water. One more minute, two, and he was going to go under.

Then he heard voices.

"Mrs. Lockheart, we're not sure we can save him."

"Mr. Wong, did Mr. McNamara file a Plan of Succession with you?"

"I'll call for a hearse. Or maybe we should just keep this hush-hush."

"It was his cousin. I'm sure of it. McNamara was an idiot to trust him."

He opened his eyes. The man who had just called him an idiot was no other than Detective O'Connor. *Funny how he gets around. Also, impressive.*

If I live through this, I'm buying him. Whatever it takes, I'll pay it.

I'm gonna need guys like him.

*　　*　　*

Then brown eyes and a surgical mask were staring down at him. They blinked, and the mask moved.

"Don McNamara, we've surgically removed your arm and replaced it with a mechanical."

He nodded, kind of. At least, he thought he did.

"You sustained several other injuries. A number of pulses to the heart and the lungs. We feel it's in your best interest to replace these organs with cloned replacements."

He made a face. At least, he thought he did. It was not exquisite news. The same thing had happened to Joey, his now-dead brother. Cloned organs were inferior to originals. Better than nothing, however.

So count your blessings, Arturino, he could almost hear his dead mamma exhorting him.

By the time Deuce was put back together, the Moon had been taken apart.

He should have expected it, should have planned better for it, but maybe he was so young he was still stupid. At twenty-seven, you still believe in one or two things. He hadn't thought that was so, and it was an embarrassing thing to know about himself. Family life tended to erase the stars from your eyes real fast.

But at any rate, the Earthside forces had taken over, at considerable loss of Moonside life and property. The casinos were nationalized, and the Families dis-Enfranchised. In short, the Moon's entire economy and way of life had been ruthlessly destroyed by a planet which did not give a damn about the satellite until there was money to be made, and the merest hint that maybe one or two Moonsiders had minds of their own.

"*Bastardi,*" Deuce said, to his mother, seated with him and Little Gino Scarlatti in a makeshift bunker a good, safe distance away from the Bonnanio trailer. Hidden among the skeletal structures of Darkside City, Hunter's massive casino city—Deuce could not now imagine ever completing it—the bunker was heavily fortified, thanks to Iniya, and also nearly impossible to locate. She'd cloaked it with all kinds of very neat alien technology. Deuce was taking notes, bet your life on that.

Little Gino was one of the Scarlatti Select of Six—they ran their operation with six leaders, one of whom was then named *capo di tutti di capi*, essentially, in English, the big cheese.

Little Gino was not him. This was not good news for Deuce. Of all the Scarlattis—the whole Family of which terrified Deuce, they were such weirdos—Little Gino probably scared him the worst. The strange, erratic guy would just as soon slit you from sternum to crotch as toast your health.

"You gotta get back in the action," Little Gino was saying to Deuce.

Deuce thought about telling this little no-account what he could do with his action, if he was so uncouth as to actually lecture a Don.

The Scarlattis had officially gone along with the Earthside takeover, and that infuriated Deuce. He had no idea how Little Gino felt about it, except that the whacked-out drug addict was smart enough to make a bid for whatever power he could snag with an end run. That is, appeal to Deuce for help privately, and then, if Deuce and his whatever-he-had army somehow pulled off a reversal of fortunes, Little Gino could benefit.

"Godfather," Little Gino said, "you got all my people backing you."

"How many might that be?" There would be no way, at present, to tell if he was lying.

"I got at least a sixth of the Scarlattis that are left," Little Gino told him.

Deuce hid his surprise. "About two hundred soldiers, or are you counting their families?"

"Soldiers, Don McNamara." Gino let himself look proud, which Deuce could see why. That was a good haul, if it was true.

Deuce considered what to say next. How to proceed. He didn't know how two hundred people could so much as follow Gino into one of those restaurants on the Strip that offered breakfast practically for free. They had to be psychotic losers like Gino.

While Deuce was pondering, Gino blurted out, "Plus I can tell you where everybody stands, just about."

Putz, Deuce thought, because Gino was raising without calling.

"The Families, I mean," Gino said. "Ask me."

"Fair enough," Deuce said casually. "Let's start with the

Chans. What happened to Yuet?" Deuce asked. "What's her deal?"

"She's gone underground. Which surprises me." Little Gino sat back in his chair and crossed his legs like he was not so nervous he might wet his pants. He tried to give off that innocent, *Excuse me, I'm used to being waited on, I'm so powerful yet humble, where the hell's my drink and bar snacks?* atmosphere.

Not one to ever show his hand, Deuce looked a bit alarmed, and said, "Hey, Little Gino, you need something to drink and a little something to go along with it."

Little Gino looked pleased, and Deuce's mother looked privately amused. *Ma, you're a chip off the old block,* Deuce thought proudly. She also knew better than to get up and get it herself. That evened them out with Little Gino: The mother of the Godfather of the Moon did not so humble herself. Not for guys like Little Gino, anyway. That left a moron like him something to aspire to.

Deuce commed someone, and one of Deuce's loyal foot soldiers name of Downtown Dallas took the runt's order with the graciousness of a cocktail waitress who had her own little side business pleasing men in a, ahem, more specialized capacity.

Deuce liked the kid, who, with a name like Dallas, had to be from some kind of mixed marriage—like the Caputos, the Borgiolis were old-fashioned when it came to preserving their Italian heritage. Dallas looked very Italian, however; sculpted face set off with a Roman nose, dark hair and eyes, and a trim little beard.

For his part, Deuce acted like he had all the time in the world; he had, however, like minus thirty seconds before his next round of painkillers. But you did not let the enemy know that.

And everybody except Connie was a potential enemy. Not a sad thing, just a true one.

Dallas brought Gino his young, dumb-kid rum and Coke and some pretzels made from real flour, not crater, which Gino probably couldn't even tell the difference. Deuce liked Dallas even better, cuz so what if the chump couldn't tell? Deuce, Dallas, and Connie could, and their class and contempt was shared in a silent mutual smirk.

Gino, ignorant of all the nuances, sat back like a fool and continued trying to impress Deuce with his gossip. Roger Smith—his brother and co-Godfather, Abraham, having mysteriously disappeared—would continue to head the Smiths' Wild West, courtesy of the government. Deuce made a mental note to drop in on Roger, very privately. Deuce had Honorary Affiliation with the Smiths, but he had no idea what kind of greeting he would receive, even without the fascist Earthsiders knowing he was there.

The new C.E.O. of the Van Aadams Family—they did not deign to call their Godfather a Godfather—the newest kid on their block, some dopey third cousin—was also going for the bennies awarded to turncoats.

"His name is *Sydney*?" Deuce asked, laughing.

"Yeah." Gino looked edgy. Clearly he did not know that the Van Aadamses originally came from Earthside Australia, and that Sydney was the name of the capital city of the country.

So Deuce said, "Kinda sissy name, *capisce*?"

"Oh. Yeah. *Sì*." Little Gino looked only mildly relieved. Maybe he was under the misapprehension that Sydney was a classy name.

Deuce was depressed. This kid was hoke city. Deuce had to cultivate some better contacts, or he was dead. When you played the high-stakes games, you wanted the best pit boss, the smartest dealer, and you did not want the other players to be too stupid. The game had to be smart, or ineptitude and plain dumb luck could wipe you out.

Wiping out was no option, not in this game. Not when you were playing with the only deck you had. And your markers were the lives of people who figured you for the guy with the winning hand.

"Okay, so we've talked about Sydney and Roger," Deuce prompted, to get the guy back on track. "What's up with the Chans?"

"Well, as I said, no Yuet," Little Gino informed him. "Sying II got blown up. No Chan has come forward. I think word's been given down that anybody tries to deal with the government, they're dead."

"So who's running the show?"

"Department of Fairness officials." .

Deuce actually winced with physical pain, and not just because the painkillers had worn off. He had never in a million years dreamed that this kind of *schiamazzo* would happen in his lifetime.

Little Gino said, "Your cousin, Angelo—"

Deuce interrupted. "*Ne o abuto abbastanza di tutte queste storie bestiale.*" Which meant, in the language, I've heard enough.

He stood. Little Gino was a mixture of extremely apprehensive and maybe the teeniest bit smug. Which was stupid, to let Deuce know about either emotion. You played this game, you better have a poker face so good the other guy wondered if you were dead.

"Okay," Deuce gritted. He looked at his mother, who said, "Deuce, you've got that other meeting."

Little Gino was not too stupid to stand up. He set down his unfinished drink and made a little bow. Downtown Dallas picked up the glass and the bowl of pretzels and exited.

"Godfather," Gino said, reaching for Deuce's hand.

Deuce let him kiss the back of it. Rings, he didn't have, except for his wedding ring, and kissing that was over the top, as far as he was concerned.

Then Downtown Dallas, who didn't realize it but had just gotten himself a promotion, returned, opened the door, and escorted Little Gino out like he was the freakin' Pope.

As soon as the door was closed again, Deuce collapsed. He whispered, "Ma, get my medicine."

His guts—old and new—were still on fire when Detective O'Connor came to visit a few minutes later. Escorted in by Dallas, who was working the courtesy angle like a pro, the redheaded detective had had quite a bit of body work done himself, no doubt courtesy of the explosion at the Stellaluna restaurant that they had both survived.

"Don McNamara," he said, inclining his head a bit, which told Deuce reams about where the guy stood—not in direct opposition, at the very least. He was an Earthsider, true, but the man had a lot invested Moonside. His career, for one thing; but when you're stuck smack dab in a war, sometimes those concerns didn't concern you so much as they once did.

"*Buon giorno,*" Deuce replied, putting at least one card on the table: Used to be they were sworn enemies, a Family man and a lawman. And not so long ago, O'Connor had tried to serve a search warrant on his home when a very pregnant Sparkle had been there alone. Well, not exactly alone; their home had been an armed camp, but he, Deuce, had not been home.

There was business, and there was messing with your family. Which could never be anything but personal.

O'Connor replied smoothly, *"Buon giorno."*

Deuce said, "My painkillers are kicking in. Just so you know."

The man nodded. He said, "You want a witness to this conversation? Your mother?"

Guy moved fast. Deuce was considerably cheered. After the strangeness that was Little Gino, a straight-arrow sharpshooter like O'Connor was a breath of fresh air.

"Naw." Deuce waved his hand. Naturally, he was covertly recording the conversation, and he could only assume that O'Connor was, too.

"I got a report on your arm," O'Connor said.

It took Deuce a minute. "My . . . arm."

"The one you lost, which was summarily replaced by a mechanical; that apparently grew back on its own, because when you lost it this second time, it was a human arm again."

"Huh. They must have screwed up my chart again," Deuce said blandly. He was livid. Whoever had let O'Connor see that report was in trouble, of the sort for which Family men were renowned.

"So I asked to see the arm," O'Connor went on. He shrugged. "Well, I didn't exactly ask."

"In the middle of a war, you had all this free time?" Deuce asked.

"The war's over." He leaned forward. "How did your arm grow back?"

Thing was, in this day and age, you could grow organs, but you still couldn't grow limbs. You could grow all the skin again, or the veins, like that. But the whole thing, no.

So O'Connor's little discovery was newsworthy, to put it mildly.

They looked at each other. Deuce didn't even blink. Poker was his game, through and through.

O'Connor said, "I want in."

"Oh?"

"I know a lot of people." He leaned forward. "People who want to get to know you, to your—and our—mutual benefit."

"Yeah, like who?" Deuce said bluntly. In the old days, no one could hold out longer than him. But he was exhausted, and the painkillers were making him lose whatever edge he still had. *God, I'm tired of all this,* he thought. Alarm bells sounded. He couldn't be tired of all this. Guys like him weren't allowed to get tired.

"These people," Deuce said.

O'Connor looked surprised that they weren't going to waltz around the room a couple more times. He asked, almost gently, "Your painkillers fully kicked in?"

Deuce was even more alarmed. Never in his life had another man cut him slack in a business setting; what, did O'Connor figure Deuce was losing his edge? That he had to be coddled?

Deuce said, "I want a for instance."

"For instance . . . Earthside factions who want in."

Deuce took that in. The picture clicked into focus, and he was relieved from the top of his skull to the bottom of his toes, which were all still his original ones. Deuce was still regarded as the Independent candidate. You had your co-opted Family guys, and your underground Family guys, but Deuce was a free agent. Somebody who could move fast.

On the other hand, so could a loose cannon.

He said, "I'm the point man for the declaration of war."

O'Connor snorted and shrugged his shoulders. "My people don't need to put their alliance with you in the papers." He leaned forward. "They could change this entire situation in a heartbeat. Believe me."

Deuce got commed. He tapped his badge and told it, "Earphone." Then he said, "Yeah."

"Deuce, it's Connie. The doctor who operated on you wants to talk to you. There's some kind of problem."

Yeah, I'll say. His staff can be bribed.

"Thanks, Ma. I'll deal with that in a few minutes."

He disconnected and looked at O'Connor. "I got another appointment. Let's meet again in, say, a few hours?"

"Whatever you want." O'Connor stood. He held out his

hand. Deuce did not shake it. O'Connor did not appear to be offended. Not that Deuce cared.

O'Connor was almost at the door when he turned back around. "You'd have to go to Earth," he said, and left.

A minute later, a bomb went off.

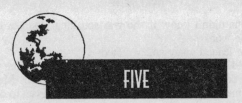

FIVE

Sparkle woke up with a start. Her body ached; she was shaking so hard her teeth were chattering. She had a headache and her bones throbbed, as if someone had drilled each one open and dropped in a cube of ice.

And yet, she was so hot she was perspiring. Heat rolled off her in waves.

We're near !kth space, she thought.

Dread engulfed her, and for a moment, she was blind—literally—with fright. Danger surrounded them. How could Hunter not sense it?

Perhaps, for him, there was no danger. Perhaps this place was lethal only for her, or for the children.

The children . . .

She leaped out of bed. The room tilted hard to the left; she lost her balance and stumbled forward, trying to catch herself. Crashing into a chair that had been pulled up beside her bed, she knocked it over and tumbled to the floor.

The chair falling made a loud, echoing noise that rattled her jaw. Her ears closed up, and she could hear nothing.

As if it were too heavy for her body, her head slammed against the hard floor. A series of cracks jagged through her face and blood spurted from her nose.

She couldn't hear. She couldn't see.

Hunter burst into the room—she knew it was Hunter, but she didn't know how she knew—cradled her, and scooped her up, carrying her back onto the bed while he commed for medical. Leaning over her, he took her hand up in his.

"I'm so sick," she tried to tell him. But she couldn't see

him, and she didn't know if she was speaking aloud or only thinking the words.

Then she leaned away and vomited.

She could see and hear again. His face swam before her, filled with concern. Real concern; she was touched. Maybe she was something more to him after all than a vessel to carry his children.

"Is it from the delivery?" he asked, meaning the babies. Maybe it would have occurred to her another time to ask him how she should know, but she did know.

"It's from here." Her voice was thick and blurred. It didn't even sound to her like a human voice.

He nodded slowly, and when she looked at him, he was clearly very troubled.

"Is it bad here?" he asked. "Is there something wrong?"

She nodded. "Very wrong. Hunter, I'm so hot. It's hot."

Then a team of medics clattered into the room, checking her over in lightning speed as if she were a trauma victim. Someone said something about a dangerously high fever. Another talked about her electrolytes. Within seconds, she was hooked up to an IV.

Hunter stood out of the way, but his gaze never wavered from the bed. Though she hovered on the verge of loathing him for what he had done to Deuce and her, she was grateful for his protective presence. Despite everything, he was still the most powerful human being on Earth and in the Moon. That must count for something where they were now. Otherwise, why would they have chosen to deal with him?

After a time, one of the medical staff said to her, "Temp's stabilized. Mrs. McNamara, do we have your permission to operate? You seem to be bleeding internally."

"What?" Her gaze ticked past him to Hunter. "What?"

He shook his head. "They can't figure it out, darlin'. But please, give your permission. We'll also repair your nose."

She thought about holding out her hand to Hunter to gain some comfort. But she was not that kind of person, never had been, and could not be now.

But he moved past the medical people and all the machines as they began wheeling in more equipment, and enormous lights, and he did take her hand. He folded her fingers over his and said, "Are you in pain?"

"No." She kept her face smooth and expressionless as he kissed her fingertips. "Just a bad headache."

"I'm sorry." He frowned. "We can't turn back."

She didn't say anything. She didn't know what to say.

Then they gave her something to make her drowsy, and placed a mask over her face; and she found herself thinking that she might not wake up, ever.

Deuce.

His face floated before her eyes, along with the certainty that he, too, was in terrible danger.

Iniya reached down and lifted a piece of the bunker ceiling off Deuce's head. About a dozen of Deuce's trusted security guys were outside, looking to find who had tossed the bomb into his makeshift home.

Deuce groaned, and said, "You know, all these explosions. I'm nostalgic for the old days, when we only blew each other up on holidays and other special occasions."

Iniya threw the piece of ceiling to the ground where it smashed against something that sounded like fine china—not that they had any, but there was some jade green casinoware somebody had pilfered from the Chan's Pearl of Heaven Casino. Deuce briefly wondered what the breakage was about, then grunted as the remote data terminal pulled him deftly to his feet.

"Are you intact?" she asked him.

He nodded. "What about Detective O'Connor?"

"Located. No longer intact."

"Damn." He smoothed back his hair, which, if it had not been white-blond already, would certainly be white by now, with all these stressful occurrences. "You were not present for any of our discussion, but did you eavesdrop?"

For all he knew, she had bugged every square inch of the Moon, and him, too. She was an alien intelligence who had access to all kinds of stuff he couldn't even imagine, much less suspect her of doing. It gave him the creeps, because if she wasn't really and truly on his side—if she was just using him to get past the doorman—he was in big trouble if she ever turned her laser guns on him.

But why break a trend? he thought philosophically. *With most people, I'm in big trouble.*

The main problem as he saw it was, he had no strong ally. Too bad Detective O'Connor had now met an untimely demise; it sounded to Deuce like some action was finally going to take place. As in, good cards. Face cards. Well, if they had sent one messenger, they could send another.

And if that one got blown up, another.

His badge vibrated, and he tapped it, said, "Earphone," and got his mother again.

"Gabriel Kinkade-Jones to see you."

Gabriel. With a name like that, he had to be a Mormon. Deuce said, "And I care because?"

"He's the new head of the MLF." His mother's voice was neutral, but even she must realize this was big news: A second Mormon had been picked to lead the MLF. That had to mean at least one faction of the Mormons had broken with the Van Aadamses. This was *molto* shocking, to say the very least: The MLF was far more violent than any Family had ever been, at least since the original turf wars had been fought a century ago.

Deuce sighed. He needed some people. He needed trusted bodyguards. He need confidants. He had a mom and a robot. Angelo, he sorely missed. *Cretino.* It occurred to Deuce that he would have to put a hit out on his own, best-loved cousin. That depressed him worse than not having any other close acquaintances.

"How's the dog?" he asked his mother.

"She's good, Deuce. She's a great dog."

He sighed as she disconnected.

"Iniya, stick close," he said. He shrugged off his tiredness and his *agita.* You grew up in a Family, you did not whine about the hand you were dealt. If you couldn't get better cards, you either bluffed or folded. That was the Life. If you couldn't handle it, then you could always opt out and work as a janitor, become one of those bums who stood on the street corners with their hands out, signs around their necks: WILL WORK FOR OXYGEN.

Actually, Deuce had helped a few guys like that. One had come up to thank him later, told him he had a job and was getting married. Where were all those guys now, the ones who had loved him so much when he'd stood up to Hunter in the early days, when everybody had been afraid of the evil invader from Earth?

Footsteps neared his closed door. Iniya rose and assumed a sort of martial stance, looking rather imposing, if he did say so. Her chassis, Mr. Wong, was slender but gave off that aura of *aiya!* quick-chop kung-fu solidness. Like the Chans. The younger generation of that Family had always been extremely into the whole *tong*-thing, karate-chop your enemy's head off first and ask questions later.

He brightened. Just before all this idiocy, he had gone to the people he knew best: the Casino Liaisons. Not the particular individuals he had himself worked with when he was a Liaison—they'd either been promoted or had died—but their counterparts.

He had gone to them, and they would have done wonderful, good things for the situation if Deuce had not accidentally declared war on Earthside. As far as he knew, that infrastructure was still in place.

Lee Chan had been the new Casino Liaison to the Borgiolis, and it was in that capacity that Deuce had joined forces with him. He had been his first, best hope. He might be again.

First order of business, though, was to get through the meeting with Gabriel Kinkade-Jones. Then he'd do what he did best—move and shake.

Deuce cracked the knuckle on his left hand. Suddenly he was itching to get the hell out of there, pain or no pain.

The door opened. Two very enhanced MLF security guards, tricked out in truly impressive battle gear, barged in and gave the room a scan. Iniya was on red alert, or whatever passed for it in her quadrant of wherever. Maybe they didn't have colors like red. Maybe they didn't have eyes. Or maybe they had lots of them.

Anyway, she had previously explained to him that Hunter Castle had outfitted Mr. Wong with all kinds of detecto stuff, including scans for hidden Peekissimos, that kind of thing. Weapons warning systems. After standing a bit like a hunting dog—which Deuce, frankly, had never seen—she relaxed and went into at ease.

"Okay, General, it's clear," one of the MLF guys said as he walked to the doorway.

And then there was Gabriel Kinkade-Jones. Who, to his
surprise, was a broad. A very gorgeous broad, he might add,
all wild-haired auburn like some old-time warrior queen in a
flatfilm about jungle legends and like that, wearing not an
MLF cammy outfit and a beret, like they went in for over
there, but a pretty darn nice stretchy black catsuit. She had
accented it with silver cuff bracelets and a heavy silver necklace, and black low-heeled boots.

Meow.

Now there's a dame, he thought.

Not that there was anything outré about ladies running
things. Gina Rille had headed up the MLF after her father's
deterioration. Papa Levi Shoemaker had rescued Deuce from
certain death, but Gina had contemplated young Signor Mc-
Namara's execution. With a heavy heart, to be sure, for she
loved Deuce. Nothing personal. Business was the nature of
their beast.

Unfortunately—or not so, for him—she had gotten blown
up when Deuce had been rescued from the MLF base. It was
a death he honestly mourned.

The Mormons tended to be an old-fashioned breed, and they
didn't usually go in for women leaders. Exceptions and all
that, to prove the rule, but by and large, it wasn't done. And
not by women with men's names.

But here she was.

"*Buon giorno, signorina,*" he said graciously, bowing as she
swept farther into the room like she was wearing a crown, a
cape, and carrying a bouquet of a dozen simulated florals.
Here she is, Miss Terrorist.

"*Signora,*" she corrected. He saw the wedding ring as she
said it.

"*Ah. Mi scusi.*" The male in him was disappointed, even
though it didn't make any sense. "Sorry for the mess. I think
your people redecorated my office."

She flashed him a faint smile as he kicked a few pieces of
debris out of her way en route to the official secret club hand-
shake. Very warm, very smooth, very strong.

Then he chivalrously located a chair and silently invited her
to sit. His brand-new guts were starting to hurt again, and he
was a bit surprised. Joey, his brother, had received cloned
organs, and he had very rarely kvetched about them hurting.

Joey was a big baby, too, and he loved attention and fussing over, especially by nurses with big *poppas*, which Hunter was amused to provide for him. So, to make a short story long, if Joey had been in even minor discomfort, he would not have hesitated to mention it.

However, Joey's organs had been grown on board *Gambler's Star* by Hunter's crack team of superdoctors. Also, Hunter had probably employed the miraculous main data terminal that connected him directly to the !kth. The main data terminal had grown Deuce's arm back for him, a feat which human medical science could not currently duplicate. So he figured he himself had gotten Grade-B guts, as opposed to Joey's top-of-the-line ones.

Oh, well, two of a kind beat out a handful of meatballs any day. In other words, mediocre guts were better than no guts at all.

"So, *signora*," he said. "To what, God help me"—he crossed himself—"do I owe the honor?"

But Ms. Kinkade-Jones was not paying attention to him. She was eyeing Iniya, that is to say, Mr. Wong, and apparently not liking what she saw.

"Is this Mr. Castle?" she asked.

"No," Deuce replied, startled. If she knew Hunter had had a makeover to look like Mr. Wong—since discarded—then she probably knew he was alive. "Mr. Castle has left the area in *Gambler's Star*."

She looked impressed. "You're telling me the truth."

"Which you know because . . ." He took a wild stab. "Bernardo Chang is your spy aboard my boss's vessel."

Her smile grew. She was enjoying their little game.

"Close, but no banana. It's Colvin Pines."

The CO of *Gambler's Star*? Deuce was impressed. *Mamma mia,* if Deuce's own spies were half as good as the MLF's, he'd be richer than Hunter by now.

"And he's sending you reports."

She frowned. "We haven't heard from him in days." She looked at him. He shook his head.

"Hunter's out of range for me, too."

This was a sore point with him. Iniya asserted that she couldn't run her simulation and directly access the !kth data terminal on board the *Star* to snoop around about Hunter, which did not make a bit of sense to Deuce. If the simulation was to interface with the !kth properly, at some point, there had to be a linkup with the !kth terminal or a !kth entity of some sort, or something. This was not a question. This was a fact. Iniya was lying to him. However, she swore that their technology was so advanced that they could, indeed, interact with another race entirely by rote.

All he could figure was that, in time, she would trust him sufficiently to share significant data with him. So the best he could do was bide his time . . . and hope that that time would be soon.

Said remote data terminal was sitting in the corner like she had turned herself off. He hoped she was recording and double- and triple-filing everything. Even if she was sending it all back to her bosses in D'innland. Or !kth-town. Or wherever actually held her loyalty.

Gabriel crossed her knees—wow, hubba hubba, thighs like rocks—and said, bluntly, "The MLF has splintered. The group who just bombed you is no longer under my command."

"I'm breaking open the champagne."

She narrowed her eyes. "The lines have been drawn among the Families. We know who is cooperating with the Conglomerated Nations of Earth and who has run for cover. It's assumed that Earthside used your declaration of war as an excuse to invade, but the smart money knows that's all it was. An excuse."

She shrugged. "The basically intelligent money, as well. However, our constituency, the Non-Affiliateds who are so disenfranchised and distanced from the system that they're living in a fantasy, believe that you, and you alone, are responsible for what's happened."

"Also, it was a miscommunication," Deuce said, raising his hand to protest his innocence. "I never intended to declare war, never in a million years." It took everything in him not to glare at Iniya, who, if she was telling him the truth, had not been the one to declare war on his behalf. Some !kth operative had done that dirty work when Deuce had been linked up to *their* remote data terminal instead of the D'inn one.

He continued earnestly, "*Davvero, davvero*, Signorina Kinkade-Jones, which in the language means that I am telling you the truth."

"I figured as much." At his questioning look, she shrugged. "You're much too smart to do something so . . . maverick."

He was touched. "*Mi scusi*, but you don't even know me."

"I know *of* you, Mr. McNamara." She gave him a sultry, flirtatious look. There was no denying that it was more than friendly. He thought sadly of Gina Rille, who had also been extraflirtatious in the beginning.

"My reputation exceeds me," he shot back.

"We'll see," she drawled. "Now. I'm here because I want you to join forces with us. I know you have supporters. I don't know how many."

Finally, a potential ally. Or else, a very interesting opponent. Either way, he won.

She waited a beat. Then she said, "Your thoughts, Mr. Mc-Namara?"

"All the good ones," he answered, "are married or gay."

She chuckled. "I'm a widow, Mr. McNamara." She cocked her head. "However, you are married."

"She left me, I think. I'm not sure." He shrugged. "We're not currently speaking."

She started to say something. Then she simply smiled. She said, "What do you know about my faith?"

"The Mormon religion, or the MLF one?"

She sighed. "That's such a misconception. The MLF is not a religious organization."

He crossed his arms. "Lady, I've been to your HQ. Before it got blown up. I talked to Shoemaker. I knew Gina Rille very well."

She inclined her head. "She cared for you very much."

"Yeah, when she wasn't trying to whack me. Listen, you wackos have me pegged for the Messiah or something. I'm supposed to part rivers and like that." He narrowed his eyes. "I call a war, the bombs come. Am I right?"

She shrugged. "I couldn't have headed the MLF if doing so interfered with my private beliefs as a Latter-day Saint."

He cocked his head. "You aren't answering my questions. You guys go in for Messiahs, too. You've got God living on some planet."

"We're all expressions of God," she replied.

"You're hedging your bet," he accused. "You guys think plain old people become gods eventually. This life is like part of school. You die, you get your report card from St. Peter. If you done good, you graduate. So you go to the next grade. Keep getting good grades, poof! You're a god."

She chuckled. "How well you put it. But I want to stress that that is not the belief system of the MLF in general."

He cut her off with a wave of his hand. "Hey. I know Family guys who say they're against the death penalty, go out and whack a guy for giving an out-of-date code on a storage facility for frozen cratersteak."

She imitated the tilt of his chin. "Which is why the MLF thinks we should replace the Family system with an independent government run by democratically elected representatives."

"Which is why the Families shudder at the thought of you guys taking over. You are incredibly naive. Anybody can buy an election. And anybody who wins one, can be bought."

There was a silence. He said, "You want something to drink? I know you Mormons don't touch the good stuff—"

"Do you have any Tycho Delight?" she asked.

He raised his brows. Tycho Delight had been Joey's hard liquor of choice. Moon-fermented, Moon-distilled, Moon-bottled gin. Very, very hard liquor.

He didn't say anything. Neither did she. He gestured to the mess, and said, "If you can find it, you can drink the whole bottle."

She laughed. Lustily. "Let's go out for a drink," she suggested. "I have a couple of armored vehicles. One for a decoy, just in case."

He shrugged. He was tired of being cooped up in what was obviously a known target, and, by the by, so much for the fabulous technology of the space brothers protecting him from harm's way. He hoped that somewhere out there, beneath the pale moonlight, somebody's alien butt was being kicked for nearly getting Mr. Big Shot Deuce McNamara killed.

"Is there any place over here we can go?" she asked, preparing to stand. She meant Darkside City, which was a nice tip of the fedora to Deuce. Sure, there were joints, and they were busier than ever, because everybody was trying to forget their troubles. Mob families through time had learned that war and strife were usually very good for business.

However, all things considered, Deuce would prefer the

slightly more anonymous setting of the original, more populous casino city located on—or rather, in—the bright side of the Moon.

"I'd prefer to go to Moonbase Vegas," he told her. "I want to get in the thick of the action. I've been repaired, in case you hadn't noticed; hence, recuperating. I'm a little behind the curve."

Or the eight ball.

"Deuce," Iniya protested. That was interesting: it was the first time she had referred to him as just plain old Deuce, and not "Deuce of Moon." She was parsing, bless her soul. Or whatever passed for a soul in her universe. She said, "Moonbase Vegas is not secure."

"Yeah, well." A human would detect the irony in his voice. So would a state-of-the-art mechanical. Not so alien dames, looked like. Deuce hoped Gabe here figured Mr. Wong was just poorly programmed, but it was hard to imagine that any product manufactured by Castle Industries was less than first-class. Also, a bit painful for the ego.

"Ma," he said suddenly, comming Connie, "I want you to get out of here. Go to the next safe house." They had them scattered all over the place.

She commed back. "I didn't want to interrupt your meeting to tell you, but my bodyguards insisted I vacate. We're on the move already."

Deuce was extremely pleased. Those boys were going to be getting a lot of goodies in their Christmas stockings, that was for certain.

With Iniya and Downtown Dallas in tow, he went in Gabriel's car, not quite comfortable with the notion but hey, there it was. He couldn't decide if he was being decisive or reckless. It would be a very small matter to whack him right then.

Well, not to him.

They sneaked through the dark alleys and hidden sectors of the skeletal foundations of Darkside City. The sight of the naked beams and half-completed caverns made him melancholy. This town was a dream he sincerely doubted would ever see fruition.

Gone were thousands of jobs for N.A.'s. Family guys who had turned their backs on their oaths to be loyal to their Families until death, now faced death. Or maybe the government takeover of the Moon would prove a blessing in disguise for them, and in all the chaos, Families would be glad to be together, period, not the end of any specific cousin, nephew, or grandmother.

Though he didn't pray much outside of church—meaning the One True Church, holy, catholic, and apostolic—Deuce prayed now, for all the people who had died, and were dying, at a time that was not their right time. Moonsiders and Earthsiders alike. Special intentions; he prayed for his father, Hunter Castle, and his wife, Sparkle, and her kids.

That part hurt a little too much, and he shut his eyes against the pain. It was a well-established fact among wise guys that strong men hurt just like weak ones, only strong men usually did something about it. What Deuce could do, he had no idea.

To Deuce's surprise, it was less of a pain in the *culino* to get from Darkside City to Moonbase Vegas now than before the war, even before the hint of war. The security at the John Gotti Memorial Airlock was lax on account of the newly imported Earthside officials had no idea what was a real Moonsider ID and what was counterfeit. The guards only pretended to scrutinize tags and papers and like that, handing them back so fast you would think they were on fire.

Deuce and Gabriel's entourage scooted through much, much faster than ever before in Deuce's entire life. So fast, in fact, that he, she, and Downtown Dallas all burst into laughter. Iniya faked a knowing grin, and everyone stayed merry.

Then they were on the strip, and Deuce stared out the tinted Kevlite window like a kid just let out of prison and sighed for earlier, easier days.

There she was, his hometown, Moonbase Vegas. The neon was blazing. Encased in the silence of the aichy, he could almost hear the bells and whistles, the drunken laughter, the couples fighting, the constant *ching-ching-blip* of the games.

The shafts and tunnels extended without number or apparent order, although part of every Family kid's education included memorizing the layout of the vast warren, including booby traps and dead ends. As with the Borgioli escape tunnel, you just never knew when you were going to have cause to get the hell out of Dodge.

The hallmark of the base was the enormous, lasered-out

canyon that contained the entrances to the six Chartered Establishments. They were spectacular combinations of holos, neon, and lunaformed rock, extending straight up like old-fashioned, Earthside skyscrapers. Who knew how high? This being the land of the big con, few realized that the actual exteriors extended maybe as high as two stories.

The rest was illusion, an eye-popping craziness of lights and signs and flash encapsulated in the most sophisticated holos anywhere, powered by the massive superconducting mesh that surrounded the city.

Before the government takeover, over 275,000 tourists a year journeyed from Mother Earth to the pleasuredome. The pleasures it housed were, by Earth standards, wrong and nasty and sexy; everything forbidden was purveyable here in spades, diamonds, hearts, and clubs. Casinos and speakeasies, dives and joints and dens; hot girls and hotter boys and all the booze and drugs you could swallow. Sex at one-sixth gravity, dirty dancing at six times the price on Earth, if you could even find it on Earth—it was all temptingly available and incredibly easy to purchase on Moonbase Vegas.

The entrances to the dens of iniquity—the casinos—beckoned in a fairly straight line along Moonbase Boulevard. Each was decorated with the official colors of each Family, which were worn on the person of its Members and Affiliates with pride, except for many who had had the misfortune to end up in the low-class Borgioli Family.

The Lucky Star shimmered with the blue and white of the Caputo Family. The Caputos, the pioneers of the lifestyle in Moonbase Vegas, the first ones to come to the Moon, had maintained extremely close contact with the Earthside entertainment industry.

As a result, they could fill their lounges and auditoriums with all the big acts, and the big audiences with the two-drink minimum, just like the old days on Earthside. Two of the most anticipated shows were the Blasts from the Past temporary clone celebrity look-alike contest and the annual Elvis Festival, recently culminated in a "Heartbreak Hotel" charity marathon for drug awareness. Which was very much a cynical in-joke among Moonsiders; sure, everyone was aware of drugs.

The Lucky Star was also home to the Moonbase Vegas

Historical Museum, where all kinds of neat stuff was put on display, including the original eagle feather and golf ball from the astronaut period. However, truth was, they were not the real feather and ball; those had been stolen years before, and each Family privately believed they possessed the originals. Deuce happened to know—for a fact—that Hunter had had them last. What he didn't know was if they had been lost in the explosion that had changed the course of lunar history forever.

Not that anyone went to look at the fakes, anyway. Gravoids. *Cretini*. If it didn't extract cash from them in a colorful and amusing way, the tourists weren't interested.

But back to Moonbase: the Tour. Next was the Smiths' Wild West, in brown and black, which looked like an old fort from the cowboy days. You could grow your own food in the (hydroponic) garden, but the mere fact that real Earthside dirt was spread across the floors—and that real animals, including horses and cows, pooped real poop on it—made Moonsiders nuts. And most Earthsiders, too, truth be told, because nature and animals and all like that was fairly exotic down there, as well.

To top it off, there was this whole Indian thing going, with teepees and broads in leather bikinis (crater, but so what?) About seventy-five years ago, the Smiths were worried the Native Americans back down on Earth might protest, but they were too busy trying to survive to care about stereotypes and like that. And by now, here in the future, nobody really knew from anything else, so nobody cared.

However, gossip was they were going to shut down "Comanche Nights," the record-breaking show at the Wild West, amid government claims that it was losing money. Fact was, there were a lot of very naked people in that show.

To the west, on Moonside Freemont Street, glittered that truly embarrassing parody of glamor, the Borgiolis' casino, the Palazzo di Fortuna. Deuce's newly classed-up taste made it even more painful to acknowledge. The Borgiolis thought that holos of the Last Supper overlaid with glittering mosaics of gondoliers, and gas movies of men and women dressed in gauzy togas dangling grapes in front of each other looked fabulous. Truth was, they were *tackissimo*.

Even more hideously embarrassing was the massive animated figure of Michelangelo's *David* in the lobby. It ran through its schtick on the hour and the half; the vast majority of its routine centered around its big-guns genitalia, har-de-har-har-har.

Meanwhile, on the easternmost end of the Strip, on Bugsy Siegel Way, the Chan casino glittered in salmon and jade.

It was surreal and hallucinatory and altogether what Deuce thought a casino should be. Thirty-foot-tall green-stone rabbits perched on either side of the coral entrance. Deuce supposed most of the paying customers didn't realize that in gambler talk, a "rabbit" was an inexperienced player or a sucker, and everyone who worked in gaming, which was still seventy percent of the permanent population, according to government statistics, thought the rabbits were a very humorous joke.

Inside, the foyer was one thermodynamic self-combustion of Chinese legends all melting into one "This is China" fantasy medley: court ladies turning into frogs and back again in hues of jade, scarlet, blue, and all your metallic shades; kites wafting in the enhanced air; scarlet, blue, and purple flowers as tall as apartment colonies jutting through the roof of the cavernous foyer, a holo-projection of an ancient Chinese temple.

Banners and pennants unfurled in slow motion, jeweled birds and monkeys scampered atop ornately decorated columns of "ivory." Chinese-maiden cocktail waitresses were got up in whiteface and red eyes, lots of dingle-dangles in their black wigs.

Next on any tour was Donna MaDonna's, the Biggest and Sexiest Lingerie Shoppe on the Moon (Fashions All the Way from Earthside Paris!) Most of the local girls—prostitution also being legal on the Moon, at least so far—bought their gear at Donna's.

Deuce was a favorite among the hookers, because when he had been a Casino Liaison he had given them lots of presents and cash in exchange for tidbits of gossip, and he had always treated them like ladies. Later, when he had more power, he paid them triple what they could make on Moonbase Vegas to come on over to Darkside City to keep the bored workers entertained. For that, he had practically become their patron saint.

The last stop on the tour was the Scarlatti casino, the Inferno. Music was their draw. They boasted no fewer than two dozen clubs inside, each featuring a different kind of music, from the very, very latest in vibratory resonances to the Shriner Shuffle, as the younger Moonsiders termed it: music with melodies, music you could hum to. Boring music, in other words.

Gabriel Kinkade-Jones turned to Deuce, and said, "So, where to?"

He looked at Downtown Dallas, and he looked at Iniya. "Comm my mother, please," he requested.

Then he turned, very seriously, to the MLF terrorist widow, and said, "A wedding chapel. I think you and I should get married."

SIX

Maybe with a feather, you could knock over Ms. Kinkade-Jones. In her armored aichy, all dressed in black and silver, she stared at Deuce, and said, "Get married?"

He shrugged. "Way I see it, if we're married, your people might think at least twice about whacking me."

"But if we think you're the Messiah, as you claim we do, we'll assume you can't be killed."

"Yeah, well, explain that to Jesus." He crossed himself and muttered, "*Mi scusi, Dio.*"

She said, "You're already married."

"As you pointed out before, and as I told you, I think I been abandoned. It can be a contingency wedding." They were legal on the Moon, since there was so much uncertainty in Family life about whether your Significant Other might have simply gone into hiding, into a protective witness program, or been killed on the job.

Before she could say anything, he added, "You're a Mormon. You guys do the polygamy thing like it's going out of style. So what's the problem?"

She grinned at him. "You're not a Mormon."

"I'm better. I'm a dedicated Roman Catholic," he informed her proudly.

He did not add that his adoptive mother had been a staunch member of the Catholic Ladies Association, which had fought hard and long to outlaw the fascinating Mormon custom of marrying more than one woman at a time.

He held up his hand. "Plus, since you're a widow, you don't have to worry about it being kosher. And if you have a boyfriend, hey, we never have to have the, uh, honeymoon. It would be a political marriage." He smiled hopefully. "Filled with advantages for both of us."

"If I really want to ally my group with the guy who declared war on Earth."

He shrugged. Exactly. He needed some up-front support, and immediately, or he was dead. Literally.

Iniya and Downtown Dallas looked suitably unconcerned about the entire matter—very professional, that—and he was very proud of them both. Especially Dallas, who was certainly getting an eyeful of the glory that was Gabriel Kinkade-Jones as she leaned forward, passed her hand over a small silver box, and pulled out a decanter of something amber and some shot glasses.

Deuce hesitated. "Um, about your name. You're not a guy with a makeover, are you?"

She laughed appreciatively. "If there's to be no honeymoon, why do you care?"

"Just curious." He grinned at her.

"No." She shrugged. "My father had six daughters."

"You being the last." At her nod, he said, "Pardon my French, but your religion is not healthy if there's such inequality of the sexes."

She raised her brows. "I'm impressed. This coming from a macho Italian."

"Only legally." He gestured to himself. "As you can see, I am the spitting stereotype of an Irishman."

"From Earthside Sweden." She poured him some of the liquid. "This is Atherton Gold, Mr. McNamara."

His favorite, favorite beverage. The smoothest hooch ever created. He took it from her and held it while she poured herself a shot. Then she hoisted her glass.

"What're we drinking do?" Deuce asked.

She gave him a wink. Moving his shoulders, he threw it back. As soon as he swallowed, she said, "Our honeymoon."

He almost choked, but he caught himself in time.

And then his gaze slid toward Iniya, and he saw that she did not look so neutral. She looked jealous, as only Mr. Wong could look. Interesting. He'd better file that away for later.

Gabriel sat back in her seat and crossed her legs. A lot with the leg-crossing. She must know those gams were prime real estate. She continued, "This type of arrangement will only protect you so far. The really devout consider only temple weddings to be legitimate."

Also interesting, that she framed her statement that way, "the really devout." He said, "So, just how many Mormons are in the MLF?"

She looked incredibly amused. "Obviously, that's privileged information. I'll share it with you after we're married."

"On the other hand, I'm the Messiah, I suppose I can get married anywhere I want."

She gave her head an amused shake. "I suppose."

His badge vibrated. "Yeah, Ma," he said. "Listen, I don't want you traveling so much, or I'd ask you to come to my wedding. Also, Annie Bonnanio, who would make a *bellissima* flower girl."

"What?" she sputtered. "Deuce?"

"Visual," he said, and there was a picture of his mother in the monitor, agape. "I'm marrying the head of the MLF," he continued smoothly. "Make sure the word gets passed, *sì*?" He smiled at Gabriel, who smiled comfortably back. "And by the way, he's a broad. Funny first name is all."

"But what about Spar . . ." She stopped, and he was proud of her, too. Of everybody, today. Maybe they'd actually live another day.

"That's so nice." She looked this way and that, obviously searching for a view of the bride.

Gabriel obliged, leaning into frame. She said, "It's so nice to see you again, Mrs. Lockheart."

"I'm so sorry about Gina," Deuce's mother replied. Now it was Deuce's turn to look stupefied, and to want very badly to ask a few questions. Was Gabriel Kinkade-Jones mixed up in the crazy Generational Protection League, the way Gina had been?

"Thank you, Mrs. Lockheart. Of course it was a terrible loss. For many."

Deuce's mother said, "And us."

Deuce was agog. Had Gina been carrying someone's child—or children—as a surrogate when she had been killed? No one was saying—not over the loudspeakers, anyway—and Deuce figured he would have to bide his time on this agenda item.

"Well, I welcome you into our family," Connie said. "I know you'll make a wonderful addition."

"And I'm so glad to be a part of it," Gabriel replied. "I know my people are eager to get to know Deuce better, too."

They made little women-have-secrets smiles at each other and disconnected.

Deuce turned to Gabriel. "Here's a pertinent question, not that I wish to intrude upon your private affairs. Are you currently pregnant?"

She gave him a coy look. "Not currently."

"Do you have any heirs who might want to whack a contingency stepfather for any reason?"

She shook her head. "That relationship is so slight, I'm not certain people even keep track of it anymore."

"The Charter Board does," he asserted.

She gave him a steady, long look.

"The Charter Board," he said slowly.

She didn't blink.

He thought, O, Mamma mia *they've sabotaged the Charter Board.*

Where that left him, he had no idea, but he figured it was basically good news . . . except for the behind-the-scenes chaos it would, or was no doubt generating. So much so that eventually the truth would no longer be hidden, and the entire lunar economy would go belly-up.

Which had to be a short-run goal of Earthside, if only to seize control on a complete and permanent basis. Then they could begin extracting cash the way the first lunar miners had extracted precious ores and collected helium dust.

So whose side is she on? He observed his fiancée with fascination, mentally fanning his cards this way, that way, calculating his odds, making book. Maybe this wasn't such a great idea, marrying her. Maybe he should just shoot her.

"Penny for your thoughts," she said, although no one alive had ever seen a penny except in a museum.

"Just wondering what you're going to give me for a wedding gift."

She tilted her head. A lot with the head. He wondered very briefly if she was a mechanical or some kind of remote data terminal herself. Come to think of it, for all he knew, every other person in Moonbase Vegas had some linkup going with some alien or mystic oracle or something. Why not? More weird things had happened in the last week than in the rest of the history of mankind, at least to his way of thinking, and that included all the wars, the invention of the Quantum Instability Circuit, and the scientifically documented fact that blondes did, indeed, have more fun.

She said, "I was wondering the same thing." In case his mind had wandered too far afield, she said, "A wedding gift."

"I'm thinking a hell of a lot of ammo," he replied. "That makes MLF girls really hot."

She laughed. Then her smile faded, and she grew very serious. "I'm going to give you guerrilla warfare."

They were silent for a moment. Then Deuce said, "Looks like we're registered at the same store."

"No way," she asserted, "are we letting Earthside make a beachhead on our world. If we don't take a stand now, we might as well capitulate. We'll be nothing but a colony for the rest of our existence."

"Now I know why I decided to marry you," Deuce said warmly.

To his delight, she leaned forward and kissed him full on the lips. The last such kiss he had received from a wife of his had been Sparkle's parting good-bye kiss, just before she, Hunter, and her three children had blasted off for parts unknown.

He opened his lips slightly, in part to see how far she was willing to take the kiss. In answer, she pressed her tongue against his and slipped her hand underneath his palm, directly centered in the middle of his thigh.

Chills and thrills shot through him, which communicated themselves to her when his damn thigh muscles contracted. He figured she would chuckle and break the spell, but the kiss grew.

Then she murmured, in a voice only he could hear, "I'm your Connie Lockheart, Deuce. I signed up, and I'm to carry your children." She smiled at him. "And I'd much rather do it in the natural way, if you catch my drift."

He blinked. "I have a say in all this?"

"You're the singularly most important man in the Moon,"

she said. "You can be a figurehead, or a spearhead, but sooner or later, your line must be continued."

With a feather, you could have knocked him over.

Sparkle dreamed:

She was a young dancer again, the star of *Venus on Ice* at the Van Aadamses' Down Under Casino. As the Moon's Women's Kickboxing Champion, as well as a precision ice-skater, she soared and spun in her towering headdress and matching thong, the diamonds dripping down her cleavage. Moon women did not suffer the indignities that the gravity of Earthside perpetuated on Earthside women. Plus, they were more amenable to rejuves and makeovers . . . any kind of surgery or enhancement was fine, and practiced with abandon. There did not appear to be any side effects or drawbacks, except to the credit stripe . . . and most, if not all, of that was paid for by the employer.

But at any rate, she was dreaming, and in that dream, she was free . . . not in a liaison to anyone; not bound in any way to anyone; just her young self, free and beautiful and optimistic. Every one admired her. No one could touch her.

No one could touch her.

Hunter Castle sat by Sparkle's bed, drumming his fingers in extreme agitation.

The verdict was not good.

How could that be, in this day and age? With his money, and his access to vast knowledge and expertise hitherto untapped by human minds, how could Sparkle de Lune di Borgioli-McNamara be failing to respond?

His medical team had braced him: The possibility was strong that none of that was going to benefit the mother of his grandchildren.

Who also happened to be the woman he loved and wanted above all others.

No modesty, just fact: He looked pretty good, for a guy his age (and he wasn't saying; that was part of his legend); he was the richest person alive; and he was currently the only person dealing with beings beyond the known universe. There was a lot to like about him.

But he was also a ruthless bastard, and as much as he

wanted to feel affection and kindness, at the center of his soul, there was a block of ice housing a devil, just like in Dante's *Inferno*. You didn't live as long as he had without knowing that ruthlessness, competitiveness, and the unending drive to succeed stemmed from some kind of pathology, as therapists liked to say.

Something such as having seen your daddy murder a man for trying to blackmail him. And told over and over that you could do better. Self-pity? No.

Self-awareness, yes.

When you were Hunter Castle, you did not go to therapists. You did not discuss your personal, private demons with anyone. You didn't fool yourself that women loved you just for you, and since you had no mother, you didn't go that route, either. You worked, and you strategized, and you picked up the next card on the top of the deck.

Again, no pity. Just reality. And the neuroses that pushed him had resulted in a pretty spectacular life. Quiet desperation? Not for him or any Castle.

He took a ragged breath and wondered how his son was doing. His only son. Perhaps someone he could actually admit to loving.

Then Sparkle opened her eyes, looked straight at him, and began to speak in a distant, hypnotic voice:

"They will kill the children. They will kill the children. They will kill—"

Then his badge vibrated, and the image of Cor-!kth fwommed into its full glory at the entrance to the room. Sparkle's eyes opened. For a moment, she stared transfixed. Then her eyes rolled back in her head, and she fainted.

The image of Cor-!kth regarded Hunter. He said testily, "Was she not adequately prepared?"

Hunter moved to Sparkle's side. He replied to the alien's holo, masking his horror and confusion, "Cor, you're a sight for sore eyes."

"I have harmed her eyes?" the alien replied.

"Just surprised her a little," Hunter said. "She'll be fine."

The alien shrugged. "We have much to discuss."

"Indeed, we do. But first, I need to see to my . . . companion."

"Has she evidenced growth in her abilities?"

Hunter hesitated. "Not quite yet."

"Very well." The alien disconnected.

Hunter sagged. Good Lord, what had he done?

It was called the Heavenly Bodies Chapel of Love. Giggling couples milled in the foyer, picking out which wedding package to stripe for. The entrance reminded Deuce of an old-fashioned wedding cake, complete with ornate frosting decorations of white exterior foam and an abundance of pastel-and-gold doves, bells, and cupids above a swirling galaxy whose stars were glittering holos of silver hearts.

Lacy curtains swagged the entrance and a bell tinkled the "Wedding March" as Downtown Dallas entered first, surveyed the place, and walked apace to speak to the management. A number of obviously drunken prospective consumers of wedded bliss craned their necks to see beyond the curtains, then gave up when Deuce pulled back even farther. They should have waited in the aichy—it was SOP—but he had wanted to see the chapel before giving his consent to be married there.

Okay, a political marriage, and completely unromantic. The average life span of a legal marriage in the Moon was 3.2 years, which made it not all that romantic to begin with. But Deuce was depressed. The wedding chapel was such a monument to poor taste, and he didn't really want to get married anyway. Sparkle, pragmatist that she was, would probably applaud this move and gladly stand aside, at least temporarily. She certainly wouldn't betray jealousy.

Not a cause for joy, that.

Downtown Dallas came back to Deuce, and said, "They've agreed to clear the chapel. They'll do it for ten thousand." He grinned at his boss. "On account of lost business."

"Give me a break. That's more than they clear in a week," Deuce said. He shrugged. "Hell. Give it to them."

Dallas nodded and went back to parley. Interest in who was behind the curtain grew among the restless and unmarried, while the preacher dickered with Deuce's guy.

Gabriel, who had walked in escorted by Iniya, looked around, sighed, and said, "I know what you're thinking. This is a terrible place to get married. But we're here, and we need to do this as soon as possible."

Deuce took her hand and gave the back of it a kiss. Things

couldn't be all that easy for her, either. Her eyes widened slightly, and her lips parted. Being a man, he couldn't help a very quick image of the supposed honeymoon. He figured it wasn't really gonna happen, but it was nice of her to give him a little husbandly respect in front of his boys.

Dallas came back with a small midnight blue velvet box and a bouquet of simulated florals. He kept hold of them as he gestured behind Deuce.

"There's a little privacy room in there. The minister suggests you wait in there while they clear the chapel. They've got one couple pretty upset."

"Tell whoever's in charge to go ahead and get 'em hitched."

"Should I get a rebate for the delay?" Dallas asked.

"Naw. It'll take longer to hash out than it's worth." Deuce gestured for Gabriel to accompany him to the privacy room.

It was actually a rather sweet place, well holoed with a rosebud wallpaper simulation. There was a real mirror.

Gabriel smiled, and said, "In the temple, these rooms are provided for brides to change into their wedding gowns."

He looked at her rosy, nostalgic smile in the mirror. "If it's important to you, we'll go pick up a gown." He touched his badge. "Dallas—"

"No." She put her hand over his. "That's a very kind gesture, which makes me feel better about this entire matter, to be honest." She shrugged. "I didn't figure on having to marry you. But it might be kind of pleasant after all."

They looked at each other and burst into laughter. He said, "Wacky world, eh, big cheese?"

She chuckled and twirled in her catsuit. "This will have to do."

"Works for me," he drawled.

They laughed again.

Outside the door, they could hear Dallas saying, "Okay, folks, thank you, yes, please clear the building. Thank you, folks."

"I wan' get married," some drunken man slurred. "Got my honey ri'here, wan' get married."

"Five gets you ten he's already hitched Earthside," Deuce murmured. "Of course, in your world, that's not a bad thing."

He heard her warm chuckle. She said, "You're a good sport. That's a most attractive attribute."

"It only gets better, baby."

After about ten minutes, Dallas knocked on the door. "Don McNamara, Donna Kinkade-Jones, the chapel's cleared."

Deuce opened the door. "You sweep it?"

Dallas was fighting not to move his gaze from his boss to the boss's fiancée. He said, "Yes, sir. Mr. Wong scanned for anything and everything. As far as we know, the joint's clean."

A good lieutenant, Deuce found himself thinking. *Tries his best, covers his butt. Acts professional.*

I couldn't want more.

"Dallas," he said, "I'm giving you a field promotion. Our side, well, we're sort of in a state of flux." Deuce flashed him a wry smile. "You're a *capo,* all right with you? I'll give you some territory, new responsibilities."

Dallas looked extremely thrilled. He bent over Deuce's hand. "You're too good to me, Godfather. It's an honor I don't deserve."

"Dallas, your loyalty to me is something I don't deserve. I know it's optional, these days, and I'm grateful for it."

"No, no," Dallas began.

Then Iniya walked up, and announced, "I'm going to sweep outside." She said it with the same tone of someone who was going to smoke on the porch.

Deuce said, "*Grazie.*" But something was up with the terminal. Could it possibly be that she was actually jealous, wherever and whatever she was?

More likely, she's calculated that this marriage is a dumb idea, he realized.

He said to his intended, "*Mi scusi, mio amore.*"

She gestured that he was free to do as he wished, and he took his cue.

Joining Iniya on the sidewalk, where a barker was shouting, "Get your marriage license here!" he lit a cig, commed for the pollution levy, and said, "On your planet, you guys smoke?"

"No." She shook her head. "But we have other vices."

"That's nice to know. Are you a bad girl or a good girl, where you live?" He shrugged. "Do you have girls there? Do you know what a girl is?"

There were a few beats . . . she was probably processing, or pushing away from her monitor out there in outer space and saying to the multitentacled green blob of slime beside her,

"Gri'pdlod, any friggin' idea what the hell a girl is? It's some damn human thing or other."

"Girl. Young female." Beep, beep, beep. "I am woman, Deuce." She leered at him. There was no other word for it. "Young woman, but not girl."

"I see." He moved his head in the direction of the chapel entrance. "And what's it about this wedding that is making you an unhappy young woman?"

Beep, beep, beep, for a long time. She said, "Unhappy. Yes, Deuce. This is too much uncertainty. Too much unknown. We have too little data."

"Yeah, well, I have a feeling that's going to be the case more and more often," he said apologetically. "On account of, my species and war, we don't do it in a very organized way."

She took a moment. Then she said, very seriously. "D'inn and !kth are at war."

"Yeah, I got that back when we were about to get blown up in the shuttle," he shot back. "And please don't be offended, for I would hate to offend a being from another galaxy this early in first contact, but why do I care? Why does my species care? Cuz, again, *mi dispiace*, we have an awful lot on our plates right now." He touched his chest in a gesture of sincere regret.

"Jumpgate." She sounded a bit irritated with him, as in, *Duh*.

"Okay, about that." He was anxious, and he slid a glance into the chapel. Gabriel looked relaxed and confident, every inch an imperious leader. "Let's talk about that a little more. Forgive me, *cara*. Perhaps it's that I somehow still fail to see the big picture."

She looked at him blankly, yet he sensed patient amusement in her expression. "The !kth are building jumpgate." She paused and said, "The jumpgate. D'inn—I am D'inn—do not possess jumpgate technology.

"!kth wish to invade you."

He crossed his arms. "For our precious metals, the fact that our planet can still sustain life, or to mate with our women?"

"Have already mated," said Iniya. She corrected herself again. "They have already mated. Long ago. Giants in the earth." She blinked. "You possess DNA of !kth. You and father. Your father."

He burst out laughing. "Get out. We're part bad guy?"

"Not humorous." She scowled at him. "Deadly serious."

"You're not joking?"

"Not joking."

He stared at her. He didn't even know how to respond.

"I gotta sit down," he said, and did so, on the curb, automatically comming for the loitering levy. In a satellite where space was precious and gambling was the main economy, you did not sit down just anywhere.

Throwing up occurred to him. Also, passing out.

"So, how do I know you're the good guy?" he asked finally. His voice was hoarse and he could barely speak.

"!kth wish to invade space . . . human space. D'inn will make peaceful contact."

"And the proof is . . . ?"

There was a long silence. Then, "I saved your life."

"So did the !kth remote data terminal, when it was hooked up to Mr. Wong. It saved Hunter's life, too. And it grew back my arm."

He thought for a moment. *For all I know, this is some kind of sting operation. Some nonsense perpetrated by Earth, or some kind of test of my loyalty, given by who knew who.*

"Arm," she said. "Your arm. It contains !kth DNA."

Her English was getting better. He wondered about the possibility of a similarly new and improved tangled web.

He lit another cigarette, and commed for another pollution levy. He took a deep drag while he pondered what he was going to say to her. He really had no idea. This was way beyond "I'm not sure you should marry a nice Mormon girl with a boy's name."

"You seem like a smart alien female," he said finally. "So you must realize that just about anything you say to me requires proof, and that said, proof cannot come from you? Or anywhere near you?"

Mr. Wong looked equally frustrated. She was really getting the hang of human expression . . . if she really was there at all, and not some *scemo* in a bunker running a simulation. It could even be some moron Scarlatti—them with all their advanced equipment; they even had some new kind of tattoo that could make you hallucinate—out to make his bones on a Godfather by completely faking him out.

But if you strolled down "what-is-reality" lane, you never got anything done. Generally, life handed you enough reality checks that it was hard to BS yourself for very long.

With Downtown Dallas at her side, Gabriel appeared in the doorway and looked questioningly at Deuce. She was holding her bouquet of simulated florals and a flouncy ivory veil had been added to her ensemble. It looked rather silly, sleekly glamorous as she was, like someone who had popped a cheesy lace doily on top of a Grecian statue of Venus.

He said to Iniya, "If you thought appealing to me for help was a good move, you must figure I'm somewhat intelligent, for my species. So you know you're going to have to do a lot better to gain my trust."

She did the head-bobbing/dropping thing, but this time, for the first time, she raised it after lowering. She must have known she'd done something clever, because she grinned at him.

"The ball's in my court," she said slowly.

Wow. Talk about picking up the lingo. Her ability to *sprechen Sie* had gone full speed ahead in just the last few minutes.

"Yeah," he said. "Your court."

She nodded again. "Perhaps it's best to proceed with the wedding. A static state is comfortable, also predictable, but unrealistic. Particularly in your case."

"You must have just picked up the revised Webster's D'inn–English Dictionary," he observed. "Your language skills are really classing up." He gestured in case she didn't understand. "Improving."

"Thank you. Thanks," she added. Her grin grew. She looked proud of herself. He grinned back.

"Why do you smile at me?" she asked.

"Oh, you're just . . ." He looked for a way to explain it. "I'm sharing a moment of friendship with you. I'm happy that your ability to communicate with me is improving."

She took that in. Or something.

He continued. "Back in the car, I thought you were jealous."

There was a pause, during which he assumed she was looking up the definition. Finally, she said, "My reaction was discomfort over an uncertain alliance in combination with ours."

"That works," he acknowledged.

From the porch Gabriel stood quietly waiting.

Deuce turned to her, and said, "Let's have a wedding."

She led the way back into the chapel.

So there he was, and damned if his mind didn't slide back to the fact that he and Sparkle hadn't had so much as a ceremony of any sort. Filled out "the paperwork," as she referred to it, and tubed it in. He was the one who had brought up wedding rings.

"If you want one." For someone in love, she had sounded pretty noncommittal.

So, what now, did he take that one off? Wear two? Contingency weddings were perfectly acceptable, and legal, but he felt sad. He didn't know where this romantic streak had come from, but there it was. God help him if anyone ever found about it.

Especially his own heart.

So Deuce and the two guys took their places at the altar which did not have so much of a religious scene as a sentimental one, with a long, white-stone sort of table covered with banks of pink and white roses, above which several velvet holos of large-busted maidens or fairies or something floating serenely across a lavender sky as the crescent Earth and various stars twinkled. The flowers were crater, nothing unexpected there, but the air was enhanced with the scent of roses. Nice touch, except it reminded Deuce a little bit of the room deodorizer him and Sparkle used to buy back when they were poor.

To the left of the altar, a very sharp-looking dame in a spangled pink evening gown sat at the keyboard and flicked on a switch. The houselights dimmed and the spots came up. There was a drumroll; Deuce took a breath; and the ceremony began.

Gabriel stood at the end of the room, awaiting her cue. The dame in the evening gown flicked another switch, and the music started, dum, dum, dum-dum, the "Bridal March," he thought it was called. To Deuce's immediate left, Downtown Dallas was properly respectful, folding his hands. Iniya-as-Mr.-Wong stood in turn beside Dallas, both acting as a kind of joint best man.

As Gabriel walked down the aisle, a traveling spot hit her. It was crazy, but he could just about picture her in a white wedding dress; even in the catsuit, she did not look so much like a terrorist as a broad on a pleasant date. Bowling, maybe, which was huge in the Moon on account of the enforced gravity lanes.

There were rows of pews on either side of the aisle, maybe ten per, and despite the moment, Deuce found himself calculating how many people it would take to fill the room. He didn't know if they charged a gate at nondenominational weddings. That was not the sort of thing you did at Family weddings, and he hadn't actually attended a non-Family one before.

Then she stopped at the end of the aisle. Her face softened. At her silent urging, he joined her, facing the altar, which now featured soft washes of grazing sheep.

Then, from the side, a man in a white-and-lavender Western suit and sparkling bolo tie jointed them. He had very shiny white boots with lavender-and-gray designs on them, and Deuce wondered where you got wild boots like that. He couldn't decide if they were in good taste or not.

The minister smiled at them both. His name tag said, "Reverend DuBois."

He flipped open a white-leather book with gilt-edged pages. *Paper.* Wow. Deuce was loving this whole deal more and more.

"Dearly beloved," Reverend DuBois began.

The words zipped across his name tag, and Deuce realized it was a prompter. Deuce was just about to repeat, "Dearly beloved," when the man went on.

"Invested friends, high rollers, and other interested parties, we are gathered here to"—he checked his watch—"tonight to witness the union of this man and this woman in a contingency liaison."

Deuce's chest tightened.

"The game of life is stacked with jokers and wild cards, and though the odds on the wheel are the best in the house, still they are not even," he continued. "Thus, it makes sense upon occasion to play more than one hand. For just as you cherish each separate bingo or keno card and play it as well as you can, still, the point is not to lose."

"Amen," said Downtown Dallas fervently. Deuce raised his brows slightly. He had not figured the man for religious.

"Now, Deuce," the minister said. The man blushed. Deuce figured it was hard for him to call a big shot like him by his first name. No ego in that thought, just the truth. You didn't get a whole lot of powerful men and women liaising in a sawdust joint like this one.

"Do you promise to play this game with an unmarked deck?"

"I do." Deuce's eyes filled with tears as he gazed at his bride.

"To enter into liaison free of markers which would in any way obligate this woman?"

"I do."

"Are you willing to throw unshaved dice?"

"I am." He was so moved he could barely speak. And though he fought valiantly to hide his feelings, he knew the others could tell.

Dallas wiped a tear from his own eye, and Gabriel's smile was gentle and sweet.

They went through their vows, the gist of which, he understood, English-speaking people had been saying for hundreds of years. He felt himself part of a grand and glorious tradition, the side-bet romance, and counted himself a fortunate man that a marriage of convenience had been bestowed upon him so early in life.

"You may kiss the bride," the minister finished, him in his Western-style suit and bolo tie.

Deuce leaned forward to give her a little peck, but she slid her arms around his neck and planted a real good one right on his mouth. To his amazement, his stomach fluttered and his, um, he got very interested in the kiss.

She whispered in his ear, "Honeymoon," and he gave what he got, chip for chip, then decided to put it all on red.

"Oh, yes," she said, sighing. "Yes, very much, yes."

As they had hoped, the wedding made headlines, in the Moon and Earthside. Calls and interview requests started coming into both their camps. "Lost" and new soldiers began appearing. For the most part, morale was terrific. The Mormon MLF'ers liked joining forces with people who were opposed to Earthside possibly forcing the League of Decency on them. The McNamara Family, as Deuce's group was being called, knew they needed allies badly. Now, with the alliance, there was a good, strong rallying point for those who had the courage to fight Earthside with everything they had.

Deuce agreed with Gabriel's request to honeymoon at MLF base camp. To make it harder for their enemies to whack them, they changed cars several times before they arrived.

It was a hero's welcome. Deuce beamed as the soldiers shouted, "Deuce, Gabe! MLF! LDS!"

"Listen to that, boss," Downtown Dallas said, looking as radiant as a new bride himself.

"It was a good calculation," Iniya allowed.

The camp reminded him a lot of the old MLF base. The lights were dim, and everything was draped in what passed for camouflage on the satellite: shadows and muted colors, to represent the myriad lights and signs in the tunnels. Most of the buildings were Quonset huts, the remainders of some old mining camp. One building was old steel storage crates soldered together. In the background, troops were drilling; in the foreground, officers waited to greet their leader and her new husband.

" 'Ten hut!" cried the sergeant at arms, and everyone snapped to attention. Gabriel saluted them, and they practically snapped their spines as they saluted back.

Deuce's personal orientation was not so martial, so he merely inclined his head as they passed in review. Then he stopped cold.

The face of a dead man stared blankly at him.

He cleared his throat. "You must be related to Brigham Young," he said.

"Yes, sir." The man still did not look at him. "I'm his twin brother."

Deuce nodded and made a note to speak privately to this guy. This could spell very big trouble, as in R-E-V-E-N-G-E.

"Deuce," Gabriel said. She handed him a goblet of something pale and fizzy.

Then another man came forward. He was all got up like a general—the MLF was known for its extreme militarism— with stars and bars and things like that. He had a rather anemic blond moustache, leading one to assume that he would have had blond hair if he had not shaved his head. Weirder, however, was that on either side of his sort of beret thing, he had Scarlatti brands burned into his scalp.

Obviously, this guy had been a Scarlatti before he'd joined the MLF. That made him possibly dangerous: The Scarlattis took so many drugs and did so many weird things that Deuce figured they were damaged goods, even if they came in out of the cold. Once nuts, always nuts.

Also, it took a lot to quit a Family. A whole lot. And more than that to leave the Scarlattis. Sure, all Families took it personal, but the Scarlattis usually declared a Vendetta against anyone who walked out. To them, it was exactly the same as turning traitor.

So, this guy no doubt had a death sentence on his head, and probably had a truly impressive drug habit to boot. Howsoever, he lifted his glass and clicked his boots like some old-fashioned Nazi bad guy in a flatfilm, and said, "To the husband of our leader. To Don Deuce McNamara, the Godfather of the Moon."

"Don Deuce," everyone chorused. Some smiled, and some scowled. Deuce took count. More smiles than scowls.

Va, bene: He was in.

Then they sipped. *Champagne*, he prayed, *even crater*. But it was some horrible, sweet concoction only a Mormon or a three-year-old would think of drinking. Nevertheless, Deuce made himself look appreciative, and Gabriel obviously appreciated his attempt.

Then another general stepped forward. Volunteerism—people had to feel important, or they had a tendency to burn out—included lots of intangible benefits like lots of medals and crap like that.

So this guy raised his glass, and said, "To the alliance of the MLF and the McNamara Family!"

Everyone drank. Deuce marveled. He had waffled on starting his own family forever and ever; fearing for the lives of his supporters, he had never filed the official papers with the Charter Board. His own brother had urged him to declare a Family. Sparkle had nearly come to blows with Joey over being named the McNamara Designated Heir.

Now it was a fait accompli, as classy people who drank wine liked to say. A done deal. No need to file papers of creation, not with a corrupted Board: The McNamara Family was a reality. And he was the Don of it, and still alive to tell the tale. But the joy, the triumph, the gusto . . . where was it?

A year ago, two, okay, six months ago, if someone had told him this might happen—had bet even money on it—he would not have believed it. It would have seemed too amazingly wonderful, the complete and total fulfillment of any young man's lunar daydream.

But now, the reality made him tired and sad. There was nowhere in his charter of being alive that stated a proviso for joy over being responsible for so much and so many; for being someone who was looked up to; not to mention being assured by a robot which might be a mouthpiece for an alien from an alien race that part of him was Not of This Earth, not From the Earth to the Moon.

Gabriel took the glass of liquefied sugar from him—mercifully—and suggestively drained it. To hoots and hollers, she let her tongue lap up the last little bit. Bride stuff, wedding stuff, he was truly thrilled and flattered.

I'm in for it now, he thought as she finished off the beverage, wondering if the suggestiveness was for show, or if she really meant it at some level. Then, to cheers, she threw her glass down, shattering it. She gave his back to him; what the hell, his shattered into even more pieces, not that he was competitive.

Then she put her arm around his waist and raised a hand. It took a while for them to quiet down, which Deuce could only take as a good sign. Angry people either yelled or sulked. No one had yelled yet. And they looked fairly overjoyed, to him.

"Comrades," she began, and they all went berserk for a couple–two minutes. "My comrades," she pressed. More craziness.

"This is my husband, who will now assume command of the MLF and lead us to victory against the oppression of the Family system!"

He stared at her as the troops went wild. She gave him a triumphant smile, and said, "C'mon. They expect us to be alone for a while."

SEVEN

The thing about growing up in a Family was that you were fully expected to become a cynic as soon as possible. Ambition, while very, very admirable, was not the same thing as believing in Santa Claus or the Tooth Fairy. The Casino System socialization was such that you were expected to figure out, at an extremely young age, that Santa Claus could not possibly be real because if so, he would be an unbelievable putz: You did nice, nice, nice all the time, you ran out of the ability and the resources to do nice.

Rule #1: You had to take in order to give.

Plus, you could not spend an inordinate amount of time trying to figure out some value system, some decision-making process, by which you decided what to give to whom. This was a given; even Holy Mother Church had codified what it meant to be a Good Joe, or a saint, or what would send you to hell. So there were guidelines within the Family, and a primary directive was:

Rule #2: Give only if you have a good chance of getting back.

That only made sense, and not even the new Family Monsignor, Tomasso Borgioli, could argue against it. The Church could make all this noise about how it was more blessed to give than to receive, but there was absolutely no evidence to substantiate that claim. No one in the entire history of the Christian religion had truly selflessly given: if it wasn't to please God the Father or impress the locals, then it was to feel better about your dear saintly self, and not so very deep down.

That was no less a selfish act than was funding the Chans

in their eternal struggle to deal drugs down Earthside, where all forms of Chan drugs were, of course, illegal. Their drugs were highly addictive and, ultimately, lethal. But the profit to be made was fabulous.

On the other hand, if you spent all your time making sure Chan drugs were illegal, and that gave you personal satisfaction, you had also gotten back a fabulous return on your investment. It was no purer a motive than dealing drugs in the first place, although no one in a Family had ever been able to convince a law-enforcement officer of that. So:

Rule #3: Do your business and leave the rest to the priests.

And that was probably the rule Niccolo Borgioli followed the most closely.

Because if he didn't leave the rest to the priests, he would never be able to stop wrestling with his conscience over the mortal sin he had just committed.

Here was the deal:

Nicky was the favorite nephew of Angelo Borgioli, who had just become the Godfather of the Borgioli Family. The Borgiolis had just come out in favor of the Earthside-declared martial law.

In other words, Nicky's betters were pretending that it was a wonderful thing that the government of the planet had come in and taken over everything. Stolen not only profit and property, but honor and the way of life for an entire civilization.

Nicky was outraged and humiliated. Always, the Borgiolis did the low-class thing. Here they had once been allied to the most powerful man in the universe—witness his logo intertwined with their coat of arms all over the place, the rushed font of CASTLE with the shield bearing the sheep and crossed fingers—and now they were back to nothing again except being a pack of grappa-stomping peasants from the Old Planet, who didn't know enough to use handkerchiefs when they had to blow their noses.

It was demoralizing; but worse, it was a blow to Nicky's honor as a *capo* of the Borgioli Family. Uncle Angelo had pledged his personal as well as the Family's loyalty to Uncle Deuce. Uncle Angelo and Uncle Deuce had fought together, saved each other's lives; and now, when the chips were down, Uncle Angelo deserted Uncle Deuce. All the Families were publicly against him, while privately rooting for him and praying he would be successful—with no arms to speak of, few men, and a very shaky power base.

Opportunism was a trait to be admired, and Nicky did. He had been brought up to. But not at the breaking of his word as a man and a Borgioli. For Nicky's word was his most prized possession. Just like any Borgioli child who had made the trip down to the Charter Board Building and declared that he was an adult who had the right to give his own respect and promise his own loyalty.

The Family lifestyle was cutthroat, but it was not without rules or honor. Otherwise, you had total chaos.

So he paced, his sort-of girlfriend, Veronica, watching him. She was not the smartest, but also not the dumbest. She loved to kiss, and she was a good dresser. Looked sharp on the arm, like a good watch or a nice pinky ring.

Nicky knew he didn't love her, but he figured she knew it, too, and that she comforted herself with the knowledge that she was the moll of one of the most eligible bachelors in the Moon. No boast, just fact: He was young, rich, and in line for Designated Heirship. Thanks to the sizzle of their former alliance with Hunter Castle, there was still some dazzle to the House of Borgioli. It was only a matter of time until people realized that the Borgiolis were still only Borgiolis, ham-fisted Sicilian peasants who had no taste and less sophistication.

So for now, Veronica would do, and if she eventually left him because she got some street cred, he would be hideously embarrassed but not terribly surprised.

But no more embarrassed than now, as his uncle sat with a contingent of Department of Fairness pigs and pretended to agree with every single thing that they said. Nicky had planted an eavesdropper in the flower arrangement—real flowers—on his uncle's desk, and if Angelo didn't know it, the Borgiolis were in worse shape than Nicky could ever imagine.

"So you see, your dealers are not giving the top card to the player in every case," one of the DOF'ers was saying to Angelo. No doubt they were showing him a holo from the Eye in the Sky, the elaborate system of spying surveillance each casino boasted. "Sometimes from the middle, sometimes from the bottom."

"Well, of course," Nicky said to Veronica, who looked up from *Fabulous Beast* and blew a bubble. It was very, very expensive to chew gum; you had to pay an arm and a leg—not literally, but almost—in levies to do it. Not only did you have pollution, but hazardous waste, and something that was not recyclable. Gum was sold in jewelry stores, like diamonds and precious gems.

Nicky kept Veronica well stocked in gum. It made her so grateful.

He said, waspishly, "Why do you read that trash?"

"For the articles," she replied. *Fabulous Beast* contained innumerable pictures of men with seriously enhanced physiques. Beefcake, in other words. The more steroid-driven, the better.

Her eyes widened slightly, and she murmured, "Oh, my." Then she looked up at him, reddened, and turned the page. "A sale at Moonbeam Appliances. How wonderful," she said, unconvincingly.

He was irritated with her, not because she was lying to him but because she was bad at it. He truly did not mind if she lied. That was part of being in a relationship, true? But how come he hadn't picked someone with a little finesse? It was like going out with a woman who brayed when she laughed; it reflected poorly on you.

And so did his Godfather.

"Oh, my," Angelo was saying. "I see what you mean. Look there. He dealt from the bottom of the deck. Shocking."

Nicky sighed with shame. How could he take this? He was a man, not a, a whatever it was Uncle Angelo had become.

"Ronnie," he said abruptly. "Listen."

She popped her gum.

"*Ronnie.*"

"Mmm?" She was lying on her stomach; now she lifted her legs into the air and crossed her ankles, letting them rock slightly. It was a fetching maneuver; at one time, it had captivated him. Now he was cranky and feeling trapped, and he wondered where the broads were who had both brains and a bod, like Uncle Deuce's old lady, Sparkle de Lune.

"He'll be fired immediately," Uncle Angelo assured the bad guys.

"And Dis-Membered," one of the DOF'ers said meaningfully.

Uncle Angelo said miserably, "Of course."

Nicky fumed. To Dis-Member someone was just about the worst thing you could do to him/her. Better you just put a blaster to their head or bury them alive in a crater. Push 'em out the airlock and say, "*Sayonara*, sucker!"

Because once you were Dis-Membered, you were an N.A. Only you were an N.A. who was once better than N.A.'s. And so even the lowliest of the low despised you. And without your credit line, your Family vehicle, your contacts, and so on, your chances of survival were tiny. Meanwhile, while you went down the drain, any belief that you were made of sterner stuff—Family blood ties—went down the drain, too. Fact was, all naked men looked and shivered pretty much the same.

"Nicky?" she said, smiling, even though she could hear the conversation just as well as he. It had no effect on her, as far as she was concerned. Her job was to charm Niccolo, and it used to be a very cushy, ah, position.

Nicky could not blame her. Thinking had not been in her job description, and he hadn't thought a thing of it when she confided in him that she wasn't too good "at that reading stuff."

"Are you saying you're tired of me?" he asked, raising his voice.

"Nick-y." She made a little-girl pouty face. "Whatever has gotten into you, honey?"

"Maybe a backbone," he muttered.

He crossed to her and sat on the bed beside her. She purred and rolled onto her side, reaching out to trail long, crimson nails down his chest. They flashed and pulsed; if you tapped her left thumb, her nails played "Moon River," an ancient folk song, in beautiful, bell-like tones.

Remembering that, and the rest of their courtship, he softened. He took her hand and kissed her ring finger—it went *bing!* so sweetly—and looked hard into her eyes.

"Ronnie, you have been such a wonderful, special dame for me," he said feelingly. "But I'm going undercover." A common enough occurrence in Families, and one for which there were all sorts of protocols to follow. "I want to put you in a contingency romance with someone else in the Family."

"Oh." She looked very sad, then very excited. "Who?"

"I haven't asked around," he confessed. "You got a short list?"

She nodded. "I'll get my purse."

She slid off the bed and swayed her hips over to the dresser. As he watched, he felt a little better. Any girl who had the foresight to prepare a short list had to have a few brains in her head.

Veronica would be all right.

"Here it is." She fished it out of her purse and waved it in the air.

Then she came back to the bed and snuggled up beside him.

"Who's number one?" he queried. "Besides me."

She fluttered her lashes at him. "You'll always be number one, Nicky. Even if you get whacked. Now. Let's see." She checked the list. "Oh, pooh. The next one down got whacked two days ago."

He tsk-tsked. "It's a brutal world, babe." He thought about asking her if she wanted to defect with him. But a woman like Veronica would say no. She wasn't maverick material.

Or traitor material.

He felt a pang. He truly loved his relative. And his Family. But Uncle Angelo was making a mockery out of everything the Borgiolis stood for: fraud, graft, corruption, and self-interest.

If he doesn't watch himself, someone is going to execute him, he thought anxiously. *But it ain't gonna be me. Better I leave than that.*

Then he stood and started peeling the Borgioli colors—red, green, and white—off his jacket. It felt as if he were peeling the skin off his own soul.

Thank God Papà isn't alive to see this, he thought sadly.

On the other hand, he would probably agree with what I'm doing.

Veronica watched him soberly. Ever since Deuce McNamara di Borgioli had made it fashionable to pretend to leave the Family, young men found all kinds of ways to achieve the greatness.

"Maybe I'll just wait until you come back," she said, yawning. "With all this war stuff, it's hard to keep track of who's available and who's dead."

He looked at her. He swallowed hard.

"Ronnie," he said, "you're a swell dame."

"You're too good for me, Niccolino."

Then, with that, he left his Borgioli bedroom, his babe,
home, and his Family.

She called after him, "You want some gum?"

"You want some real champagne?" Gabriel Kinkade-Jones
di Borgioli-McNamara asked her husband, of almost equally
long lineage and vintage.

"You're how old, twenty-five?" he asked her.

She looked at him. "And you want to know why?"

That was a good retort. They'd probably get along fine, him
and the contingency missus, if he didn't whack her first.

"You tricked me. No way am I overthrowing the Family
system."

"Then why didn't you say so back there?" she asked him,
moving her shoulders as if it was no big deal.

"Right. In an armed camp of religious fanatics, I'm having
my first spat with my wife."

"Well, I did trick you," she admitted. "But it was practically
a joke. I expected you to protest." She raised her hands in
imitation of him. "Waiwaiwait, forgetabout it."

Despite his agitation, he couldn't help but guffaw. She reminded him of his brother, so it was probably a good imitation
of Deuce himself.

"I'm gonna have to make a clarifying statement ASAP," he
said.

He made a show of rubbing his hands together as they
strolled toward a small Quonset hut flanked by two guards.
They snapped to when she came within saluting range.

"Real champagne, huh? With, like, alcohol and everything?"

She nodded and opened the door, gesturing for him to go
in first.

O, Mamma mia.

Satin sheets and dozens of pillows and a mirror above the
bed. Real flowers on the nightstand. A silver bucket, and a
magnum of the bubbly—Crescent Moon, no less—nestled in
the center of cubes of real gleaming ice.

"Do I surprise you?" she asked him, amusement and something else . . . mmm, he knew what that something else was
. . . lust . . . in her voice.

"Every second," he admitted. He sighed. "Now, about my

statement regarding the overthrow of my own preferred personal way of life."

"Later, Deuce." She planted another big one on him.

He chuckled. "Okay, Delilah. Just don't cut my hair while I'm asleep."

"Wouldn't dream of it," she replied, lifting the champagne from the bucket.

Deuce figured he shouldn't drink it. There was probably a mickey in it, something to knock him out or kill him. She had really pulled one—or two, or three—over on him. He needed to fix things immediately.

He picked up the two glasses and walked toward the bed.

What the hell.

EIGHT

Nicky stood for a moment in the Family parking structure and realized he would have to leave his car behind. It was a wicked, low-slung Nebula, sleek and shiny black. He loved his car.

For the first time it really dawned on him what he was doing. He almost staggered from the impact. He was leaving his Family; everyone and everything he loved would be lost to him forever.

But if he didn't fight for his way of life, the Earth would take it from him anyway.

Heartsick, he turned from the Nebby and looked around at all the Family cars parked in neat rows, shields up. They were voiced for their owners only, and a trusted chauffeur or two. The wrong voice tried to access a vehicle, they were all set to detonate.

He was not certain how to get out of the structure on foot. He was nineteen. The structure had been up his entire life, yet he had always driven into or out of it. He had no idea where the escalator was. The realization completely unnerved him, as did the stories circulating about Van Aadams girls so pampered and spoiled they had no idea how to wash their own hair.

Once he got out of the structure, he wouldn't know what to do next. He didn't have the slightest idea how to use public transportation, but he would have to. The thought just about gave him hives, which he was certain he could catch on an M.T. Only N.A.'s and tourists used mass trans, and apparently, they were used to using it Earthside, and it didn't bother them at all. A Moonside Family Member would rather die.

Literally. And it had happened, the dying from it, according to cautionary tales that circulated among the Family Members. More than once.

Plus, although the Borgioli assets had been restored by the government in return for Uncle Angelo's cooperation, Nicky wouldn't be able to stripe his credit card for so much as a toothbrush, or his uncle would know where he was. As he started thinking about food, lodging, and the simple necessities of daily life, the pile of onechips he had lifted on his way out of the Family compound seemed pitifully tiny.

Losing his nerve, he started to go back. His heart was pounding. He broke into a sweat. His early life had been one of privilege, no matter that it had been spent among the trashy, lowlife Borgioli Family. It was still a Family, and he had been highly placed in it. He had not been in the first circle, but the old regime was gone—the Godfather, Don Alberto, was dead; his daughter and Designated Heiress (and Hunter Castle's wife) Beatrice, had committed suicide; Big Al's favorite nephew, Joey, was also dead; and Deuce, of course, had opted out.

Now Uncle Angelo had taken over, bringing prestige and elevation to his branch of the Family. He had no children of his own. He also was unmarried. The logical course of action would be to Designate Nicky as his Heir. But if he did that, the pressure to whack Angelo for the good of the Family— and the good of the Moon—would be too much for Nicky to handle.

Maybe Angelo would understand that. If he did, he would privately respect Nicky for leaving even if he had to order a hit on him publicly. Nicky wondered how hits would be conducted now that the Charter Board was off-line. His entire life, the Charter Board had kept a real-time, running total of all the debts, dishonors, Vendettas, pieces of action, side bets, and so on that the Houses perpetuated amongst themselves. It had presided over all the meetings of all the Godfathers, Van Aadams C.E.O.'s, and the Scarlatti Select of Six. In intra-Family affairs, the Board was arbiter, negotiator, judge, and jury.

Or had been. Now all it was was a wall-sized bank of dimmed lights in an extremely fancy sit-down room with a round table the size of the Sea of Tranquillity divided into pie

shapes by color, one pie for each Family plus Castle Industries. Just before the war broke out, the MLF had been pushing
hard for a referendum for an "Independent" slice—independent being just about the wrongest word to describe a situation
that ever came down the pike.

Freakin' terrorists.

It was the MLF, in fact, that had claimed responsibility for
sabotaging the Charter Board. Nicky was still trying to decide
if it was a good thing or a bad thing. Without it, the Earthside
DOF could not run the economy efficiently. But except for
the running tabs it kept on everything, the Charter Board was
more of a checks-and-balances kind of thing than a governing
body. The Families had internalized all the nuances of dealing
with each other for over a century, and they could probably
continue to do so without the Charter Board.

So, a good thing. Of course the MLF would never see it
that way. They hated the Families.

Not a problem, as the feeling was more than mutual.

It perplexed him and every other Family Member and Affiliate how the N.A.'s could possibly believe the MLF was
operating on their behalf. That once they were in power, they
would give a damn about the little guys. The Families employed them, fed them, clothed them. Mass trans in the Moon
was absolutely free, and unmonitored. There was free public
education, funded by the exorbitant taxes imposed on the casinos. Aside from an occasional accidental shooting during a
Vendetta or small war, the civilians were protected from street
violence. Okay, and now and then, a bombing.

Could they claim the same Earthside, with their poison air
and their food with radioactivity and like that?

It still wasn't too late, Nicky figured. He could turn around
and no one would ever know about what had almost just happened here.

His badge vibrated. He startled, then tapped it.

"It's Ronnie," she whispered. "If you haven't gotten out of
here, run for your life. Your uncle just figured it out."

Nicky disconnected without saying a word.

And he ran.

*   *   *

Gabriel rolled over, waking Deuce, who, by necessity, was a very light sleeper. His blaster was in his hand by the time she finished moving, and she smiled calmly.

"It's just me," she whispered.

"Yeah. Figured that." He slipped the blaster back underneath his pillow.

She sighed and touched his face. "Well. That was pleasant. Not the blaster part. The other part."

"I thought so." He took her hand and kissed the tips of her fingers. "*Grazie, cara.*"

"So, you'll take over leadership?" she asked languidly, stretching.

He groaned. "Why can't I find a nice Italian girl, settle down, get fat eating spaghetti?"

"How dull." She chuckled at him and moved her head. "But as for the spaghetti part, now that you mention it, I'm starving."

"You're a woman of appetites."

She rose from the bed in all her beauty. No doubt about it, she was a looker. All those muscles, no flab, she worked out probably as much, or more, than Sparkle had in her showgirl days. She sashayed across the hut, more than aware that he was following every move, and put on a hunter green bathrobe. Her auburn tresses were spectacular against it; she put him in mind of Quintana Roo, the ingenue on *Phases*, everyone's favorite soap opera.

Then she opened the door to the Quonset hut and said to one of the guards, "Powers, can you ask O'Hara to get us some sandwiches? Whatever the kitchen's got."

"Yes, ma'am," the soldier responded.

She shut the door and leaned against it. "If it's meat, it'll be crater. We save our money on provisions. But our bullets are the finest money can buy."

"Oooh, you make me hot when you talk that," he said dryly. Then he got up out of bed and wondered if it was bad manners to ask how about the shower facilities. Operations like this, they conserved water sixteen ways to Friday. Back when he and Sparkle had just started out, they used to shower together to save credits. And they had crater everything. Only time he got to have real coffee, for example, was when he did his nightly casino rounds in his capacity as Borgioli Liaison.

"You want to take a shower with me or alone?" he asked her, deciding what the hell, if he was the big cheese around here, he could throw his weight around.

She blinked, then grinned. "With. I don't have private facilities, however."

"Don't matter." Actually, it did. Deuce was a modest sort of guy. "Lead the way."

She cocked her head. Then she crossed to a hanging rack of clothes and took a plaid bathrobe off a hanger.

"This was my father's," she said. "He died recently."

"My sympathies," he said, crossing himself. "May he rest in peace with God and His angels." He kissed his thumb.

"Thanks." She looked very sad, and he was moved. He wondered if his own kids would feel sad when he died. If they would know they were his kids.

If they would know when he died.

"But you guys don't believe we really die, do you?"

She looked at him. "I have faith," she said. She searched his face. "But I would really like to *know*."

"I wish I had answers for you, honey."

Her features were unreadable. "Perhaps someday you will." Then, as if catching herself, she added, "We believe in divine revelation."

"But you're not religious fanatics," he quipped. Then he held out his hand. "I'm sorry. That wasn't polite."

"But it was honest." She sighed.

There was an awkward silence. Deuce put on the bathrobe and slipped into his black boots. Gabriel made an amused face at his appearance.

"Once a fashion plate, always a fashion plate," he assured her.

She stepped into rubber sandals and reached for a metal ammo locker. Inside were shampoo, soap, her toothbrush.

"And an extra," she said, handing him an unopened box.

"Hey, neat." He was pleased.

She led the way back out. Deuce was self-conscious but you should never let the soldiers know that, not in this dame's army or anybody else's, so he sauntered along, not minding the good-natured chuckles he caught as they passed by.

"Not a lot of joy goes on around here," she said, maybe apologizing.

"You marrying me was joyful?" he queried.

She gave him a come-hither look. "You seemed pretty happy."

"Laughing all the way to the firing squad." His stomach growled. "Soon I'll be hungry enough for cratermeat."

"You've gotten soft."

They both chuckled at that one.

Everywhere they walked, soldiers snapped to attention. She gave them as sharp a salute in return. Very commanderish. Deuce wondered what her game was, handing him her nut. There were a number of advantages for her, the most obvious being, he took over the important function of standing in the spotlight. Possibly, someone might be fooled and shoot him instead of her. And he was going to have to do a lot of hustling to undo the damage her little announcement had no doubt caused.

"By the way," he asked, "I'm assuming you did not use birth control."

"And this is my fertile time," she replied, looking very sly.

He wondered if she should tell him that Iniya had insisted he was part space brother. Speaking of which . . .

"Where are my guys?"

"Being treated like royalty," she said.

"After we clean up, I'm seeing them."

"Sir, yes sir." She said it without malice, without hesitation.

She gestured to the right. Curtains of canvas tarp were suspended from a metal frame. Water was spewing rather unenthusiastically from a spigot, and someone was inside, moving around vigorously. There were a couple of grunts, maybe a groan, or a moan . . .

"Excuse me," Deuce said. "Could you two snap it up? Or three, or whatever?"

"Oh, my God," someone muttered.

Deuce nearly burst out laughing. It was Downtown Dallas who now poked his head out of the curtain and stared, red-faced at his boss.

"Padrino, mi scusi," he said.

Deuce waved his hand. *"Va bene."*

Dallas visibly relaxed. *"Grazie molto, Padrino."*

He disappeared back behind the curtain and started whispering urgently to someone else. Deuce grinned from ear to ear, which he should not do. Dallas had a responsibility to stay alert and on his toes when he was with his Godfather. But maybe love was in the air . . . or it was spring?

"You were too easy on him," Gabriel chided gently.

"Hey." He gave her a look. "You abdicated, remember? Go make the pasta.

"*O Mamma mia,*" he said, making as if to shield himself from her glare, "you'd better register those eyes as lethal weapons."

"Is everything with you a joke?"

"No. Just the parts that are funny." He grinned at her. "Tell you what, *commandante.* You deal with your personnel and . . ." he snapped his fingers. "Oh, yeah. You dealt with them by putting me in charge of them."

She looked like she wanted to say something, but she didn't say it. Deuce continued, "I half expected some kind of coup this morning. What's your game?"

"Nothing we can discuss here," she informed him.

He toyed with the sash on his bathrobe. "Y'know, I get the distinct impression that you're used to getting your way. With everyone. And I also am receiving some kind of psychic vibration that those days are over."

She shrugged. "Okay. As your Connie Lockheart, my job is to get pregnant and continue your line. I can't do that if I'm in the line of fire."

He was still puzzled. "But you put *me* in the line of fire instead. Is the plan to make a little Deuce and get rid of the big one?"

Now she really looked like she wanted to say something. But she shook her head. She batted the curtain, and said, "Show some respect, for God's sake! Your Godfather is out here in his bathrobe!"

"I'm sorry, Mrs. McNamara," Dallas blurted, emerging fully dressed. The chippie beside him was a dish, a redhead in a silk kimono and a pair of slippers with feathers on them.

"O'Hara," Gabriel said angrily, "I told Powers to send you for sandwiches."

"Ma'am, yes ma'am," O'Hara said, snapping to attention. "He told me he would find someone else, ma'am."

"At ease." Gabriel was obviously mortified. "Go put some clothes on."

"Yes, ma'am. Sir," she added, saluting Deuce.

He saluted back. Said to Dallas, "You'd better assist in the operation, soldier."

Dallas said with mock seriousness, "Sir, yes sir."

The two left. Deuce turned to his bride, and said, "Let's get wet. Of course, you look madder than a wet hen. Not that I've ever seen a hen."

She regarded him. "You could if you went Earthside."

He stared at her. "What are you saying?"

"Let's get cleaned up. We're going to have a few sit-downs today."

"Earthside," he persisted, holding on to her arm. She looked down at it, back up at him. He didn't let go.

"Sit-downs." She lowered her voice. "We cannot assume that we are not under surveillance."

"By your guys?" He tried to feign shock, but why bother? It didn't surprise him in the least that the MLF—even decent people like the Mormons—might be spying on their own big kahunas.

Family Members tried to get away with it, too. In a Family, you did that and got caught, you were whacked. Deuce did not know the protocol among God-fearing terrorist subversives.

Whatever; he stood aside and let her go into the shower first. Any number of people around her might want to whack him, and here he was with nothing for protection but their fearless leader, who had retired. A sitting duck and a lame duck at best.

Quack.

Just then, as if she had read his mind, Iniya strode up. She said, with Mr. Wong's voice, "I'll keep watch, Don McNamara."

"*Grazie,*" he told the remote data terminal of the alien broad, who might or might not be what she said she was, or half a dozen other things, including a ticking time bomb and/or proof positive that he was under way too much stress.

"*Prego,*" she replied easily, as if she'd been saying it all her life.

Gabriel took Deuce's hand and led him into the shower.

She took off her robe first and put it into a little cubicle to keep it from getting wet, then held her hand out for his.

He didn't move. "Sit-downs. Earth."

"Get clean," she said. He didn't know if that was supposed to be some kind of double entendre or a joke or what. He didn't really care. He was getting tired of the game-playing and of this woman's seemingly endless delight in throwing him for a loop.

"You got a hostility problem with my gender, on account of your father wanted you to be a boy?" he asked her.

She turned on the water but deflected it away from him. "In here, I'm fairly certain we can talk." She pointed to the water. "Yuet Chan is coming to talk with us. Or you, rather. I was to select a safe and neutral location for the sit-down. She claims to represent some very powerful Earthside forces, and she gave me some credentials that made me think she was telling the truth."

She held out her hands in a kind of "don't-blame-me" gesture.

"I don't know all the details. I'm pretty much a go-between."

She smiled at him and touched his cheek. "It has to do with some kind of space thing. A gate. I don't know. I told them I didn't want to know until it made sense for me to know. Knowledge can be a dangerous thing in the Moon."

Deuce wanted like anything to call Iniya in there. He stood in his robe, stubbornly refusing to part with it, while Gabriel spoke earnestly beneath the flashing sound of the water spray.

"The meeting is when?" he mouthed, not even chancing a whisper.

She covered her hand and let him see "seven." He had no idea what time it was, and only the vague thought that it might be a Tuesday.

"Let me wash your back," she urged. She stood naked like it was no big deal. Maybe it wasn't, for her. Maybe she'd slept with all kinds of guys all over the Satellite to further her ends.

But he took the robe off anyway, quite aware that he was disarmed in the most profound way.

About that time, the shooting began.

*   *   *

Sparkle was blind.

Moreover, she was certain that the !kth aliens had caused it. There was something about her that threatened them; it must have something to do with her intuition, which was better than that of most people.

And everything inside her was screaming to get her children and herself the hell out of there.

But now, she was blind. And too hot. The room was stifling.

And then Shiflett, the physician's assistant who attended her shortly after the birth, appeared in her room while she was staring and seeing nothing but black, and the stars and comets people see when they press their fingers against their closed eyelids or stare into blackness for too long.

"Ms. Sparkle?" he called softly, perhaps not wanting to startle her.

He did anyway, and she fought down panic. She had always heard that when you lost one sense, the others amplified. If that was true, maybe that was why she was so aware of the heat in the room.

The doctors were still not convinced that the blindness was permanent. She had overheard one using the term, "hysterical," which she understood to mean "psychological." She was not offended. She hoped it was true. She hoped her sight would return as immediately as it had vanished. She didn't care how it happened. She had three children; she was in what she knew to be enemy territory. She didn't care if they carved her eyeballs out of her head and replaced them with artificial ones, if it meant she could gather her children and leave.

"Shiflett," she said, when she could speak, for she was overcome with both relief and terror. Who knew why he was there?

She reached for him, gesturing to come closer. When he placed his fingertips against his ear, she whispered directly into it, "What do they look like?"

"Demons," he answered without hesitation.

Her stomach rolled. Chills raced down her back, and she was afraid she was going to scream. Instead, she swallowed hard. Her throat was closing up from fear.

"They want to kill my children."

There was a pause. He said, "How do you know?"

"I get feelings. I always have. Not consistently, and not whenever I want to. But about that, I am positive."

"All right." Clearly, he had made some kind of decision. "Your husband saved my life. And Bernardo Chang, who's aboard. His, too. We'll do whatever it takes to get you out of here."

She choked down emotion. She was not one for that kind of thing. Her mind was already racing down the corridors of several possible escape plans. She didn't know enough about their situation, about Hunter, about her condition, about the demons. About anything.

She started to say something, but Shiflett cut her off. "I'll be your eyes. Bernardo, too."

She nodded, feeling as though she were hanging in space. She had a quick memory of making love one night with Deuce in their apartment, all the sashes and restraints removed, so that they floated and caromed all over the bedroom.

They had laughed until they cried. Earthside tourists couldn't wait to try sex in the lighter gravity, and they were terrible at it: at least half of them got black eyes, and their bruises were so bad that a local term for tourists—besides "rabbits"—was B&B's, for "Black and Blue's."

Now she felt heavy, and dizzy, and terrified. He took her hand and she squeezed it, hard. She said, "Thank you," which was not an easy thing for Sparkle to say.

In the distance, a baby wailed. She tensed, and said, "Are they keeping them from me?"

"No. They're acting like we're one big happy family," Shiflett replied bitterly. "I don't understand how Hunter got mixed up with them. The crew of the ship is cracking. Everyone's frozen, they're so afraid. Except for Mr. Castle."

He added, "But he's terrified for you. For your health. He asks about you constantly. He's been screaming at the doctors."

"Get my children out first," she insisted. "I'm expendable."

"I'm not sure your babies would agree with you," he answered reluctantly. Then he caught his breath, and said, "Someone's coming."

The door opened.

She had never felt more alone.

Ronnie had her ear to the door, but she didn't even need to be within ten feet of the door to listen to all the shouting behind it. Nicky's Uncle Angelo, the Godfather, had just found the good-bye note Nicky had written.

Nicky had not told Ronnie he had left a good-bye note, and she thought exactly the same words that the Godfather shouted:

"How stupid can he be?"

Oh, God, Nicky, you're gonna die, Ronnie thought miserably.

"He's just confused. It's the war. He doesn't know which way to turn," a woman wailed. It was Nicky's mother, Ariana. Ronnie couldn't stand her, and the feeling was mutual. If she could have, the woman would have locked her precious son in a tower until he died from old age, to keep him safe from all the *puttanas* who only wanted him for his Family connections.

I love him, Ronnie thought indignantly, blowing a bubble in her nervousness. No one, but no one, could kiss like Nicky Borgioli.

Plus, he had given her wonderful presents: a beautiful new watch, a lot of very slinky dresses, a charge card at Donna MaDonna's lingerie store, not to mention satin sheets and velvet pillows for her bed.

I'm gonna miss him like crazy.

She blew another bubble.

I wonder if Angelo has a girlfriend?

Or room for another one?

"You always make excuses for him," Angelo continued. "That's why he hasn't amounted to anything."

"What, what? Angelo, how can you speak of him like that? He looks up to you like a father!"

"Because he's a coward who abandons his Family when we need all our muscle. Because he's such a moron, he simply leaves without discussing his concerns with me first. This is not the Borgioli way."

Oh, yeah, it is, Ronnie thought. *It's exactly the Borgioli way.* The Borgiolis were known all over the Moon and back Earthside for their lack of Family loyalty. When you belonged to such a loser Family, you could not really count on ties of blood and Membership to get you anywhere. So you had to hustle, and backstab, and flip-flop, and turn—do whatever it took. Angelo had operated like that, and now he was Godfather.

How soon they forget, she thought angrily.

"I wash my hands of him," Angelo cried. "I'm putting out a hit on him. No one disgraces us like this."

"*O, Dio mio,*" Ariana wailed. "No, Angelo, no. He's my only son. My baby."

"He didn't spare a thought for you when he left, did he? Abandoned you?"

"Angelo, don't even say it like that. I have my own money, my own connections. I don't need him to watch my back. I'm situated just fine."

"No son should ever walk out on his mother."

Unless she's Ariana Borgioli, Ronnie thought. *Then he should do just like I said: run.*

"He's just a child."

"Ariana, for God's sake, he's nineteen years old."

"Angelo, please don't put a hit out on him. Let me find him. Let me talk to him."

"It's too late. He has shamed the Family. If he hadn't written the note . . . if Back-Line Tony hadn't found it, I could look the other way. But that means either I gotta whack Tony on the off chance that he hasn't discussed it with anybody, or make an example of my own nephew." He sighed. "Do you think I like doing this?"

Ariana was sobbing. "*Per favore, mio fratello.*"

Veronica sighed. No use begging. Anyone with half a brain could see that Angelo's mind was made up. And if anyone had half a brain, it was Ronnie (Veronica) di Musso, daughter of a Borgioli Affiliate.

The problem was, her father was very sick, and there was a possibility that Affiliation might be terminated upon his death. If she didn't have a connection of her own, they all might be on the streets, N.A.'s without any transferable job skills to offer: Her father was a mechanic, that is to say in Family parlance, a professional hit man.

What if they tell him to hit Nicky?

Papa's sick, she reminded herself. *Too sick to work.*

Then there was the distinct sound of a blaster going off. Ronnie couldn't help it; she screamed.

Then men were charging her, one throwing her to the

ground while another threw the doors open and raced into the room.

She shouted, "I'm not armed!"

Then Angelo Borgioli shouted, "*O, Dio!* My sister's killed herself!"

NINE

The news spread fast: Donna Ariana, Nicky Borgioli's mother, had killed herself for one reason and one reason only: to lay on Nicky's Uncle Angelo a deathbed obligation to protect her son. It really classed up everyone's opinion of her, and it lent Ronnie a kind of leg up in the organization, that she had been the squeeze of a guy whose *mamma* would do such a thing for him. A broad like that was worth taking notice of.

Ariana's funeral was pretty nice, considering the postwar economy, with its emphasis on limitation. She still got a good, satin-lined box, decent makeup, and like that. Plus, real flowers. After all, she was the sister of a Godfather. If you couldn't manage real flowers for a dame like that, what good were you for the rest of your Family?

The funeral trade was huge in the Moon, because of the Family lifestyle. There were funerals every day of the year, including Christmas, Hanukkah, and New Year's. Everybody was fully equipped to attend them; all Family Members and Affiliates had a closet full of black clothes, nice stuff, and Ronnie was no exception: Her dress for Ariana's funeral was her very favorite, except for her evening gowns. It had tiny little black-velvet sleeves, then scooped down nicely in front. There was a cluster of black roses at her cleavage, and more around the hem, which came to mid-thigh. Also, a little half veil and a choker of very nice craterjet beads. Nicky had promised her real ones someday, but now she doubted that day would ever come.

The service was held in the sit-down room of the Borgioli

compound, since somebody had blown up their chapel. One of the most disgusting things about that was that the little drawers with everybody's ashes went up with the rest of the consecrated joint, and so there were these great big heaps of dust and bone mixed in with the wreckage of the chapel itself.

It was a terrible mess, and there was no real way to separate out what was what and who was who. So it had all been scooped up and put into several bronze containers, each with several hundred names etched on it.

Ronnie could not remember anybody ever blowing up a chapel before. It was not nice at all. It was not the kind of thing decent human beings did.

So the Department of Fairness had probably done it.

The service for Ariana di Borgioli was brief, for a Catholic funeral mass. Then the cremated ashes were carried solemnly from the sit-down room to the chapel, which was still being cleaned up. Ronnie walked way back in the procession, not really having any official status, but also no one was pretending she hadn't been sort of quasi-related to Ariana.

Angelo's new friends, the DOF lackeys, got booed when they arrived after the services for the reception. They looked a little shaken, and pale for people who lived on the surface of a planet with a sun. What did he—and they—expect? A welcoming committee?

One of the DOF guys sidled up to Ronnie while she was pouring herself a glass of champagne. He was an unwelcome intrusion: The Borgioli men were eyeing her, trying to decide whether to approach her or not. If she could make up her mind in time, she would have a new protector by party's end, of that she was certain.

Unless this moron kept her possibilities at bay, simply by breathing in her vicinity.

In a black suit and wearing a black mourning band around his upper arm, the DOF gravoid was young and, okay, kind of cute, with dark hair and big eyes like Nicky's. The free-fall drugs that Earthsiders took to acclimate themselves to the lower gravity seemed to have worked. He had on gravity shoes, but he didn't have that green look a lot of nonlunar types got when the dizziness really got to them.

He approached respectfully, and said, "Miss di Musso?"

She sipped her champagne. "Yeah?"

"I know this is a hard time for you," he began.

She narrowed her eyes at him. "Yeah."

"But we were wondering if you could help us find Nicky. Now that it's safe for him to return . . ."

She almost laughed in his face. "Whatever gave you that notion?"

The man was taken aback. He said, "The deathbed obligation—"

"Is to not whack him. Signora Ariana didn't say anything about making sure he's happy, well fed, or keeps all his limbs and internal organs intact."

The man blinked. "Oh. I guess we misunderstood the nature of the obligation."

"Guess so." She shrugged.

"Boy, I'm thirsty," he said brightly, looking around.

"There's champagne."

His cheeks turned slightly pink. "I don't drink alcoholic beverages."

"So it's true." Her tone was harsh.

"What is?"

"That you're all really League of Decency, masquerading as other things."

"Is that what you people believe?" He sounded very surprised. "But the separation of church and state—"

"Is a nice con," she said bitterly. "A fantasy at best, maybe, depending on how cynical you are. And so is mob wives wanting picket fences and husbands who come home in one piece at 5 Moon Standard Time every night, plus real flowers in their flower boxes. But two miles down on Moonbase Vegas, it ain't gonna happen."

She threw back her champagne and turned to go. He touched her arm.

"I'm not League," he insisted.

"I still wouldn't tell you where the can is, much less Nicky Borgioli," she retorted. "And if you ever lay a hand on me again, I'll break it."

He jerked his hand away and held them both up, as if to show her he was unarmed.

"Please. I pose no danger to you," he said.

She sneered at him in derision and stomped off.

Wimp.

As she sailed across the room, she collided with the God-father himself. Her empty champagne glass fell from her grasp; Angelo neatly caught it, set it down, and handed her a fresh one.

She nearly died of a heart attack as she took it from him. The only reason she was safe from Angelo was that she had no idea where Nicky was. If she had known, she would have gone into immediate hiding. Her presence here was an announcement that she had nothing to conceal. *Nothing to know, no need to blow.* It was an old Family saying.

She was saying it to herself now, over, and over. And over and over. It was okay to be here. She was on solid ground.

"*Padrino, mi scusi*," she said in a rush.

"Veronica. A sad day, eh?"

Was it a trick question? Ronnie suddenly wondered how she had had the brass to show up here. Well, showing was important because she wanted to show respect, and also to show that she had no reason to be afraid. But hanging around . . . unnecessary, and foolish.

"Don Angelo," she tried again. "A sad day, yes. Very sad. I'm so sorry about . . ." She took a breath. "Signora Ariana didn't like me. Basically, she thought I was a *puttana*."

She was aghast. Mamma mia, *why did I say that?*

Angelo was likewise astonished. His mouth opened, and he just stared at her for a moment, and then he laughed.

He took her arm and led her away from the others, into a corner where he sipped the champagne he had given her, made a face, and said, "This stuff is terrible. It's practically crater. I'll blow away the caterer."

Then he cocked his head and folded his hands over his chest. "Ariana didn't like me, either. My own big sister. And I sure as hell didn't like her." He crossed himself. "May her soul, precious to God, rest forever with the Virgin Maria and all the angels."

"Amen," Veronica said, also crossing herself.

Angelo took another sip, grimaced, and set the champagne down on a nearby table. He said, "Well, Signorina Veronica, I must say, you're a breath of fresh air."

She shook her head. "Don Angelo, I swear. I don't know where Nicky is."

"Him. What a punk." Angelo sighed. "I suppose you are nursing true love forever for him?"

"No way," she blurted.

He laughed again. "Smart girl." He regarded her seriously. "Do you have a new *amore* yet?"

She was thrilled beyond words. None other than Angelo Borgioli, the Godfather of the Family, was going to advise her, tell her who to go with among her choices. She took a moment to organize her thoughts, although her mind was racing.

"Not yet," she said. "I'm still assembling the deck."

He nodded. "What about an ace? Got one?"

"An ace?" She was all ears. After all, nobody was better connected than a Godfather. "Such as what?"

"One of me. A Godfather."

She was thrilled. "Oh, do you know someone—" She stopped. Her heart skipped at least six beats in a row. "Don Angelo, *you*?"

He shrugged, conveying an attractive mix of modesty and *duh*. She waited him to say something, until she realized the obvious: that he was waiting for her to ask the real question.

So she did. "Why me?"

"Why not you?" he asked. "You're young, beautiful, and clever. Plus you know how to dress for a funeral." He eyed her appreciatively.

"Godfather, you're too kind," she breathed.

He held up a finger. "One condition."

"I don't know where he is," she said anxiously.

He smiled brilliantly at her. "And let's keep it that way, *sì*?" He raised a brow. "Ancient history, for both of us, all right? That is my condition. See, I don't want to cause him pain. I won't seek him out. But if I see him, I won't hesitate to do everything short of killing him."

"I understand."

"Ariana wasn't very smart with the wording of her obligation. It doesn't hold me to much."

"I thought the same thing," she admitted.

He smiled at her. "Nicky loves you, in his way. But he's a boy. A woman like you, you need a man. A full-blooded man."

She dipped her head to hide her red cheeks. This could not

be happening. It was like something out of a storybook. A miracle.

"*Sì, Padrino,*" she murmured.

"*No, no, cara.*" He closed his hand over hers and gave her a gentle squeeze. "For you, I am Angelo. Simply Angelo."

She caught her breath. She didn't think she could do it. Call him that. Act like he was a normal man.

"Angelo," she repeated.

It was surprisingly easy, after all.

She smiled.

"Angelo."

"*Sì,* Veronina?" he asked solicitously. He laid his hand over hers. "What would you like? Shall we go somewhere more private? To celebrate?"

"*Sì,* Angelino," she said boldly. "That's what I would like."

They began to leave. Then Angelo stopped and pointed to her mouth. "And, my darling? No more gum, all right?"

"Of course." She took the wad out of her mouth, smiled at him, and stuck it underneath the table. He watched approvingly, nodding when she showed him her empty fingers.

Together, they sauntered from the room. Ronnie was so amazed, she could barely walk a straight line. But Angelo put one foot in front of the other, as if he had done this kind of thing a hundred times.

That made her feel a hundred times better.

Italian men were so . . . *Italian.*

But she was a little wistful about no more gum. It was such a delicacy, in the Moon.

But so were Godfathers. Far rarer.

Far more difficult to obtain.

"What are you thinking of, *cara?*" he asked, as they left the party.

She smiled adoringly up at him. "I was thinking about how much I love you."

He patted her hand and gave her a warm, Italian smile. "That's good. That's so wonderful."

Despite her triumph, Veronica felt a little sad for Nicky.

Putz.

Deuce was enjoying a crater hamburger cross-legged on his marriage bed, the burger not so bad after all, except maybe not for breakfast, when Iniya came in. She crossed the room, and said quietly to him, "I have an incoming for you from D'inn. We need privacy."

"Okay." He glanced toward the tent flap to the right, where his bride had disappeared to do something bridely, he assumed, or else plan a raid; and gestured for Iniya to join him outside.

The soldiers snapped to attention, and Deuce realized he really was going to have to make a statement soon, but also realized that he seemed to be in no hurry, which was telling. He wasn't a psychologist; but hell, someone announces that you—yes, you—want to cause the downfall of your own preferred way of life and you don't initiate damage control immediately, well you kind of wonder what's up with yourself, don't you?

"Incoming is arriving," Iniya told him.

Then, KABLAM!

Someone hit her with a laser grenade, and she went flying.

Deuce, miraculously unhurt, shouted, "Damn it!"

"What happened? What's going on?" Gabriel shouted back, racing toward him from the tent. She tackled him and threw him to the ground, completely covering him with her body, as he had done with his mother.

In that moment, he began to think seriously about loving her. She seemed like a very nice girl. Thoughtful, at least.

"My robot," he moaned. Footsteps crashed all around them. Men and women shouted orders.

"Pieces," she yelled into his ear.

Deuce sighed.

Everyone scrambled for a few hours, searching the camp and the outlying tunnels, the perimeters, and so on. Now he and Gabriel were holed up in a maximum-security bunker which was none too roomy, staring at the pile of crap that had once been Mr. Wong.

Like those statues of the guy staring at a skull, Deuce held the triangle-shaped remote data terminal, which had been operating out of Mr. Wong's skull. It appeared to have survived without so much as a scratch, if he correctly remembered what it looked like.

"Hello?" he said to it. He didn't know how it could communicate if it had no instrumentality. He tapped it for a moment, wondering if it was wondering the same thing.

His bride looked up from the headcracker she was polishing—Deuce had always loved broads who could clean their own weapons—and said, "Hello."

He realized she thought he was talking to her. He had not let her in on any of his secrets about guys in outer space and robot linkups and all like that. Nor did he include it in his plans for the near future. She was too sly and slippery, this girl. She would be an excellent shell-game dealer.

"That Scarlatti guy who was here when we arrived," Deuce said. "Blond moustache."

"Carmine?" she queried, making her headcracker go *cha-chung* as she checked the homing device.

"He good with electronics?"

She gazed at the remote data terminal, obviously clear on where he was going with his questions. "This is something very new," she said, inviting him to share.

He still did not.

"I'll send for him," she said, philosophically. He was impressed that she not only accepted his unwillingness to reveal his cards, but she seemed to understand it.

She started to get up. He stopped her by raising his hand.

"I'll send for him," he corrected her.

He walked to the door, opened it, saw that the old twenty dozen guards were gone and the new twenty dozen guards were in place, including a freshly scrubbed girl with freckles who looked no older than sixteen.

He said to her, "You know Carmine Scarlatti?"

She turned six shades of crimson. "Oh, sir," she blurted. "We're just friends."

Ah, youth. "Let's just keep that between us, okay, honey?" he suggested kindly. "Go get him, okay? I've got an interesting little project for him, is all. *Capisce?*"

She nodded, still incredibly flustered. She was so cute Deuce almost hugged her, but then she would probably really go off the deep end.

He gestured for her to scoot along; she snapped to and saluted. Bemused, he did the same, and watched her hustle off.

Then he turned to the next guard over, who was an older male with bristly sideburns. "I want a sit-down with all the *capos* and like that. The highest-ranking officers. The really big cheeses. I want it in two hours. I want it wherever you hold those things around here."

"Sir, yes, sir." The guard made a valiant attempt to snap his own spine, he straightened so hard, and off he went.

Deuce watched with satisfaction as two more guards appeared like magic, and took the places of the ones he had sent off on business. He looked at each in turn—two guys, young, kinda cocky, and said, "You know who I am?"

"Sir, yes, sir," said the one on the right. His face became impassive and unreadable. Very soldierly. "Deuce McNamara, sir."

"I'm your CO," Deuce continued. "Officially and for real, too."

"Yes, sir." No expression.

"Accent on for real."

"Sir, yes, sir."

"Private," Deuce added, glancing at the guy's markings on his sleeves. "You ever killed anybody?"

This time Mr. Big Shot missed a beat. "No, sir."

"I have."

The man's expression did not change, but Deuce could tell he was processing the new information.

He leaned back into the tent. Gabriel was watching him with a mixture of amusement and pride. He looked at her with a mock frown, and growled, "You. Pasta."

She chuckled. He wondered if she was pregnant with his baby. If it really did have little bit of space brother in its DNA.

"Spread the word. I'm taking over."

"Sir, yes—"

Deuce shut the bunker door, armed it, voiced, "McNamara. Queen's to Queen's Level Three," and sauntered back to the bed.

"You ain't going to like what I'm going to do to your organization," he informed her. When she kept grinning at him, he got a little edgy, and said, "What?"

"I have a bet on you," she drawled, leaning back on her elbow. "And I know I'm going to win."

"The bet is?"

She picked up the remote data terminal. "When you're ready to swap secrets, let me know."

It was his turn to chuckle. He liked this broad. He really did. "It's a deal."

His brand-new MLF-supplied comm badge vibrated. He tapped it, and said, "This is General McNamara. I want a full-dress uniform delivered to the security bunker. Also, fatigues and regular everyday uniforms. Shoes and all the gear as well. Here are my sizes." He rattled them off.

"Yes, sir, General McNamara." The voice on the other end was hushed and excited. "Sir? I have just received word that your mother has arrived."

"Very good. Have her escorted here." He paused. "How's she doing?"

"A little rattled, sir. She has your dog, sir."

"What's your name?" he asked.

"Stefano Scarlatti, Don McNamara."

"Oh, yeah?" Deuce brightened. "Andreas's boy?" Andreas Scarlatti had been the *capo di tutto di capi* of the Select of Six before the *Star* had blown up. The young man on the intercom was the closest thing to a prince the Scarlattis—or any Family—had. And he had joined the MLF.

"Yes, sir, Don . . ." He corrected himself. "General, sir."

"I'm having a sit-down in two hours," Deuce said. "I want you there."

"Absolutely, *Padrino*. Whatever you want. You just say the word."

Deuce smiled at the use of the language. Maybe you could take the boy out of the Family, but *davvero, davvero*, you couldn't take the Family out of the boy.

"In fact, I could use a private meeting with you right now. You want I should speak with your commanding officer?"

"That would be best, Don . . . General."

"Don General. I like that. I think that's how I'll style myself." He nodded to himself. "Okay, put your *capo* on."

"*Sì.*"

The *capo* was a dame; that is to say, a woman officer person. Deuce went through the motions of requesting permission, blah-blah-blah, when they both knew that she had better let the Scarlatti kid go to Deuce or there would be hell to pay. In triplicate.

But rank's got its privileges, and soon the kid and Deuce were meeting in the bunker. Gabriel had had her oh-so-predictable change of heart about Deuce being the only guy in charge: How did you turn over your entire organization to anyone, much less someone you barely knew? So she was there, very official in one of her uniforms.

Deuce was, too, in military green and gold, sparing a moment's pause in front of the mirror for the boy he had been less than three years ago. Then, he had been a Casino Liaison so ashamed of his Borgioli colors that he had only worn them during work hours, like temporary tattoos. In that kid's wildest dreams, he had never been the head of a Family, much less on speaking terms with anybody in the MLF.

Or the son of a man who, a robot was telling him, was not completely human.

"Okay, see, this is a remote data terminal for some pretty advanced stuff," Deuce said, embroidering the truth a little. Or rather, avoiding it. "It's something private. A prototype, just for us."

Stefano nodded. "I can see that, Don General."

Gabriel leaned forward curiously. Deuce watched her scan the remote, saw her coming up empty.

"I want to put it in a mechanical body."

There was a rap on the door. Deuce's badge vibrated, and he took the call.

"Sir, it's Carmine Scarlatti," a voice announced. "Shall we pass him through, sir?"

"Hold on." Deuce put the badge on hold and turned to Stefano. "What do you know about this guy?"

"Maverick," Stefano said without hesitation. "Loose cannon. And a true Scarlatti, when it comes to cutting-edge technology. I'll be honest. I would be good help for him, but he would better at doing what you want."

"Really." Deuce cocked his head. He looked impressed. "You're a smart kid."

Stefano smiled. "I got some street cred, that's all, Don General. Carmine, he's got the gray matter."

"Then you help him. And you watch him. He gets hinky, you come to me."

Stefano looked excited. "*Sì, prego.*"

"I'll have you transferred over to my personal staff."

The kid was about to burst. Gabriel looked concerned, making a kind of "no-no" gesture Stefano couldn't see. Deuce acted as if he didn't notice, and he was a bit irritated with her. You never pulled crap like that in a Family meeting; you never knew who had mirrors or surveillance equipment or like that.

Deuce turned on his badge, and said, "Send Scarlatti on in."

The door chuffed and whooshed as the locks undid; there were all kinds of other stuff they were doing on the other side, including the retinal scan and fingerprint readout and all like that. In this day and age, you could scan just about anything about a guy. Including if he was human, and Deuce wondered why in his whole life, nothing about his supposed weirdo DNA had ever come to light. Maybe nobody had known how to notice it.

Whatever. Now was not the time, for here came Carmine, with his brand and his trademark glassy stare. Also, a ring of spackled holes on his bald head from the removal of neural enhancers, which of necessity were embedded in the scalp when they were applied. Deuce supposed that to join the MLF, you had to have them removed. As they allowed you to hallucinate at will, he supposed that was a pretty good rule.

"Okay, here's the deal," he said. "This is a remote data terminal, very different, very prototype. It was housed inside my former employer's butler."

"Mr. Wong got blown up?" Stefano asked with dismay.

"Yes."

"May his soul rest with the angels," Stefano said feelingly, crossing himself, "if he had one."

Carmine made a quiet sort of snort as he respectfully took the data terminal from Deuce and examined it. He swore softly in dialect, glanced guiltily at Gabriel, who appeared to take no notice, and held the object up to the light.

"Don . . . um, what we are calling you, sir?" he asked.

"Don General," Stefano supplied, and the Scarlattis grinned at each other.

"Fitting." Carmine looked reluctant to give the terminal back to Deuce when he held his hand back out. "But Don General, that is one weird thing. Did my Family make it?"

"Your ex-Family?" Gabriel corrected him.

Deuce cleared his throat. "Tell me if you think you can put this in a new body."

"Well . . ." Carmine scratched his little puttied circles in a kind of unconscious, rhythmic motion. With a pang, Deuce remembered that Sparkle used to do that to her belly when she was carrying the twins. He always thought she was caressing her unborn children, loving them, but then another woman had told him that when the skin stretches, it itches like crazy.

That took some of the romance out of it for a while, but he was so crazy-happy that she was pregnant that he decided to go with the caressing notion. Maybe God made the skin of mothers-to-be itchy so that they would caress their babies.

You never knew the ways of Divine Providence: why one guy who guys tried to whack survived time and time again, and them some poor mook who's only crossing the street gets mangled so badly not even medical science can rebuild him.

Why a well-meaning guy like Little Wallace Busiek died, and really foul creeps lived to be two hundred. Maybe God had an itchy trigger finger and some guys just wandered into His crosshairs.

But these were questions for Family Monsignors and like that. Survival was his game, not what came after it.

"Okay, resuming," he said.

Everyone was looking at him. He realized he'd kind of drifted off there. He was bone-weary. But now was not the time to take a vacation. If he had thought he'd had duties and responsibilities before, he had been like unto a little child.

"I want you two to put this thing in a robot, only don't tell anyone about it." He looked at Gabriel. "Can you set them up and deal with all the security?"

"Sure," she said, nodding emphatically.

That's my contingency wife, he told himself, with immense pride.

"We'll call it Project Iniya," he said.

"What does that stand for?" Gabriel asked. Man, her hair was gorgeous. He wondered if it was galvanized, or what.

"It's a family pet name, little F," he said. She looked mildly confused, although the Scarlattis knew he was talking about the nuclear family, as opposed to the casino big-F Families. The language, again.

Just then, he was commed again.

"Your mother's here, sir."

"Show her in. No scans," Deuce said. He didn't want anyone to paw over his mother.

After all the airlocks and timelocks and disarming and like that, his raven-haired mother stood on the threshold, in MLF khakis, which on her curvy frame were stupendous. The jaws of the two Scarlattis dropped. Deuce knew she must have had a rejuv, especially since Earthsiders looked older than Moonsiders of the same age, because of all the Earthside heavy gravity.

"Hello, dear. I heard the news." As Moona Lisa leaped from her arms and joyously raced to Deuce, she gestured to the data terminal. "Poor Mr. Wong."

Deuce squatted so the dog could lick his face. "What else did you hear?"

She shook her head. "That you've assumed command of the MLF. The Families are crazed. Every single one has declared Vendetta."

He took that in. "Not surprising." He looked at Gabriel. "So, your plan was?"

"I want to reunite the MLF. We've splintered. We're arguing among ourselves."

"And putting me in charge will certainly make that happen." He frowned in complete bewilderment. "You are whacked, Gabe."

"You've been called the Godfather of the Moon," she argued. "I fully intend that once you find your way around here, you will unite the Moon against the Earthsiders. This is the awkward phase. But no one else can do it, Deuce. It's you, or we will be fighting a long, hard, cold war that"—she glanced at the Scarlattis—"that we stand a good chance of losing."

They didn't looked shocked. In fact, Carmine gave her a long, appraising look, and murmured, "*Brava.*"

At her sharp expression, Deuce cut in. "Well said."

She didn't know Family ways too good, which surprised him. All the Families had seminars on the MLF. Obviously, they had not kept up with all the changes, though. He'd been surprised by all the recent Mormon activity. And if he been surprised, he could only hope that everyone else had been, too.

Especially now that it was his group doing all that Mormon activity.

So he rubbed his hands together, and said, "Gabriel, I need someone to debrief me before the sit-down, bring me up to speed. I got a lot of stuff to learn in, oh, eighty-three minutes."

She looked at him and smiled happily.

She said, *"Bravissimo,"* with just the most perfect accent. Like she was Family born and bred. "Deuce, *te vojo bene assai."*

I am yours.

For the first time, Deuce thought they might actually win this war.

TEN

The sit-down.

It was being held underground, as in, underneath what everyone tended to think of as the ground on the base level of the MLF camp. Tourists never understood how Moonsiders could make this abstract geographical leap, since all of Moonbase Vegas was at least two miles down in a maze of tunnels, caverns, and passages to begin with. But Moonsiders could, and did, to the extent that some people felt claustrophobic in the "basements" of various buildings. This made no sense at all, but neither did a lot of other things the Earthside government spent a lot of money studying and theorizing over.

The bunker was heavily fortified, and no wonder: Deuce had no idea the MLF was so top-heavy with high rollers, and not just people with lots of spangles on their epaulets. Family *capos*, lieutenants, the *consigliere* of the Smith Family, who had drawn up Deuce's Honorary Papers of Affiliation. It was like holding a royal flush.

He noted Gabriel's proud smile as he took in the crowd of maybe fifty, realizing she had neglected on purpose to brief him in detail on the makeup of the organization. When they'd gone through their rundown, he had figured she hadn't had time to go organize the stats for him, even though it was pretty much tops on his list—after what kind of weaponry they had.

Now he saw through her omission, and he thought, *Wow, honey, thanks. What an amazing wedding present.*

He had the same visceral sense of quick, startled pleasure as when everyone jumps from behind the sofa on your birthday, and yells, "Surprise!"—after your wife or somebody else standing next to you makes sure you're unarmed. For this was an MLF he could deal with. It was a group he could lead. He knew at least a third of the people in this room by name. Family men and women, people who knew how the real world worked.

Seated a bit apart, his mother beamed at him, communicating her understanding. She was a sharp cookie, his mom. Looking all spiffy in her fatigues, all that black hair . . . she was not your typical chubby Italian *mamma*, knitting socks for the Catholic Ladies Association charity bazaar.

"Okay," he said. "First order of business. You all know General Kinkade-Jones. For the record, we have entered into a contingency liaison. I'm her husband."

Hearty congratulations passed around the room. Some of the people there looked honestly happy. Deuce took note of who they were. Mostly Family Members, as he would have expected, thinking to themselves that finally, they had someone they understood—and who understood them—in their midst.

"*Grazie*." He put his hands up to still the murmur. "Second order of business. As you all know, she has requested that I take over leadership of the organization."

The Family people looked happy. But if looks could kill, he'd be stuffed in a crater by now, with how some of the other people in the room were glowering at him.

"Let's be honest, *paisani*." He smiled, ignoring the bristling at his usage of Italian. "Those of us who grew up in Families, it's going to take a long time to forget our old ways. And I'm wondering if we *should* forget all of them. *Davvero, davvero*, there's a lot that's good about our former lifestyle."

Gabriel listened intently. He could almost hear her willing him to go on, over the shifting around in the gray Kevlite-derivative seats and the disapproval so evident on the faces of those he figured for N.A.'s. Like they were thinking, *Those bastards are going to try to steal the MLF from us, too.*

"There is also a lot that is rotten in the Family economic and political system, however," he added, with ringing confidence. "But here's the deal. We are in a war now, and we don't have time to worry about our differences, Families, Affiliateds, Independents. But if we pretend they aren't there, it'll be like not trying to think of a white polar bear." Which Deuce had never seen in his life, except in gas films and flatphotos.

He got more agreement.

"In my brief time here in MLF territory, I have seen that those of us soldiers—and I include myself—who grew up in Families have not truly left many of our Family ways behind. When one Scarlatti salutes another, he sees more than a superior in the MLF. He sees a cousin."

The Family people nodded. The others looked worried. A few heads swiveled meaningfully in Gabe's direction, and she kept her gaze fixed on Deuce.

"I don't know so much about your training in the MLF," he lied, "but in the Families, we get some history classes along the way." Yeah, beaten into them by nuns, if they were in one of the three Italian Families—Scarlattis, Borgiolis, or Caputos.

"The thing is, nothing unites people like a common enemy. Before Earthside came calling, the Families and the MLF were each other's enemies. For a very long time."

He started walking around the room, eyeing everyone who was seated, the way he had seen guys do in war movies.

"I'm guessing most of you still think of each other as the enemy you'll get back to fighting after we get rid of the temporary one."

Both Carmine Scarlatti and some kid who looked just about as weird as Carmine did, nodded in unison.

"That ain't gonna cut it," Deuce said bluntly. "Cuz when you're in a battle, you gotta be able to count on the guy next to you, or both of you are dead."

That wasn't literally true. When he was in the Borgioli Family, Deuce had fought in plenty of situations, and he had rarely, if ever, trusted the guy next to him. But his speech sounded good, and the guys were buying it, so he kept going.

"So here's what needs to happen. This is what I propose. This is the day the music dies, my friends." He stared at each man, woman, and the occasional mechanical. "We need to find a way to establish that we are Moonsiders, period, the end. We are not Families and N.A.'s. After we get our satellite back, things are going to have to be different, or we're all going to die."

"Overnight, that's not going to happen, us being like, all cozy," Stefano said bluntly.

"I agree." That was Giuliana Caputo, the grand-niece of the current Designated Heir, Salvatore.

"Yeah, but we can *act* like it's going to happen," Deuce insisted. "Otherwise, and I kid you not, we are going down. The entire Moon. We might as well cave now, get the best terms we can."

Then something struck him like the proverbial bolt of lightning, not that he had ever seen lightning. He recalled what the data terminal had said when Iniya had first contacted him: *This Earth, Moon conflict only.*

In other words, this was not the big kahuna. The alien had barely acknowledged that this situation might even be a problem, in the bigger scheme of things.

He kind of vagued out as he considered what was going on. All the faces, staring at him, depending on him. Maybe he was getting sidetracked. Maybe it didn't matter who ran the Moon, as long as their space was protected from the bad guys.

He cleared his throat, thought about bringing that little matter up, then realized that no one in the room had reason to believe a single word about alien invasions, except him.

But Angelo did. Angelo, who was now in Vendetta with him, and Deuce didn't even really know why. Oh, he knew the Families' party line—that a Godfather had defected to the MLF and was therefore traitor scum, worthy of being taken out, etc., but he also knew Angelo had been there when he had made first contact. His Borgioli cousin could not deny the reality.

And yet, by pursuing Vendetta, he was denying it.

"Listen," Deuce blurted, then clamped his mouth shut in frustration. If he went there right now, he would sound like a crazy person.

Everything was happening so fast. *I want one of those lives like they have on the viso scan*, he thought. Where everyone had nice clothes, was relaxed and extremely attractive, and all they have to worry is what kind of wine to drink: Callisto or Miranda? To drive a brand-new Nebby or a "pre-owned" Sidereal?

He sighed. Real life was pretty darned difficult. No wonder half the population was addicted to Chan drugs.

However, everyone in the room was waiting to hear whatever it was he wanted them to listen to. He had to say something.

"What I propose for now is this. I'm more than open to discussion on it. We'll divide up into the groups we really feel that we are a part of, only we'll call them divisions. We'll have the six casino divisions, the Mormon division, and the originally N.A. division." He glanced at his wife. "Any other divisions we need?"

"That's good," she said.

"That's the way it's going to be, then."

There was something to be said for Godfathers, and monarchies, and other despotic systems: The people had both a king, and a scapegoat, rolled into one. It was an important role.

Vital to the survival of his people.

And there were his people; every person in this room. Even the ones who hated Deuce's guts.

I am *the Godfather of the Moon*, he thought dizzily.

"Don General, let's be frank," said a woman whom Deuce assumed to be a Smith by her beautiful mocha skin—the Smiths having assimilated the Mitchells and the Badrus, who had been the Families with dark-skinned Family Members and Affiliates. Unless she'd recently had a makeover, or used a colorant. Neither of which was considered fashionable.

"We're never going to think of everybody as the same. We've been conditioned for centuries to think of everybody not of our Family as the enemy."

"Then we have to redefine what the Family is," Deuce said earnestly. "We have to become the Moon Family. *Famiglia della Luna*."

There were snorts of derision, but an equal number of people got real quiet. They were actually thinking about it. To be totally and completely honest, Deuce wasn't sure he could go there himself.

But then, neither could Moses.

Talk about your Messiah complex.

But if he couldn't mass them against Earth, how could he mass them against an alien invasion?

Maybe this is the best thing that could have happened to us. A warm-up round.

He felt weary beyond his years, deep inside his bones, and

down through the core of his soul. His new guts hurt bad.

Maybe that's because they don't contain !kth DNA, or the right amount, or something, he realized. *Our doctors don't know about it, didn't manage to accidentally include it in the cloning process.*

Maybe my body will reject my cloned organs.

Is rejecting them right now, hence the pain.

Maybe I'm dying.

The thought stunned him, and for a moment he panicked. He was only twenty-seven, in a time when people lived, as a matter of course, to be 227 and much, much older.

Then he rallied:

If I am dying, I'll make sure it was worth it.

There was a kind of exhilaration in thinking that way; in a perverse, wildman kind of way, dying while leading a war would be dramatic and exciting.

Not really, he told God.

In case He was listening.

Deuce was less sure of that now, than he ever had been before.

From the Captain's Log of Gambler's Star:

I'm trying to remember the first time I saw the !kth on the screen and then the holos. They must have appeared to be unbelievably repulsive to me. But I'm used to them now.

They're telling me that Sparkle has been so traumatized by a blurry first view while she was half-asleep and recovering from the delivery of the twins that she has made herself go blind. Knowing as I do that she has what is termed "an approachable mind," I can fully believe this. Sparkle has a gift in her ability to catch glimpses of the future and have intuitions about the present, but this must mean her brain is built differently from other people's. Therefore, it may be that there is something about the !kth environment that is harming her, physically and/or mentally.

I don't know if the !kth know about her gift. They play their cards closer to their vests than even I do. Which is really saying something.

I can't say I'm sorry they and I have made contact. No one else out here reached out to me, and they had plenty of warn-

ing and ample opportunity. And who knows? in the end the !kth may prove to be the best thing that ever happened to mankind, despite my current sensations of unease. I still believe we can exploit this relationship to our benefit.

Mankind's, I mean.

Who am I to judge?

Hunter Castle
Aboard ship, 2145.1

Deuce gave everyone at the sit-down a chance to talk. Most of them gave brief, canned speeches about being happy—or well, not so much—with the new state of affairs, blah-blah, and Deuce made like they were all really saying something other than "I want in on the action," or "You want my vote, you gotta prove yourself."

Deuce was okay with that. Either way. He wanted loyal people, and he wanted people smart enough to know that loyalty was a valuable commodity that they could buy and sell. Also, that currently, he hoped he had the deepest pockets of whatever currency they wanted to be paid.

The point of the meeting was simply to meet and start thinking of each other as *fratelli*, not to form a strategy or a battle plan or any of that. Though it may have seemed to someone else that it was far more important to mobilize than socialize, Deuce needed to be certain of his ducks before he lined them up in rows. Casino Liaisons were people persons, and it was people who would make or break the rescue of the Moon, not how many pulsars or blasters each side had, nor how long the conflict could continue.

Accordingly, he had planned for food, and even a bit of booze, which apparently, had been off-limits in Gabriel's Mormon administration. And not crater, not today, so along with the Bad Moon Brew, there was Tycho Delight gin, Atherton Gold, and a vast assortment of overly sweet beverages for the Mormons. Pretty soon, Scarlattis and Smiths were drinking Lunar Landers, Blastoffs, and other assorted, well-enchanced beverages, together.

Gabriel looked not so pleased; Deuce sidled over to her, and she frowned at his innocent expression.

"What if we were attacked right now?" she demanded.

"All liquored up? It wouldn't hurt as much if we were all killed sober. Which, *mi scusi*, is pretty much what would happen if someone attacked the base right now, no matter what condition the guys were in."

As she began to object, he bulldozed. "Some schmo was able to get onto your base, kill my robot, and get back off the base without detection. Or else they were working from within. Either way, it does not bode well.

"So," he said. "We let everybody have a couple more drinks. Then, when this group sobers up a little we'll give some drinks to the guards I've posted all over the base. Then they'll sober up and we'll really, truly get to work."

"It doesn't feel right," she insisted. "It's stupid."

"Short-term lunacy," he agreed, flinching inwardly. He said that word, lunacy, his *mamma* always washed his mouth out with soap. "*Mi scusi, signora*," he murmured. Amused, she inclined her head like a duchess. So call him old-fashioned. Some dames were ladies, and that was the way it was.

Then he continued. "Long-term, you just watch. All these guys who drank together are gonna be watching out for each other a few smidges more than before."

He nodded for emphasis. "Trust me. Before a big battle with another Family, even a hit, this kind of thing brings a Family together. Even the Borgiolis, to an extent, and that's really saying something."

He looked at the door, and his mouth dropped open.

"Deuce?" his bride asked shrilly.

But Deuce was speechless. Surrounded by soldiers with their pulsars pointed at him, Nicky Borgioli stood in the doorway, covered from head to toe in blood. He raised a hand to Deuce, and said, "Asylum, *Padrino*," and collapsed.

About that time, Deuce's comm badge vibrated. He said to Gabriel, "See about the boy. Make sure he's not, like, wired to explode or anything."

He touched his badge and said, "Earphone."

"Don General," came a static-filled voice. "Yuet Chan is here with an Earthside delegation. She wants to parley."

His stomach did a flip. Speak of devils; if there was a delegation, at least Earthside wasn't planning on massacring his people, unless Yuet—or a reasonable facsimile thereof—was serving as the bait to verify his whereabouts and flush him out. Iniya had insisted the meeting was going to be on the QT.

He said, "I'll send—"

"She wants to see you and Mr. Wong, sir. Only. She says you and he have some kind of private understanding about her topic of discussion."

He nodded thoughtfully, even though, of course, the soldier on earphone couldn't see him.

"Okay. I'm on my way. Get a bunch of guys around the perimeter. I want headcrackers and blasters aimed every whichway on her and her goons. I get so much as a scratch, shoot to kill."

"Yes, sir."

Gabriel looked up from Nicky Borgioli's prone form. She stared at him a long time. Then she said, "He's almost dead. I've called for medics."

Deuce crossed to the kid and stared down at him. "Nicky, who did this? Your uncle?"

"Dunno," Nicky said thickly. Then he shook his head. "Uncle Angelo . . . Mamma put on him a deathbed obligation. For me."

"He wouldn't break that, not for anything," Deuce said. "Nicky, guys are coming to take care of you. I grant you asylum if you promise to join us and fight against your uncle." He took a breath. He really liked this kid, but he had to make sure this was a straight deal. For all he knew, Nicky got hurt knifing a sentry.

"*Sì*," Nicky murmured. He slumped.

"Get the damn medics!" Gabriel bellowed.

Deuce cocked his head at her. "Y'know, you're going to make a hell of a mom," he said.

Then he went to his mother.

"Connie," he said, "we don't know each other, not really. Things are going to hell in a handbasket around here, and I'm not sure there's any point to most of what I'm doing here. But I'd feel a hell of a lot better if you blessed me as your son before I leave this bunker."

Her face was very soft. Her smile was tender. She raised her hand, and whispered, "In the name of the Father, and of the Son, and of the Holy Ghost, I bless you, Arturo Borgioli, known as Deuce McNamara, as my only son. You are the light of my existence. Go with God."

Then she made the sign of the cross over him. Deuce's chest tightened. He cleared his throat, and said, "Thanks, Ma. Take care of Moona, okay?"

She embraced him.

"I'm so proud of you, Deuce. You're a credit to the Moon, and to our family." Her eyes shone.

This time, his throat wouldn't clear, so he flashed her a smile and squeezed her hand.

"If something happens to me, Mom, you turn to Gabriel. And if you see Sparkle someday . . ." He sighed. "I don't even know where I'm going with that thought."

"Ah, Deuce." She cupped the side of his face. "Life has been hard for you."

He shrugged. "Exciting. And I wouldn't have it any other way."

She kissed his forehead. "My given name is Minerva McNamara. You have my last name." She looked a little embarrassed. "I don't know why I didn't tell you before."

"I'm glad you told me now." His voice was hoarse and he could barely speak above a whisper. "All my life, I've wondered why such a name. Mamma Maria told me I came from a long line of crooked Irish Earther cops."

"I'm from a line of very Irish Earther honest cops," Connie—Minerva told him with amusement "Maybe Maria wanted to spare you the pain of being carried by a woman with a mundane heritage."

"Yeah," he said soberly. He was bitterly disappointed. Then he brightened. He could still hope. Old-time Irish police officers had usually been dirty, no matter what they came home and told their wives and mothers. Maybe it was just a hopeful little fantasy on Minerva's part that they were clean—or maybe, unfortunately, it was true.

"Listen to me. If there's any fighting, I want you to go with your bodyguards. Do whatever they tell you, even if it seems strange. They're professionals, and they'll give up their lives for you. Let them do their job, if it comes to that."

She frowned. He frowned back. "Let them. Cuz if you die and they don't, I'll whack 'em anyway."

"You talk so big," she said. "I don't believe you'd hurt a fly."

"I have hurt flies, and worse," he retorted, wanting her to

be very clear on what he was, and wasn't. A chill went down his spine. The last woman he'd spoken those words to—those exact words—was dead.

"Mamma, I want you to be extremely careful." He tried to will her to understand how important she was to him. "Accent on extremely."

"I understand." She leaned forward and kissed him softly. "I promise. I will."

"Okay." He glared at her two bodyguards as they came over to her. Dallas was one, and then there was Joe Dorset—a regular American name, nothing to do with Families or other entanglements. Dorset was a former Castle employee brought from Earth, and Deuce figured he would be a good bet as a loyal watchdog.

Once again, he was in a position he was comfortable with, and one that he fully understood: There was practically no one around him he could trust. That was the wise guy's way, and despite what anybody said to the contrary, it made the most sense. Live any other way, and you were a putz . . . and dead.

"All right," he said again. He glanced around the room. He needed not a bodyguard, but an honor guard. Someone to impress upon Yuet that the MLF wasn't just for psychotics anymore. He would meet with her alone, but he wasn't just going to go up there like a sitting duck—quack quack. She had something to say, she could say it or she could walk away in a huff because he hadn't colored exactly within the lines.

Just about then, the medics showed. They immediately started doing doing things to Nicky and Deuce felt somewhat better about the kid's chances. That much blood, though—it was everywhere, and even now, pooling on the floor, it was not looking good.

He crossed himself. Then he nodded at Stefano, who was watching him. The young Scarlatti immediately began making his way through the crowd. At Giuliana Caputo. He took in the Smith consigliere. He saw no Van Aadamses in the crowd, so he moved on to the Chans. A very solid-looking Wei Chan, much-distant cousin of Lee, answered his gesture and hurried over to Deuce.

Deuce crouched beside his wife, who was holding Nicky's blood-drenched hand, and put his hand on her shoulder.

"How's he doing?" Deuce asked softly.

"Just fine," she answered loudly, but as she looked at Deuce, her eyes told a different story.

"I want you to go upstairs with me," he said. "I want Yuet to see you with me. See that you're not my hostage or something."

Reluctantly she rose. Staring down at Nicky, she whispered, "He's so young."

"A lot of 'em are," Deuce said, meaning the dying faces he had seen in his time.

The Family lifestyle was violent in the extreme. So was the MLF way of life. It was a road few opted out of, though. They just put up with the dying and hoped Lady Luck favored them with a kiss. That when their number was up, it was quick. To hope for painless as well was more than one could reasonably ask for, however. And as for dying in bed—such fairy tales were for *bambini*, not Family guys.

He wondered if the N.A.'s realized that even though they were shafted in a lot of ways, they were fairly well protected from death by violent means? No guarantees; and most Family Members and Affiliateds didn't hesitate to shoot a civilian in the heat of battle. But most of the time, the civilians had sufficient warning to get out of the way.

Most of the time.

Deuce's stand on the subject—that civilians were off-limits, and he would rather take a bullet than juice an innocent Joe on his way home from his nine-to-five—had been a private one, because it was that kind of soft thinking got you whacked by your own side. They worried you were too soft for business, so they got rid of you before you screwed up. Deuce understood. Therefore, he kept his eccentricity to himself.

Now he looked at the face cards he'd dealt himself—one from each Family except the Van Aadams, and the Queen of the MLF—and said, "Okay. We're going up. I want you to stay with me long enough for Yuet Chan to see us. Then I want you to leave when I tell you to."

Wei Chan looked startled. He said, "Has she taken over?"

Deuce shrugged. "I don't have any recon to that effect. And if she has?"

Wei smiled sheepishly. "I guess it doesn't matter, does it. Old habits die hard, Don General."

"I hear you completely," Deuce assured him. His look took

in the others. "That was exactly my point earlier in the evening. We all still identify with our Families, to some extent."

Everyone looked pensive a moment. Then one of the medics shouted, "We're losing him!"

Nicky was gagging on his own blood. His legs were thrashing. It was terrible to see.

"Deuce." Gabriel put her hand on his arm. "Do something. Please."

He blinked at her. "*Mi scusi?*"

She swallowed and stared at him. "You can heal him."

"Oh, for heaven's sake," he blurted. "Gabe, not you? You don't believe all that nonsense, do you?"

She took a deep breath. Her mouth worked. "You are the one," she said deliberately. "The signs have been there. We've followed your life . . ."

"*O, Mamma mia.* This is too much. I'm shocked at you, Gabriellina."

"Just touch him," she begged. "Save him."

"Why should I have to touch him?" He closed his eyes and touched his forehead. "Abracadabra, you're healed!"

"We've stabilized him," one of the medics informed the room.

Gabriel's eyes glistened.

With an exasperated sigh, Deuce headed for the supersecured stairs. No escalator down here, no lift. Nothing that could be sabotaged or that could break down.

He said, "I'll go first. You aren't here to protect me."

"I think we all know why we're here," Stefano said in a dazed voice.

Gabriel, however, was radiant. And why shouldn't she be? She was married to the next holy martyr of the one true and universal catholic psycho ward.

The stairway was heavily fortified. The lights were encased in Kevlite, as were the various cables and coils. Deuce heartily approved.

It was also short, and they were upstairs in no time. The guards on the other side of the door opened at Deuce's voiced code—"Liberty, Equality, Fraternity"—and let them out of the bunker.

Armed MLF soldiers were massed in front of the gates. Lights blazed down on the figures, casting everyone in sharp relief. Deuce had never seen Earthside daylight in real life, but he'd seen tons of gas films, and the sight before him was similar.

Yuet was truly splendid in a jade-and-salmon gown of silk and satin, and a Chinese headdress with lots of sticks and dingle-bobs. No doubt about it, the Chan Family were the best dressers of the Families.

But the Earthside "delegates" with her were not what Deuce had expected: soldiers, to be sure, but not uniformed in the customary black with a green-and-blue oval in the center of their chests. A derogatory term for Earthside Conglomerated Nations troops was "bull's-eyes."

No, these guys looked like Chan guys. Which, to Deuce's way of thinking, was much better.

"General on deck!" someone shouted, and all Deuce's troops snapped to attention, rifles clicking and clacking. It was thrilling. No wonder these guys got so into this stuff.

However, he hid his excitement behind a mask as he walked between the rows of guys and gals and marched straight up to the gate.

"You were supposed to come alone, with Mr. Wong," Yuet chided him.

"Yeah, so?" he flung at her.

She looked around. "Where is Mr. Wong?"

"You wanted to talk privately?" he continued.

She didn't look very happy. He didn't care.

"Yes."

He turned to the nearest high-ranking guy, and said, "Open the gate for Madame Chan, and Madame Chan only."

They passed the word all over the place. Then the Kevlite gate went *ka-chunng*, and Yuet stepped across the threshold and onto enemy territory.

"I have your guarantee of safety?" she asked.

It was a little late, seeing as he could personally gun her down where she stood, but he nodded.

"And of privacy?"

Meaning that all his Peekissimos and other surveillance devices would be turned off for their sit-down. A bit naive of her, perhaps, but he nodded. In this case, that was a given; he was not in total share mode with the MLF, especially if she wanted to talk to him and Mr. Wong.

She saw the faces amassed around him and gave him a strange little smile.

"Most impressive," she said. "Well-done."

He wanted to say that he didn't do it, but he'd been handed the deck, so he simply shrugged.

Then he added, "May I present my contingency spouse, General Kinkade-Jones di McNamara."

"Of course. It's been all over the media." She bowed. "My best wishes, General."

"Thank you, Madame Chan," Gabriel said smoothly. "Deuce is everything I could want in a husband," she added meaningfully.

"I can well imagine." Yuet smiled at them both.

Wrong, Deuce thought, *unless you have ever been married to Buddha.*

Deuce said, "We'll be out in a short while, darling," kissed Gabriel, and escorted Yuet away. Gabriel looked not so pleased; perhaps she had expected to be included at the last minute.

Deuce took Yuet into the same hideaway bunker they had hidden in after the assassination of Mr. Wong. Yuet looked around unhappily, and said, "Where's the remote data terminal? I was told to include Iniya in our discussion."

Oh?

ELEVEN

In the language—that is to say, English, this time—Deuce looked at Yuet Chan, and said again, "Oh?"

Yuet shrugged. "Why are you so surprised? Did you think you were the only person in the universe besides Hunter Castle to know about this?"

"Yes," Deuce replied honestly.

She laughed. It was a deep, rich laugh. Deuce thought about the kiss she had planted on Sparkle back when she assumed the Godmothership of the Chans. He hoped some of that affection might have been transferred to him on account of his being Sparkle's husband. But now, with the contingency thing . . . some people didn't approve of that so much.

"I've always liked you," she said, and that settled that.

However, he didn't relax. He said, "Who told you about Iniya?"

She looked further amused. "You always rush things. When you were in my House"—that was to say, her casino—"I offered you tea, despite the fact that an attempt had just been made on my life."

"Yeah, well, you Chans, you're set up for that kind of thing. Trust me, you don't want to eat or drink anything around here if you can help it."

At this, she really let go with a belly laugh, and Deuce grinned at her.

He said, "Did you know that once I snuck past all your Peekissimos and stared at your paintings of naked Chinese girls on the walls?"

She looked shocked. "How did you manage that?"

144

"Door was broken. I just strolled down the corridor. I think one of your stepbrothers was getting ready to take you out. It was when your esteemed mother was lying at death's door, God rest her soul." He crossed himself.

She softened. "I'm so sorry about your brother, Joey. You know I didn't have anything to do with that explosion."

"*Sì.*" He made as if to tap his badge. "If you would care for some tea, I'll comm for it."

"No, no. I trust your judgment." She grinned at him. "But it's very impressive to see you with a choke hold on your impatience. When you were Liaison to our House, you were nothing short of impetuous."

"Hey," he said, mildly insulted, "I was younger then."

"By three years."

"Yeah, well, I've been living at lightspeed since then. I'm about a hundred and sixty in Deuce McNamara years."

"May you live a hundred thousand more."

He inclined his head. "Same to you, Madame Chan."

"So." She folded her hands. "I am here on behalf of the same intelligent people who attempted to reinstate me as God-mother of the Chan Family."

He blinked. "The Eight?"

"The Eight," she agreed.

"The Eight, who also know about Iniya."

"Where is she?" she pressed.

He sighed, unsure how much he should reveal. What the hell. "Mr. Wong was destroyed. The terminal appears to be intact."

She paled. "Have you hidden it well?"

He shook his head. "I gave it to a couple of Scarlattis to put in a new casing."

"No," she blurted. "Not Scarlattis. They'll figure it out." She frowned. "How could you do that?"

"Hey, I didn't know anyone else knew about it. I knew they might figure it out, but I sure as hell couldn't access it by myself."

"Oh, Sparkle," Yuet said, sighing.

"Oh, Sparkle, what?" Deuce asked sharply.

"Your wife has an approachable mind," Yuet explained.

"English, please?" he requested, trying to sound polite . . . and not at all impetuous.

"She can interface with some of the other species without using any kind of data terminal. Directly. Mentally." She tapped her forehead with her extremely fashionable, long red nail. "It's why she used to have those paranormal experiences."

"I see." Maybe Sparkle was part !kth, too. Maybe that was why Hunter had wanted her to carry his children, so that they wouldn't die inside a totally human mother.

For the first time, he realized that if she had carried Hunter's kids, and he, Deuce was one of Hunter's kids, his wife had given birth to his half brother and his half sister. And little Stella was his half sister, too.

Maybe he would start having visions himself.

The idea gave him the creeps.

"Don General, are you all right?"

He bristled. This broad knew an awful lot about his business. She even knew his new title. He gave her a little half-hearted wave so he could lie to her about being fine and wished he could be alone for a few moments. It amazed him that he hadn't thought about all this before. *Distracted*, he told himself.

His guts hurt. They hurt bad. He wondered if Gabriel got pregnant, would the baby live? Would there be something wrong with it?

"You really don't look well," Yuet Chan said. She reached to touch her badge. "Should I comm for help?"

Sweat beaded his forehead. He wasn't due for a pain pill, but he sure could use one. But like any Family Member, he knew how to control pain. It had caught him by surprise, was all.

"No. Let's keep going. How do the Eight know about Iniya?"

She didn't look happy about his refusal of medical aid. Still, she settled back into her chair and folded her hands. She looked like an old-time Chinese Empress. Not that Deuce had ever seen an Empress.

Or maybe I have, he thought, watching her. *Yeah, I sure have.*

She said, "How do you think?"

Twenty questions, he was not willing to play. But it only took him a moment to say, "She contacted them?"

"Her father did," Yuet said, looking pleased with him, like she was proud of her little pet Godfather of the Moon.

Her father?

"So . . ." he said, leading her.

She shrugged. "One could surmise that she's the second-in-command."

"Of the entire D'inn, ah, group?"

Again, she shrugged. "We can only go by what they tell us." She raised a brow. "What did she tell you?"

He hesitated. So far, Yuet had been only moderately forthcoming, and there was no way to know if she was bluffing about what she already had on the table. Sparkle used to be able to tell sometimes if people were lying. It was also how she played the stock market. Sometimes she used to help Deuce cheat at cards, but not often, and only when it was someone who could afford it.

"Yuet, I must speak frankly," he said. "You sicced O'Connor on me. Then, at the big sit-down, you showed up, and the room blew up. I know the MLF did it, but you were there, and you also know who the D'inn are and that I know about them. The playing field is far from level, and I need you to throw a little more my way."

She nodded. "All right. I understand your hesitation. And I applaud it."

He didn't even blink. He just waited.

"This is what we've been told." She looked uncomfortable, as if she didn't quite know what to do with her hands. They had been sitting in their MLF-issue chairs in the dingy bunker, nothing to look away at, nothing to use as props.

He commed his badge and said, "Hot tea, on the double. Also, if we have cookies, bring them."

"Yessir, Don General."

"How very kind," Yuet said graciously.

"You'll be sorry. The food here is *immondizia*. It's like they think they're more virtuous if their grub is crummy."

She chuckled. "That's religion for you."

Ah, so she knew about that, too. He wondered if she knew about the whole Messiah deal.

She added, "The !kth are trying to build a jumpgate. Your former employer is helping them. They're building it so they can invade our space. The D'inn want to stop them."

He crossed his legs. "So the D'inn can invade our space instead?"

She shrugged. "They don't have the jumpgate technology. Instead, they're trying to build a ship that can travel from our space to theirs, and vice versa. The !kth tried that, but the ship didn't make it. I believe the wreckage of that vessel is what Castle built into *Gambler's Star*."

She was right about the *Star* and the crashed alien vessel, but Deuce didn't let her know for a minute that he knew it. There was no percentage in it.

"The !kth also tried forcing the creation of a hybrid human, which was someone aboard the *Star*, but they don't know who it was. Apparently, it didn't work."

That Deuce also knew more about than she did, unless she was holding back. That unsuccessful hybrid had been Jameson Jackson, and his corpse had ended up in Deuce's freezer in his garage. Beautiful, blonde Dr. Clancy had been murdered because she'd discovered the secret during Jameson's autopsy. It was also she who had taken the data terminal out of Jameson's chest.

Deuce suspected Mr. Wong of the murder, or maybe even Hunter himself. At any rate, the doctor was dead. And a damn shame, too.

He had really liked her.

Then his own boys had set half of Darkside City on fire, trying to get rid of Jackson's body before Detective O'Connor successfully served his search warrant on Deuce's penthouse. Now O'Connor was dead and the other half of Darkside City would never be built.

Meanwhile, the blast that had killed O'Connor had also taken out the doctor who had commed him about his arm, and all the records on said arm.

Damn aliens. The rogue sector of the MLF might have taken credit for that one, but his money was on the things from another world.

"So they're building a ship, and why are they telling us about it?" he asked Yuet.

"They need some help." She looked like that cat with the canary. "The Eight have been working on interstellar travel for quite a while."

The Eight had become almost mythological. People didn't

even know if they still existed. They had never come forward, never made themselves known. Now, he was hearing they had some fancy-schmancy technology he could only dream about.

What about fancy-schmancy weaponry, too?

"*O Dio*," he whispered, half to himself.

"Indeed." Now she looked like a high roller who was just about to break the bank. In their line of work, the one with the most information was the one with the biggest, er, smile.

"We come in where?" Deuce asked. And then he knew: the data terminal.

"You must hate this," he said. "Coming to me for help."

She looked blasé. "I know you killed Wayne Van Aadams. But it was Wayne's own Uncle William Atherton Van Aadams and Hunter Castle who colluded to put the blame on me. Not you."

"True."

"And Sparkle loves you." She looked pained. "This contingency wedding . . ."

He held up a hand. "I wish that were true. But Sparkle doesn't love me." As she opened her mouth to protest, he lifted the hand a couple of inches. "This, I know. Let's leave it at that."

She pursed her lips. He squinted at her, and she sighed in defeat.

"Back to the subject," he said. "What I got is the data terminal, but all you have to do to get it is whack me, and so?"

"Iniya trusts only you," Yuet said frankly. "Her father can't convince her to work with anyone else."

"Her father?"

She shrugged. "I assume that she's his lieutenant."

"And are they the official government?"

"They say they are."

"And I'm the only guy for her." He folded his arms. "What, she's in love with me?"

"I have no idea." She sounded rather prim. "But you need to come Earthside and—"

He widened his eyes. "*Mi scusi?* I'm a little busy right now."

"With something smaller than you are." She stopped his protest. "You know it, and I know it. Who controls the Moon isn't going to matter if the !kth invade and we're all subjugated or wiped out."

"You Chinese. You're so emotional." He grinned at her. "Ever wonder if it's someone just scamming us? Like the Scarlattis, with some new weirdo hallucination machine or something?"

"I worry constantly. Especially since I've never seen the remote data terminal. I've had to accept its existence on faith." She moved her head, and all the dingle-bobs dingled. She reminded Deuce of the mobiles they'd made in art class, back when Joey and he used to fight constantly, and he could never imagine a world without his brother.

"But Earthside. I don't know." It could be a tremendous setup. "Why don't I just send Iniya along with you?"

"She told us she's voiced herself to respond only to you."

Deuce was not so sure about that. She'd never mentioned it to him. Plus, she'd been blown up, so to speak, and who knew if the voice feature was intact, if it had ever existed?

"Yeah," he said, and moved nonchalantly. If he'd been alone, or with one of the other Liaisons, he would have lit a cigarette. He looked at her. "You smoke, or is that against your drug-free policy?"

"Against my drug-free policy," she said, without rancor.

"You must love it Earthside, them with all their thou-shalt-nots."

"When I'm not in prison for a crime I didn't commit, yes, I do."

Thoughtfully, he chewed the inside of his cheek. "You're never going to let me forget that, are you?"

"No. Because *I* won't."

"Forewarned, forearmed." He pulled out a cigarette. "Thank you."

"I already told you, I don't blame you," she insisted. She studied the cigarette. "Give me one, too, if you please."

He was puzzled. "I thought you just said you don't smoke."

She reached forward with her classy-looking talons and plucked his Lucky Sea out of his hand.

"The hell with it," she said, smiling at him.

He lit the cigarette and commed for the pollution levy. She took a deep drag, held it, exhaled.

"Divine," she admitted.

He got out another, and they smoked together in companionable, if not altogether serene, silence.

Finally, he said, "Okay, I'll go Earthside."

At which point, Yuet Chan, Godmother of the great House of Chan, which had survived down the centuries as a dominant and highly respected mob family, burst into a fit of coughing and tamped out her cigarette.

"Good God, that's a foul and loathsome habit," she said, as tears welled in her eyes.

Deuce hadn't laughed so hard in ages.

The nice men in the Castle suits came to the door of her family's new apartment with more food than usual. Annie Bannany grinned at the wrapped box of toys in the beefy arms of one of the men.

There were always toys from Mr. McNamara for Annie and her brothers and sisters. Dolls and blasters and minipads with new books on them. Annie had more stuffed animals than the rest of the kids who lived in the trailers on Copernicus Way combined. She was the envy of all the girls at school, with her dozens of fashionable outfits and shoes, and her very own, custom-blended hair galvanizer.

Good things were happening to Annie even though bad things were happening to the Moon. Earthside soldiers were occupying it. Her mother had explained what that meant—that the Earthsiders were acting like they owned the Moon, when everyone knew they didn't.

In secret, she and her mother did all they could to help Mr. McNamara, who was trying to get the Earthsiders to leave. People came to have secret meetings at their trailer, and sometimes they left stuff for them to take care of. Her mother said they should both be very proud that they could help the cause.

Annie was proud. Mr. McNamara had changed her life forever. Without him, she would have starved to death, or maybe even been killed on the road when she had run away from home.

But he had saved her and brought her home, and made her family rich.

So when the men knocked on the door, and said, "Uncle Deuce sent us," she let them in right away. Even though she had never called Mr. McNamara "Uncle Deuce."

Her mother was at the entertainment complex that she managed. Her brothers were at Moon Scouts, and her sister, Lunette, was visiting wounded soldiers. She was home alone with Cynthia.

The four men tromped into the house. One of them was fat, and one was tall. The other two were very young, almost boys.

The fat man said, "Hey, kid, where's your ma?"

Something was wrong. She didn't know what, but she felt deep down in her bones that she and Cynthia were in terrible danger.

She did as she had been taught when she was home by herself, which was to say, "My mom's taking a nap."

The tall man pushed her roughly out of his way. She bobbed into the wall, unhurt but terrified, and watched as he marched down the hall. He knew without asking where her mother's bedroom was. He knew everything about her house.

She inched in the opposite direction, ignored by the other men, who moved into the living room. One closed the front curtains.

She slid into the front bedroom, which she shared with her two sisters. Cynthia was sleeping in a crib, even though she was almost too big for it.

Placing a hand over her sister's mouth, Annie shook her gently. Cynthia's eyes flew open and she started to cry, but Annie let her see who she was and put her finger to her lips.

Cynthia was only three, but she was pretty smart for a little kid. She nodded and batted at her sister's hands. Annie realized her sister couldn't breathe, and she pulled her hand away.

"We have to sneak out of the house," Annie whispered. "There are bad men in the house."

Cynthia whimpered, but Annie shook her finger sternly.

Moving quickly on her feet, she bounded to the bedroom window and opened it. She was lucky that the seal was cracked, making it easy to force. Even though he had had their toilet fixed and their stove replaced, her mom had been embarrassed to tell Mr. McNamara about all the things that were wrong with their trailer. His company had built it.

They had not done a very good job.

It was a simple matter to pick Cynthia up and drop her outside; the weak gravity made it easy and safe. The little girl half floated, half drifted toward the walkway as Annie scrambled out of the window and let herself go.

Cynthia landed on her feet with a squeal, and waved up at Annie as she came tumbling after, like Jack and Jill.

Both girls screamed as a looming figure cut out part of the lighting array, and scooped them both up.

"Here they are," the figure said. It was the tall man.

As Annie and Cynthia struggled and screamed, he carried them toward a waiting car.

The door opened. The girls were handed to outstretched hands. They shrieked as the door slammed, and the car carried them away.

Deuce was livid.

The note from Angelo was frank and to the point: *I have the Bonnanio girls. Give me back my nephew, or they die.*

Annie's mother, Leslie Bonnanio, was coping as best she could, but as she paced in the bunker Deuce could tell she was on the verge of total hysteria. Nearly a father himself, he understood completely how crazy you could go worrying about your children. He spent almost every waking moment nuts with background worry about Sparkle and her kids, and they weren't even his babies.

This was beneath any Godfather, but beneath contempt for Angelo, who had once been a good man. It was unforgivable. In the Family lifestyle, wives and kids were off-limits. You had a beef, you dealt with the beefee and no one else. To use someone's children was unthinkable.

But to use a civilian's children like this, threaten their lives . . . unpardonable.

Angelo had crossed the line. There was no going back now. Nothing could ever be good between them. Not even if he released the kids and begged forgiveness of every decent human being on the planet. He had turned himself into a monster that had to be shot on sight.

Deuce would kill Nicky before he allowed him to return to such a man.

Meanwhile, Deuce's two Scarlattis—to the dismay of Yuet Chan, who did not want them anywhere near there—had nearly completed their installation of the remote terminal de-

vice into a new chassis. It started out as a joke, but Deuce
wasn't laughing. The new body was quite the, uh, party doll,
just something Carmine had lying around. Built for sensuality,
the android form was really something, with measurements
most women could only protest against as false standards that
their daughters wanted to live up to.

So, before Deuce could tell the boys to cease and desist
their efforts, Iniya was—at last—inside a female body.

And what a female body.

What was even more ... distracting ... was that the alien
intelligence behind the remote data terminal acknowledged
just how sexy her new body was. She thought it was pretty
funny, in fact; and she professed to be "fascinated" by the
"biochemical reactions" in Deuce as he regarded her for the
very first time.

She had long, dark hair that tumbled over her shoulders—
and *Mamma mia,* what shoulders!—and enormous brown-
black eyes that drew him in like some kind of python that
hypnotized its prey. She was wearing a slinky new black-and-
silver catsuit, with black flat-heeled boots and not much else.
They'd thrown the laws of aerodynamics out the window
when they'd designed her chassis.

Suffice to say, she was not built for speed.

But she was all there; and as she walked out of the base-
camp operating room, she regarded Deuce with a bit of humor,
and said, "Hi, honey, I'm home."

Deuce cleared his throat. It was great to hear her sounding
like a dame. A very sexy dame.

"And you've got a father, and you told the Eight you'd only
work with me."

"Yuet Chan has been busy, I see." Her android eyes stared
at him, and he shifted uneasily. Somehow, when she was inside Mr. Wong, she had seemed less foreign. He didn't know
how to explain it to himself, and it didn't really matter. But
seeing her in this extreme version of a woman made him realize there was a chance she wasn't a woman at all. Maybe
she was some thing shaped like a pineapple with tentacles.
Maybe it took eight male pineapple-tentacled things to create
one of her, and only one of her fathers was on their side, while
the other seven were getting ready to invade.

Maybe that was a little detail she had neglected to mention.

Or that she breathed cyanide gas back on Planet Zero.

She said, "Have you agreed to go Earthside?"

"Yeah," he told her, "but I'm not real happy about it." Which was not entirely true. He had always wanted to go to Earth, but on a pleasure trip. With lots of discretionary funds and no responsibilities.

"We know how important the Moon is to you. But your presence is vital. Otherwise, we would not ask this of you."

"Your English sure has picked up," he observed. "How do I know you're still you, and not some Scarlatti simulation? Or for that matter, a !kth program, guiding me to do exactly what they want?"

"That way lies madness," she said.

He was astonished. Also, highly suspicious.

"What happened to I robot, you Tarzan?"

She cocked her head. "We're an advanced species. Surely, you're not surprised, after everything you've seen, that I can learn your language quickly?" She shrugged. "Not to mention the fact that we've been capturing your father's remote transmissions to the !kth since he started working with them. We had a rich basis upon which to build a grammar."

"So why the Dick-n-Jane when you first revved up?"

When she looked at him without comprehension, he said, "Your English was not so good at first, for someone who had prior access to it."

She looked slightly abashed. There was no other word for it. Except maybe, *essere colto con le mani nel sacco.*

He was intrigued. What, she hadn't done her homework? She was a bad learner? Maybe later, he would ask. She got such a charge out of putting him on the spot. Well, two could play that game.

And speaking of numbers rackets, he wondered if, despite what Yuet Chan had said, his little long-distance pal was sashaying around in a hubba-hubba body down Earthside, too. So he said, "They want you to accompany me to the mother planet. You need to? Can't you just hook up into some terminal down there?"

"No," she said. "This terminal is the only one."

"Seems kind of foolhardy not to build another one."

She shrugged. "Perhaps. But Hunter Castle received this one

via the !kth. It was only because it was damaged that I was able to get in contact with you."

"So, do you and the !kth speak the same language?"

Her face hardened. "No. Not at all."

Aboard the command ship, Iniya pushed back from the console and clasped her hands. She yawned and stretched. She was exhausted.

Deuce was in bed with his contingency wife, and Iniya's surrogate was asleep in a Quonset hut with two female MLF soldiers. The soldiers were uneasy around her. At the console, she smiled. It was the same the world over: Beautiful women made other women squirm.

She wondered if she would ever actually meet Deuce McNamara face-to-face.

Now, as she stood, her father stood behind her. She jumped.

"Father," she murmured, pressing her palms together and bowing, as was the D'inn custom.

He wore the robes of state, which shimmered and danced as he responded to her greeting. Over his face was the mask he had worn since she was a child. She had never seen his true features.

And once she had put her mask upon completing her rite of passage, no one had seen her face, either.

That was also the custom of their people.

"How is the man?" her father asked. His name was Foriniyar, and he was the leader of this quadrant. Three *maissins* of ships lay under his command.

"He is well." She rubbed her fingers, which was the gesture for smiling. "He is pleased with the new body."

He rubbed his fingers in reply. "With that one, I'm not surprised. Come. Dinner's ready."

Unsure to whom he was referring—the man, or the body— she gathered up her own robes and followed after him.

Something about all this is wrong, she thought. *I feel as if I have been dreaming. I don't feel fully present.*

Her father gestured for her to hurry.

TWELVE

*Immediately after the tribulation of those days the sun will
be darkened, and the moon will not give its light . . .*

MATTHEW 24:29

Sparkle could still not see.

But she knew the time for escape had arrived. Since her
blindness, something had happened to her mind. She didn't
know how to describe it, but it had . . . opened in some way.
Blossomed. Perhaps the intense heat had caused it.

She had established contact with the !kth at a mental level.

It was horrible. Whenever her psyche touched that of a !kth,
it recoiled in revulsion. She had been told the !kth looked like
demons. What no one else appeared to know was that they
also thought like demons. Their minds were brimming with
hatred; it was only with supreme effort that they didn't attack
each other. The humans, they could barely tolerate. Their
loathing was so strong that Sparkle felt it as physical pain. It
was a churning, living hatred, seeking a target, needing an
object.

They were going to send operatives to kill her tonight, as
soon as Hunter had looked in on her and gone to bed.

Her heart was pounding as she lay in darkness, having no
idea if the room was blazing with lights, or if they were turned
off. She jumped at every sound; despite the fact that the stateroom bulkheads were baffled, noises still filtered through on
occasion.

She was blind, and practically friendless, and she had to find her children and escape with them.

They were in as much danger as she was, for an entirely different reason.

The door to her room hissed open. She lay rigid and terrified. The instinct to open her eyes was incredibly strong, but she kept them closed. Her sole advantage was surprise, and even there, she wasn't sure how much of her own mind they could access. Desperately, she pulled up images: her showgirl days; kickboxing tournaments; anything but the fact that if she was going to die, she wouldn't go out without a fight.

"Mrs. McNamara?" a voice called softly. "It's Shiflett."

She opened her eyes, even though everything was still as black as before.

"Why are you here?" she whispered.

There was a pause. "I thought you commed me."

Ice washed down her spine. "No."

Still holding his hand, she struggled to her feet. She didn't even know if she could walk. With one lurching step forward, even assisted by Shiflett, she felt like crumpling to the floor. Her groan was low, but he heard it.

"Maybe you should get back in bed, Mrs. McNamara."

"Shiflett, did you hear my voice when I commed you?" she asked, forcing herself to stay calm. But she was shaking. Her legendary icy reserve was shattering.

He thought a moment. "I really don't remember." Then he laughed sheepishly. "I'm a little baffled."

"Are you sure I commed you?"

"Didn't you?"

She took a deep breath. "No. But I have to get my children off this ship. Our lives are in danger. And if you were called here—"

"Wait." He gave her hand a squeeze to stop her flow of speech. "I don't remember your comming me."

Had she reached out to a human mind, then? Had he reacted to her distress? She didn't know what to do, what to think.

"How do you know you're in danger?" he added.

"Believe me when I say I do." She clasped both her hands around his. "You've got to help me save my children."

"Is Mr. Castle—"

"Has nothing to do with this," she said in a rush. "We can't let him know."

There was another pause. "All right."

She wanted to fall on her knees and thank him; instead, she said, "We can't take anything. We just have to leave."

"You mean right now?" He was obviously taken aback.

"Yes." She started to walk forward, urging him to keep up. "Where's the door?"

"But we don't know where we are," he said, tugging at her. "We're in foreign space."

"Then get us to a shuttle and cast us off," she snapped, fear rising. But he was right. They were in alien space. She had no idea how to get back to the Moon.

The panic overwhelmed her for a few seconds. She began hyperventilating.

"Take me to the bridge," she said. "Hurry."

"Mrs. McNamara . . ."

"Am I a prisoner?" she demanded, her voice rising.

"No one's guarding your door, if that's what you mean."

"So I'm feeling better. I'm going for a walk." She stomped forward, then cried out as her knees buckled. She was weak, exhausted, and in pain.

"Sparkle—"

"Damn it, Shiflett." She grabbed on to him. "Give me something. Give me a Chan upper."

"I don't have—"

"Don't lie to me."

He sighed. "All right. I brought my bag."

He walked her over to a chair and sat her down. Then he riffled through something, and said, "Okay."

There was a *pffft* and a wisp of air against her shoulder. She immediately felt better.

"I put in some stronger painkillers, too," he said. "But the pain is there for a reason."

"I'm not having some kind of fever dream. If I don't get us out of here, they'll kill me and my children. Tonight."

"It's too risky."

She squeezed his hand painfully, heard him gasp. "My husband saved your life. You owe us." That was the way it worked in the Moon. Shiflett, being an outsider, might not realize that that was one debt you did not welsh on. Or you might as well have died in the first place.

He sighed. "Several crew members have been talking about mutinying," he admitted. "They'd probably help you."

She didn't have time to be jubilant.

"Let's go."

"I'll hide you."

"No. It might raise an alarm. Besides, I want to be there when you talk to them," she insisted.

He sighed again.

Nicky Borgioli had been patched together and lay in Uncle Deuce's own bed. He was captivated by the notion that he was going to have a scar running across his chest, at least until such time as there was enough time to clone some skin and graft it on. Or else, polish out what was there.

It had taken a while—and a lot of explanations and re-explanations—for him to accept that he had sworn to Deuce to join the MLF. That was like asking him to renounce Catholicism and become a Satanist. And one could argue that he had made the vow under duress, since Deuce had withheld medical treatment until Nicky had agreed.

However, as Deuce had gone on to explain about the aliens and the jumpgate and the ship and like that, and then had him talk to Iniya and Yuet Chan, he figured that if they were all *pazzo*, at least they were treating him well. They babied him and cared for him, especially that gorgeous mechanical broad who claimed to be the remote-control device of a woman from another planet. Plus they had offered him a free trip to Earth, even if it might include a few fireworks and/or death.

Speaking of, the way things worked in Family life, his turning into such a miserable traitor did nothing to his real uncle's deathbed obligation. No matter what, Angelo could not kill him, nor engineer his death, nor simply stand aside and allow someone else to kill him. If Nicky died before Angelo did, no matter how it happened—even in an accident, or direct, one-on-one combat—it would cause Angelo a grave dishonor. And frozen financial assets or no, honor was the real currency in the Family system. Even among Borgiolis.

So, as strange as it all seemed, here he was, following Deuce right into the arms of the MLF, Casino Families Enemy

#1, and Angelo, as Godfather, could not order a traitor's death for him. Which was what would have happened if his dear mother had not sacrificed herself for him.

Life was a mystery.

Deuce had forbidden anyone to tell Nicky about the hostage situation with Angelo and the Bonnanio children. He was afraid Nicky would offer himself as trade.

Angelo might not outright kill his nephew, but if he was capable of threatening civvie kids, he was capable of maiming and/or imprisoning Nicky for life. It had not been unknown for those saddled with a deathbed obligation such as this to purposely deprive the object of their vow of oxygen long enough for them to become a vegetable, and then hook them up to life support.

It had been very careless of Donna Ariana—God rest her poor soul, since suicide was still not real cool with Catholic priests—not to be more specific about the obligation. Better, almost, that she had not made it at all. It rendered her sacrifice practically meaningless, and it made situations like the kidnapping of little Annie and her sister more likely.

Leslie Bonnanio was safe on the base, heavily sedated, and Deuce sat by her bedside in her private room in the infirmary. Tranqued as she was, her forehead was still wrinkled with creases. She was in obvious distress, and her dreams were not pleasant ones. That was a sin; sleep should be a safe place for the innocent, even if they had nowhere else to find it.

"I will find them," he said to her.

Then he rose and moved quietly out of the room. She whimpered once, as if to beg him to hurry.

He strolled outside, his head bowed. He wasn't exactly hiding from his troops—he had to ask no one's permission to go anywhere and everywhere—but there would be a lot fewer questions if he just did his thing.

So, as he entered the guard gate, Stefano, who had been assigned duty for just this reason, nodded and opened the airlock. As previously instructed, he wrote in the logbook, "*PFC Carmine Scarlatti, permission to leave, as per Don General McNamara.*"

Deuce gave him a salute, and said, "*Grazie tanto, fratello.*"

"Go with God, *Padrino*," Stefano answered fervently, making the sign of the cross over Deuce.

In response, Deuce cracked the thumb knuckle of his left hand. Hey, any port in a storm.

Once outside, Deuce ducked into a crawl space and took off his uniform. Beneath, he wore a black one-suit. He pulled a black watch cap down over his white-blond hair. He had a pair of gloves in his pocket, but he would wait to put them on until he was closer to the objective.

Any of the MLF mucky-mucks could see him, they would doubtless demote him. In the Moon, he was kinda sorta the leader of the free world, and said leader was not supposed to run around putting himself in jeopardy for two little kids. The best thing you could say about it was that it was dashing, but dashing you were supposed to leave to the superhero types, like Devon LaDare on everybody's favorite soap opera, *Phases*.

However, he wasn't going in alone. He hefted the hard round object in his palm. It was one of the D'inn's supereffective disappear-o bombs. He had two more in his pocket. He had hooked Iniya into one of the base's munitions manufacturing devices, better known as a blaster baker, and she had churned out about a dozen of the little suckers before she informed Deuce that she couldn't make any more because the baker had run out of a crucial ingredient, which nobody had ever heard of before and didn't know how to get more of.

So then the base knew the robot chick could make amazing bombs, and the jig was up maybe a couple of feet, what with the seriously, ah, enhanced mechanical babe making secret weapons for the home team. Speculation was rife, but luckily, that was still all it was, since facts were scarce. Plus, given Deuce's background not only as a formerly loathsome Family man, but the former second-in-command of the richest and most powerful man alive, Hunter Castle, nobody was very surprised that he had access to cool bombs made by gorgeous women and like that.

He was also packing a superjuicer, a couple of blasters, and a portable headcracker. Armed to the teeth.

Plus, he had backup.

He walked farther down the tunnel, well away from camp,

before he hit his comm badge. On a secured line, he said, "Lee Chan, come and get me."

As prearranged, Lee Chan poked the nose of a fast-paced two-seater out of a perpendicular tunnel and swooped around to pick up Deuce. He stopped on a dime, not that anybody used them, and the passenger door popped open.

The car said, "Welcome, Mr. Unidentified Passenger."

"Hi, Lee Chan." To the car, he said, "Thanks."

"You're very welcome, Mr. Unidentified Passenger."

Nice car.

"*Buona sera*," Lee Chan replied, in Italian to honor the Godfather. Deuce felt a little bad for the way things had worked out: Just before the war—Deuce had invited Lee Chan to act as an emissary to several of the Casino Liaisons, which gave him a huge leg up in the prestige sweepstakes. But now most of the other Liaisons were either dead or out of a job. The Earthside government guys had replaced them with their own people, to the icy amusement of the Families: No one believed any of the casinos would be solvent by the end of the next lunar phase.

So Lee Chan was the emissary to plenty of nothin'.

Still, he had the friendship of Deuce McNamara, which could either make you impressive or dead, depending on who you were strutting your stuff around.

They descended Sinatra Way for a few levels, then proceeded over to Corleone Court. Against the left side of the corridor, there was an unilluminated neon sign for *Venus on Ice*, Sparkle's old show, and Deuce's chest tightened. But he drowned out all the *chiasso* in his head to focus on the matter at hand.

They went down, down, to the C&C's—Cables and Coils—the "bottom" level of the navigable tunnels. Deuce had found treasures down there—a lost crate of toilet paper, a box of dresses, no doubt from freighters which had lost part of their cargo. Or else, from thieves who had filched them from the loading bays.

All that stuff had been small potatoes, from which he had very seriously graduated when he began to work for Hunter.

It was with a start that Deuce realized that a crate of toilet paper would still be rich cargo indeed for the MLF. That in some ways, he had descended the ladder of success. So he kept his eyes peeled, and not grudgingly. He was a professional; if you worked for an outfit built on scarcity, you dealt and played a hand based on scarcity.

Then a van floated into their field of view and flicked its lights on, off. Lee Chan grunted and pointed.

"That's ours," he told Deuce.

"Good work." Deuce was pleased. It was a very unnoticeable vehicle, not too sleek, not too rickety. Fifty witnesses could see that van and remember nothing about it.

Lee Chan commed the driver on a secured line; trouble was, in this day and age, you couldn't be guaranteed that anything was secure. The Scarlattis had never stopped improving their surveillance equipment, and now Earthside was here, with all their fascist Peekissimo gear.

On the slightly less dismal side, no one had ever assumed security was total in the Moon, not even since the building of the first casino by the Caputos. You couldn't move into total paranoia, but you could take precautions. Everybody had, and everybody still did, so he didn't suppose he could blame that on the government.

Meanwhile, Lee Chan murmured, "There's a bad moon on the rise."

The comm line crackled with static. Then a voice replied, "Moon River, wider than a mile."

"Okay." Lee Chan grinned at Deuce. "We're up." He said to the aichy, "Switch to auto pilot. A new driver will arrive in approximately three minutes. Greet and accommodate his or her ergonomic requirements."

"Yes, Lee Chan," the car said dutifully. Then it added, a bit pensive, "Have a nice day."

Deuce and the Chan Liaison cracked open the doors and gingerly got out. Deuce had a blaster in his hand, armed for killshot, and he moved with great care and deliberation. After all, Lee Chan could have been bought. So could the guys in the van. You never knew, until it was way too late to share the secret with anybody who could do anything about it.

They walked slowly, skirting the headlight beams of the other vehicle. Deuce was nervous. His guts hurt. He remembered a time when he wouldn't have been able to describe what nervous felt like. In his youth, he had been edgy, sure, and even scared; but nervous had not been in his vocabulary. He had been one hunka-hunka derring-do.

No more. Once you accumulated a pot, you got antsy about losing it. Deuce had a lot to lose now.

The van driver came abreast of him. He wore Borgioli colors, but Deuce didn't recognize him. As he neared, the guy's cheeks reddened, and Deuce went on alert. He made sure his blaster was ready for business, but he kept his face pleasant and untroubled.

When they stood face-to-face, the other man dipped to one knee, grabbed Deuce's left hand—sans blaster—and touched it to his forehead.

He said, "God bless you, Godfather."

Deuce raised his brows. "I ain't your Godfather. I ain't anybody's Godfather."

"*Bugie!*" the man exclaimed, which, when taken in a different context, would mean he thought Deuce was a liar. "You know and I know, and you must help us free—"

"Easy, easy. Don't get all worked up," Deuce said, slightly alarmed. "I don't deny that I got responsibilities."

"And the power to fulfill them," the man replied fervently. He had the fever: Deucemania, or whatever you wanted to call it. It had happened to Deuce before. The folks infected with it either found satisfaction in Deuce's accomplishments, or turned on him with truly amazing hatred when he failed to meet their excessive expectations.

"All's you gotta do is drive our car away, okay? Take it somewhere safe."

"Can I join you?" the man asked. He smiled hopefully. "Not on your secret mission, but can I get into the MLF and fight with you?"

Deuce took a good look at the guy. He was younger than Deuce. He was also thrilled to be involved in something so . . . nerve-wracking. Deuce was reminded of Little Wallace Busiek, his number one fan; now number one dead fan, because he had loved Deuce's exciting life too much.

He looked at the guy and thought, *Do I have a legitimate right to know more about what's good for this guy than he does?*

No one had pulled any punches with him, Deuce. But on the other hand, he had never ducked one. And he had blocked plenty. This guy . . . he wasn't so sure he would even know what hit him.

"They got a lot of rules," Deuce said. "They don't trust Family people too good."

The man raised his chin. His dark brown eyes gleamed with lunar patriotism. "I don't care. I want the damn Earthsiders off my rock."

"Fair enough." Deuce chewed the inside of his cheek. "You meet my representatives at Dutch Schulz and Milky Way tomorrow night at seven, okay?"

Deuce was fairly certain he wouldn't send anyone there. If this guy had the stuff, it wouldn't matter. A real go-getter would make his way to base camp. They needed bodies, to be blunt and ice-cold about it. Not cannon fodder, but not far from it.

Or what's a heaven for?

He felt a little too old for this man's game, even though he was not even twenty-eight.

The man said, "I'll be there," like they were rendezvousing to elope, and hurried over to Lee Chan's two-seater. He climbed in, blinked the headlights once, and soared off into the neon sunset of a billboard promising DOUBLE SLOTS!

Lee Chan murmured, "Poor schmuck."

Deuce decided then and there that there would be no one to meet that guy tomorrow night at Dutch Schulz and Milky Way. Deuce couldn't do that to him and live with himself.

He had his rules: Innocents were always exempt.

He and Lee Chan got into the van and made for ground zero like two bats out of hell.

And Deuce had seen hell, thank you very much.

Very clearly.

Shiflett said, "Thanks for showing." Then he turned to Sparkle, and murmured, "It's Chang. He's here."

"Mrs. McNamara," Bernardo Chang said, with alarm in his voice. "What are you doing out of bed? You're not well."

Shiflett lowered his voice and whispered in Chang's ear.

There was a silence. Sparkle set her gaze in the direction where she had heard Chang's voice, daring him to disbelieve her.

To her intense relief, Chang said, "All right. I'm in."

For the first time, she really, truly thought they might get out of there alive.

She said, "We need to find out where we are, and how to get home."

Chang said, "I know a lot of that already. I stowed away on the *Star* for a long time, and I listened in on an awful lot of private conversations."

Sparkle tried not to feel too elated. Forcing herself to stay calm, she asked, "Would it be possible to return to our space in a shuttle?"

"Properly outfitted, perhaps." Chang touched her shoulder. She started; he said, "Sorry." Then he added, "But it'll take some time."

She swallowed hard. "How much time?"

"I couldn't really say." He was silent for a moment. "Perhaps a week?"

Sparkle kept calm. She had to, for the sake of her children. "I don't have a week. I don't even have one night."

Shiflett whispered, "Someone's coming. Mrs. McNamara, stand perfectly still."

She did as she was told, holding her breath, tensing as she felt the arm of Shiflett, to her left, and Chang, to her right. Both stiffened and tensed. She caught their swift intake of breath. *What?* she wanted to scream, but there was nothing to be done but to freeze.

She hated what had happened to her. She was used to being in charge. Her beauty had always put her in charge; and in the low gravity of the Moon, and with the possibility of rejuv, there would be no end to that beauty. Which was strange: If anyone could be so beautiful that it became a source of power, why didn't more people achieve it?

Maybe it's like happiness, she thought, but she didn't let the thought go any further than that.

Because, as always, survival was more important than happiness.

Nothing was more important than survival.

Nothing.

Except my children.

Her heart was pounding. She wanted to tear away from their arms and run to her babies.

The men exhaled.

"It's all right," Shiflett announced.

She caught her breath and said to the two men, "You have got to get us out of here *now*. To get to me, the !kth will kill anyone and anything aboard. But they want to do it without arousing Hunter's suspicions. They need him."

And then something new hit her, with such force that she literally staggered backward:

More importantly, they need his grandchildren.

Because they contain !kth blood.

"Mrs. McNamara?"

Something dark descended over her; she couldn't see, couldn't breathe; she was losing consciousness. She flailed, fighting hard, and moaned, "No."

The world became a flat gray line that stretched into a horizon on either side of her peripheral vision.

Then there was nothing.

Deuce and Lee Chan parked the van in an alley near Borgioli headquarters and walked down the streets like they had nothing better to do than stuff their hands in their pockets and gossip about broads. Deuce marveled that other than several destroyed buildings now hidden from tourists by holo-projections, there were few obvious signs of the total Earthside domination of Moonbase Vegas. Just a few soldiers on street corners with superpumpers, most of whom were greeted warmly by the Earthsider tourists.

"It's so nice to have some law and order up here," one woman simpered as she postured at a tall, dark, and handsome soldier. "We were afraid to come here until you people took over."

"Thank you, ma'am," the soldier replied. "It's an honor to defend your right to gamble safely."

Deuce and Lee Chan exchanged looks. What was safe about gambling in a casino, both of them would like to know. House odds were house odds, which meant the deck was always stacked against the player. If the average rabbit played long enough—adding inexperience in with ignorance—he was bound to lose his shirt. Maybe taking it off himself made it seem less like he'd been robbed.

As the soldier looked up—perhaps sensing their disgust— Deuce smoothly rounded a corner into an alley, walking with purpose. Liaisons learned how to hang out without appearing to do so; the key part of the word "malinger" was, after all, "linger."

Just as coolly, Lee Chan followed his lead. They sauntered down the street, just a couple of Moon guys hangin' around talking, Deuce moving even more slowly when he heard the heavy fall of boots behind them. He recalled there was some new *schiamazzo* about papers and IDs, which he foolishly had not bothered with. He wondered if Lee Chan had done his homework, and figured that he had. When you lived on the edge of legal, you made sure you didn't take unnecessary chances.

Words to live by, you moron, he told himself.

The footsteps receded, and Deuce breathed again. He glanced at Lee Chan's inscrutable face. If the guy was freaked out, he hid it well.

They walked another ten minutes or so. Deuce murmured, "You're sure the van's locked on to us?"

"Yessir," Lee Chan said placidly. Then he pointed, and said, "Showtime."

They faced Borgioli HQ. An aichy was landing on the roof. Deuce wondered if it was anyone he knew. He wondered if he was going to kill anyone he knew.

One thing was for certain: He wasn't leaving without those two little girls.

Then his guts seized, and a shudder of pain ran through him.

Not now, he thought, and pulled himself together.

"Are you okay, Don Deuce?" Lee Chan asked, frowning.

"Never better," Deuce shot back. "Let's go kick some Borgioli butt."

Lee Chan smiled brightly, showing all his teeth. His eyes gleamed like a tiger's, which Deuce had seen. The Chans had this wild side. Sometimes it was scary how crazy they got in battle.

But he figured that, right now, it was going to prove to be very, very useful.

THIRTEEN

In Angelo's private quarters, Ronnie sat with the two little girls and thought, *This is bad.*

The girls were huddled together, wide-eyed at the opulence and terrified about what was going to happen next.

Ronnie couldn't let Angelo waste them.

Tears streamed down her face. She had on a real silk peignoir, which was another word for a fancy bathrobe, and real diamonds, and on a small table beside Angelo's huge bed, a vase of real red roses filled the room with an unbelievable scent. It was heady and delicious, but it was making her sick to her stomach.

No. What Angelo had done was making her sick. This was against the rules. Taking civilian babies hostage—what a monumental dishonor, not only to the entire Borgioli Family, but to all the Families. And of course, to hers. She had not yet accumulated enough honor that she could lose any of it lightly. Was Angelo truly so angry at Nicky that he would do this awful thing to make him come back?

"Wanna go home," the little one, Cynthia, wailed. "Wanna my mommy."

"It's all right," Ronnie soothed.

The other girl narrowed her eyes. "Don't lie to her," she snapped. "It's not all right. She's not stupid. She's just little."

"It's just pretend," Ronnie said desperately. "Nobody would really hurt you girls."

The child just stared at her. Ronnie felt herself redden. Her name was Annie, she recalled. Bonnanio. An Italian name. Was Angelo in Vendetta with the family for some reason? But

170

that was ridiculous. It still wouldn't explain why he had taken the girls hostage.

As if he had read her mind, Angelo strode into the room, all business and no pleasure, like he was about to conduct a sit-down. He was alone, which, given the situation, was a little unusual. Usually when you were keeping hostages, you kept them safely locked in the bunker, and you kept yourself surrounded by goombattas. Ronnie figured it was a statement about how little he thought of her. Either that she was invisible to him, or harmless.

That, or else that he trusted her, and it couldn't be that. He'd be a fool to trust someone he hardly knew. She was just a plaything to him, an object, like the roses on the table. Which, okay, you had to consider the lifestyle. And maybe once she would have been content with that. But Nicky had thought she was a pretty special broad.

She had *un piccolo* self-esteem now, and she wanted to keep it.

Still, she rose nervously, feeling guilty for what she was thinking, and said, "Angelo. Hello, darling."

He nodded at her. He didn't look so good, which was a cause for alarm. As long as she was liaised with him, her wagon was tied to his star. If he went supernova during this very stupid blunder of his, her worth would plummet. Some of the Family men who had approached her at the party, for example, would back right off.

"Any word from Nicky?" he asked.

"No," she managed, as evenly as she could.

He sighed and gestured with his hands as if to say, whatta ya gonna do? *Forza maggiore.*

"Veronica, I know this is mortifying to you. I'm sorry."

He looked at the children. "You have to know, nothing bad is going to happen to you," he said. "I'm only pretending, to get my nephew to come home."

He turned his gaze back to Ronnie. "So if you know his plans, his destination, I want you to tell me. He's in grave danger out there, and it's my job to protect him."

His eyes were filled with pain. She was confused. If Nicky's mother had not committed suicide, her son would necessarily be dead by now. A Godfather did not allow a prominent Fam-

ily Member to walk away without retribution when he left the
Family without permission.

Her eyes widened.

Had Ariana committed suicide?

No one had heard her deathbed obligation except for Angelo.

She tried to replay the events in her head. Angelo had
shouted something, or Ariana had. Ronnie thought she would
never forget those awful moments for as long as she lived.
But now, they were a blur.

"What's wrong?" Angelo asked gently.

She swallowed and shook her head. He took her hand and
kissed her knuckles.

"I know this isn't what you bargained for," he said. His face
was so kind. He was a young and handsome man, and a Godfather to boot. She couldn't help the way her heart melted. It
had been stupid to think he'd whacked his own sister.

"I'm sorry," he continued. "I know I've acted disgracefully,
and caused dishonor for the Family." He shook his head. "It
was wrong to give in to the government. But since we're the
Borgiolis . . ." He didn't finish his sentence.

Instead, he raised her to a standing position, and said,
"When this is over, I'll make sure you have whatever you need
to make a new liaison with somebody, if you want. Money, a
letter of recommendation . . ."

"Angelo, you're too kind," she said in a rush. She was
touched to her soul that in all this turmoil, he would think of
her future. She added, "Don't even think that I would want
that."

So when the bad guys burst in from the balcony, through
the airlock, and into the room, and shouted "Freeze!" it made
perfect sense to her to pull the blaster from her cleavage and
throw herself in front of her protector as she fired.

His agonized shout of, "No! Ronnie!" was the last thing she
ever heard.

But it was the best thing she ever heard.

Because she got the distinct impression that Don Angelo
Borgioli cared more than a little that she was dying. That was
definitely something to go out on.

Even if your star was falling.

Then something glowed in front of her. It was brilliant, a

moonburst of silver. She lifted a hand toward it, or thought that she did, and whispered, "I'm coming to you, Holy One."

Her body began to dissolve.

I'm going to Heaven, she thought, overjoyed. *Me. What a miracle.*

Veronica died.

Angelo stared at Deuce. He said, "Holy One?"

Deuce ignored him. He didn't know what to say, anyway.

The two little girls were shrieking and sobbing, running to Deuce and throwing their arms around his legs. Lee Chan was on Deuce's right, poised for action, but it appeared to be all over.

"Hey, Annie, hey Cindy," Deuce soothed. He looked up at Angelo, and said, "You bastard."

Angelo lifted his chin. "Me? You married the MLF."

"They're the only ones with the guts to fight Earthside," Deuce said. His tone was defensive, and with good reason. He was dodging the issue, and he knew it. There were plenty of good Family people, still in Families, who were more than willing to enter into a guerrilla war against the oppressor.

Angelo sighed and bent over the dead girl. He closed her eyes.

"She was a sweet kid," he said. "I'll never get over Beatrice, but Veronica, she was special in her way."

"Is that really why you did all this? Beatrice?" Deuce asked, as he picked up both the girls, and told them, "Ssh, ssh, Uncle Deuce is here."

Deuce glared at his cousin. "You brought dishonor to the entire Family, and the whole Family system. I could have double-crossed the MLF. For God's sake, they weren't going to declare war on the Families. Just work on clearing out the Earthsiders and the worst of the sympathizers."

"Like me." Angelo's voice was filled with bitterness.

"What were you thinking, *parente mio*?" Deuce underscored the fact of their being kinsmen, relatives by blood, to point out how wounded he was by what Angelo had done. By the look on his face, Angelo understood.

"Where's my nephew?" Angelo asked.

"Safe. From you."

"He doesn't . . . need to worry," Angelo finished in a faint voice.

"Then you're not fit to run the Family. And you know it."

Angelo's face went white. He stood for a moment in obvious torment. Then he crouched down and grabbed the dead girl's blaster. He aimed it at Deuce.

Lee Chan took up a martial-arts crouch.

"Uh-uh," Angelo said, aiming the blaster at the Chan Liaison. "Just take the kids."

Deuce said, "I'll tell everyone you contacted me to give them up." Before Angelo could protest, he added, "In the long run, it'll work in your favor. I'll make up a story. I'll make you look good. What's the word? Magnanimous?"

"You were always trying to class up," Angelo said harshly. His dark eyes seemed even darker. Angelo was a little older than Deuce was, but he didn't look it. He was the kind of guy girls just tumbled for.

Deuce longed for the old days, when they were *paisani* just looking to get ahead in the Family. Family kids had the same kind of unformed notions as other kids: Some dreamed of becoming hit men, others of being *capos*, and some dared to dream the Godfather dream. Those were usually the ones who became Godfathers. Deuce, being adopted, had never really dared to go there. Even for him to be considered a full-fledged Family Member, and not just an Affiliate, had required a ruling from the Charter Board.

Of course, at the time he'd been practically engaged since birth to the Godfather's daughter, Beatrice.

Whom Angelo had loved, and who had killed herself rather than live another second without Deuce.

"You got a lot of reasons to hate me," Deuce said to Angelo.

"I don't hate you, Deuce."

"Then why'd you try to whack me?"

"Not you. The broad. Iniya or what'sit." Angelo glowered at him. "She's a plant. A setup. There's no such thing as she's claiming."

Deuce blinked. "You were there, Angelinino. You heard her."

"I heard what Hunter Castle's robot was programmed to say. And how convenient that he managed to get out of the way just as the Moon was conquered." He shook his head. "You've been suckered, Deuce. Admit it."

The little girls were still going crazy as Lee Chan tried to pry them off Deuce. It was hard to keep your dignity—and your aim—with shrieking babies clinging to you.

"Hey, hey," Angelo said, waving to them. "You're okay now. Everything's fine." He sighed and pressed his badge.

"Yeah. Get Lucia. The hostages need some . . ." He looked at them.

Deuce said, "Pancakes."

Annie looked up at him and broke into a huge smile. When he had first found her stumbling dejectedly down the street in the middle of the night, she had confided her dream of pancakes for breakfast.

He had made sure that she had awakened to them the next morning, safe in her very own bed at home, with her very relieved mother at her side.

"Pancakes," he said again to Angelo.

"Pancakes," Angelo muttered thoughtfully. He laughed again, a gallows laugh. "*Pasticcio*." Which in the language literally meant "pie," but really meant, "a real mess."

Deuce said, "Angelo, it will be all right."

At long last, the door burst open. Three very seriously enhanced Borgioli bodyguards raced through the doorway. They had superpumpers against their shoulders. But they were no match for the trio of blasters already aimed at them. They went down before their thumbs hit their triggers.

"*Grazie*," Angelo said feelingly to Deuce and Lee Chan. The three men took a moment. No real bodyguard would have waited so long to come to the rescue of his boss. No, those three must have been waiting to see if the trespassers who scaled the balcony wall were going to succeed at assassinating their embarrassment of a Godfather.

Angelo absently kicked one of their outstretched arms out of his way as he knelt beside Veronica.

"She'll need a good funeral," Angelo said. "Very classy, with a real nice laminated coffin for the cremation."

Deuce saw a tear slide down his cheek. As a general rule, Godfathers did not cry over arm candy like her. Angelo must be feeling pretty alone, to go to pieces like this over a broad he scarcely knew.

He wanted to say something of comfort, but he kept his big mouth shut. He and Lee Chan each took charge of a little girl, and the little darlings laid their heads on their shoulders, clearly traumatized. Cynthia was staring wide-eyed and sucking her thumb. At least she was quiet.

"Let's go out the front way, like we're okay here," Deuce suggested. "Obviously, your enemies are watching the balcony."

"Obviously," Angelo said glumly.

He said to Angelo, "Can you guarantee us safe passage?"

"I think so." Angelo was busy gathering up Veronica's body in his arms.

"Can you do it now?" Deuce persisted.

Angelo said, "I think so." He shifted the dead woman in his arms such that he could tap his comm badge. He spoke in Italian, and he was telling his boys that two couriers were here for the girls, and it was all fine, blah-blah, and to prove it he would walk them out.

Deuce kept his watch cap on and his head bowed as they walked through the vast and extremely tacky Borgioli House. He used to run down these very halls with Joey and Bea, Big Al shouting at them not to damage the marble floors. Hah. Crater was all they were, only Big Al would never admit it. The man had pride. No brains, but pride.

"Mr. Deuce," Annie said in a loud voice.

"Ssh, honey," Deuce cautioned, the back of his neck prickling as she spoke his name. "It's okay. We'll talk all about it. Some people, before they die, they see things. It's called a hallucination."

"But—"

"It's okay, honey. I know you're scared." He remembered the first time he had been confronted with the reality of death: when the head of his Uncle Carmine had arrived in a box during the Family celebration of the Feast of the Assumption.

Her voice rose. "But it's just that—"

"Ssh," he pleaded. "It's all right now, Annie. The bad guys are whacked, I mean, they have gone to Heaven to be with the Virgin and the angels. And their dogs, if they had dogs that died before them," he added, grabbing at any straw to calm her down. "And kitty cats, and like that."

Angelo found it in himself to say, "Amen. Yeah, and if they had rabbits, also."

"No, it's not that," she insisted.

"It's okay. Everything will be okay," Lee Chan said.

"I have to go to the bathroom!" she shouted.

Oh, fabulous. He gave her an anxious little pat. "You're gonna have to wait, baby."

She screwed up her face. "I can't. I have to go *now*."

She wasn't lying, and she proved it.

Deuce sighed.

The leader of the free world had a unique set of occupational hazards.

FOURTEEN

The last thing Deuce took care of before his makeover was trying to figure out if Angelo was right about Iniya. It had occurred to him from time to time that it/she had rather conveniently shown up just as the war was breaking out—a war that Hunter, an Earthsider, was furious about.

Okay, so the weird area in the hold of the *Star* had looked like the remains of a crashed alien ship. And the strange liquid metal-producing machine had pretty much regrown his arm and healed his psyche in a lot of ways.

More than a lot of ways, actually. He was a different man since that machine had washed him in that strange rain inside Hunter's ship. More peaceful with a lot of his, er, life issues. Definitely more confident.

Or had that been all him? You get your very own arm back, you're pretty cheerful.

Deal was, there were definite pros and cons to being a decisive individual. If you made the wrong move, people said you were either hair-trigger or foolhardy. If you did the right thing, people praised you for being intuitive and clever.

Problem was, everyone but you got to judge you by hindsight. Armchair quarterbacking taken to the nth degree, and who ever resisted that?

It was decision-making time again. Iniya, pro or con? His money had been on her authentic alienhood, but even from the git-go—after the initial shock wore off—he couldn't be sure. But that was the pro/con part of the equation; you assessed the information as best you could, then you made your best guess, and then you freakin' did something about it.

That's where the peanut gallery came in—kicking back with a Bad Moon Brew and pontificating on if your best guess was good enough. Howsoever, the time for history to be written was now.

So. Iniya. He had to go with the scenario he felt most comfortable with.

Ding: He was insane, and it was all a dream.

"Are you ready, Don General?" said the masked face leaning over him.

"*Sí*. Do your worst," he told the surgeon as he settled in for a nap on the operating table, laughing a little because the anesthesia was taking effect.

"My best, Don General," the surgeon assured him. "You will be my masterpiece."

"That sounds painful," Deuce murmured, and began to drift.

There was this dream:

The people in the dream were kind of Asiatic-looking, like Mr. Wong, only they were almost luminescent. Kind of like their bodies were thin, or not really there. And they were playing a game, betting on something.

It was something to do with him.

He was standing in a big room, and they were staring down at him like he was a zoo animal, and he said, "It's not funny," and that made them howl with laughter.

Which really pissed him off.

When Deuce woke up from the surgery, he looked like a very dark-skinned man with curly black hair. He was extremely attractive, if he did say so. He was thrilled. He loved his broad, flat nose, and his lush lips, and his extremely high cheekbones.

The surgeon said, proudly, "West Indian, with a strong soupçon of Masai," which Deuce had no notion of what that meant. But it looked great.

And then he saw Iniya.

Her makeover had taken place at the same time as his. Gone was the trashy party-doll look. She was, in a word, Madonna-like, dark-eyed, dark-haired, exquisite. The kind of woman a man assumed he could not have because she was too perfect for this world.

He saw her while she was asleep, still as death, the android form recuperating from the shock of being fitted with the remote data terminal. The operation had been assisted by the two Scarlattis, who had been rather insulted that Deuce thought their package needed replacing. In case she needed any retrofitting, repairs, that kind of thing, he had lied to them to placate them, explaining that her cover had been compromised and that was why the makeover.

Truth be told, he was still dismayed by her appearance. People would notice her. She was that gorgeous. He should have explained to the surgeon to make her more unnoticeable, not more so. Maybe it was something to do with the original Iniya. Maybe she was so beautiful you couldn't help but make her robot beautiful.

Anyway, here they were, unrecognizable unless the MLF surgeon and his team were on someone's payroll, which you always had to assume.

But you did your best and moved on, and so Deuce slowly moved around as the anesthesia wore off, saying, "And both of us will take Earthside gravity okay, right?"

"Absolutely, sir," the surgeon assured him. "I injected time-release freefalls subcutaneously, as we discussed."

Next Deuce looked in on Nicky. The kid looked great, fairly unrecognizable despite the fact his makeover had not been as extensive as Deuce's and Iniya's. A new hair color—nice auburn highlights, like Gabriel's—and a slight reshaping of his features. The MLF had refused to fund a full redo.

Nicky was getting dressed. He said, "Hey, Godfather, don't I look great?"

Deuce affectionately shook his head. Nicky was growing on him. After Deuce had reunited the little Bonnanio girls with their *mamma*, Nicky had raged for hours, claiming that his honor was forever besmirched because he hadn't gone to rescue them. Deuce reminded him that he hadn't known about the kidnappings, but the fact that Deuce had kept them from him threw Nicky into an even bigger tizzy. This eventually worked in Deuce's favor; Nick felt so beholden to Deuce that he reaffirmed his vow of allegiance.

"To you, not the MLF," he added. "I'll do whatever you tell me to do. Fight for them, fight against them, whatever. I'm in your debt."

"Then come Earthside with me," Deuce said. "I need the backup."

Nicky, of course, was ecstatic at the invitation. Ah, youth.

At twenty-eight—Deuce's birthday had come and gone without any fanfare—*il Padrino* felt positively ancient.

Reunited with his contingency wife, Deuce sat down and told Gabriel what he was up to. She had known about the makeover, of course, but he'd let her assume it was a simple safety measure. Occasionally, big shots got makeovers, then let someone stand in for them while they issued orders from the sidelines. Deuce disabused her of this notion as it applied to his own case in fairly short order.

She fairly much went *pazzo*.

"You're supposed to help us get the Earthsiders out of here," she insisted. "Not go down there and help them."

He shook his head. "Honey, just because you spun the wheel, don't make me the marble."

"Deuce, you agreed in front of all my troops." She was wild-eyed.

He shrugged. "If you need something official, I'll issue a statement putting you back in charge."

"I'm pregnant," she shot back without hesitation. "With your child."

"Man, lady, you don't have any scruples, do you?" It was meant as a compliment, but she obviously did not see it that way.

She burst into tears. "But I'm carrying your child. The child of our new hope!"

O Dio. Dames, he thought. *Pregnant dames.*

He was not without tenderness toward her. In the Family, the mother of your children was a very special woman. You put her on a pedestal so high, her head was in the clouds. And he was the one who said they should get married, and he knew she was his Connie Lockheart when they did the honeymoon thing.

So he folded her into his arms and kissed the top of her head, feeling extremely protective of her while at the same time marveling that this was the same person who had been in charge of the entire MLF. Sobbing against his chest.

"I'm not usually like this," she insisted, as if she could read his mind. She raised her chin and sniffled.

"But you are now." He deliberated a moment. "Who was your cabinet before I showed?" Then he remembered most of them had been killed in various explosions. That was half the reason, turned out, she had come after Deuce. For more fire-power.

"Okay. So. You got any generals and like that you want to run the joint while I'm gone?"

"I can do it."

He regarded her. "Your condition, you should pardon my bluntness, is very delicate. Your hormones are whacked-out. As you yourself must surely realize."

She sighed. Then she said, "Okay. I'll concede I could use one or two really strong seconds. There's a whole cadre of people who would do a good job. I'll make a list."

Deuce thought a moment. Then he shook his head. "I don't need a bunch of pissed-off, passed-over militants running around armed." He grinned at her. "And if you can say that five times in a row, I'll stripe you a million credits."

"Stop stalling."

"My mom and Leslie Bonnanio."

She stared at him as if he were completely out of his mind.

"They'll be the figureheads," he assured her. "You'll be the real power."

"My troops will never buy it."

He touched his nose. He loved his new nose. He said, "Mine will. The Families default in favor of a direct line of succession."

"I know." She crossed her arms. "But not us. They'll rebel."

"Wrong. Because you, Ma, and Leslie are going to give 'em what they want," he told her.

"Which is?"

He smiled at her. "A good fight." He held up his hand before she could sputter out of control. "And the blessings of their very own private Messiah."

Deuce was right on both counts.

He called a big rally of the whole base. As soon as he announced that he was going Earthside to drum up support for the cause from "disaffected persons who wish to remain nameless," the troops, almost to a person, looked at Gabriel. She sat calmly, aware of the gazes upon her, and kept her attention riveted on Deuce.

"While I'm gone, of course General Kincade-Jones di McNamara is in charge," he said. Everyone looked at him like, "Duh."

"And in the Family way, I elect my mother, Connie Lockheart di McNamara, to stand in for me. Also, Leslie Bonnanio."

The women, who had been prepped, looked on placidly as the grumbling started.

"Anyone not happy with that arrangement can have a meeting with me. I'm leaving for Earthside in two days."

But one guy stood up angrily, and said, "This doesn't make any sense. Your mother and that other woman have no battle experience."

"They most certainly do," Deuce retorted. "Ma, tell 'em."

She blinked at him. Then she said, "I've been running the Connie Lockheart organization for decades. As such, I've been the target of countless assassination attempts. We're thousands strong."

Leslie Bonnanio looked nervous. "I've been running a covert operation from my house," she said, keeping her voice strong.

"Here's the deal," Deuce cut in, to make it look like she had more credentials and he was interrupting her recitation of them. "These are broa—people I trust. I'm still the boss around here, and these are the three I want. Anybody has a beef with that, they're free to let me know. Also, they're free to go. Which then, I'm saying, so much for loyalty."

He pointed at the women. "These people, I'm sure of their loyalty. So, give them your respect or pack your suitcase."

There was more grumbling. There were more protests. Deuce found it all incredibly boring. Also, rude. You did not act this way in a Family meeting.

Not if you wanted to live through it.

However, he understood that MLF ways were different. And for all they called him "Don" General and believed he could dance on the head of a pin, they didn't have the first notion of how you treated a real Family Don. Or a Messiah, he supposed. So he excused them all—at least eight hundred thousand times, cuz of him being so holy and all—and let them argue and all like that, until they wore themselves out.

Taking a quick frown and scowl count, he figured they were gonna lose about a quarter of the troops. Maybe more, even. However, it could not be helped. And since he doubted they planned to leave in order to fight for Earthside, it didn't matter much. If they went off to conduct the war in their own ways, that was fine with him. In fact, better. The more Earthside was harassed, the happier Deuce would be.

For her part, Yuet was pretty agitated that he wanted to wait two more long days before taking off for Earthside. Despite the fact that part of his concern was for his subcutaneous free-fall drugs to kick in—she chided him for being timid about the Earthside acclimation process—she was wild to get him to the mother planet for a big sit-down with the leaders of the Eight.

He figured she must have a time limit to accomplish her mission before she was replaced. He was sorry about that, but it wasn't his responsibility to make sure her life went smoothly. He had to do what he had to do . . . and on the timetable best suited for him.

Because you did not leave your wife, even if she was contingency and one kickass lady, without making sure she was looked after. That was standard male practice if you were Italian. Stuff like that drove the Women's Association in the Moon (WAM) really crazy but hey, there it was.

You also took care of as many variables as possible. And that included organizing and spearheading as much of the guerrilla warfare against the enemy interloper imperialist take-over pseudo-government tool of the League of Decency as possible.

So Deuce sent out several war parties, which were bent on blowing up the remains of the Charter Board as well as causing general mayhem on the Strip. Bombs were scheduled to go off in poorly guarded sectors—first assuring that no civilians would be harmed—and he was rather shocked, actually, to learn that the MLF didn't have a very strict policy about avoiding injury to noncombatants.

Although, why shocked, he wasn't sure. He was even more convinced that the Family way was the best system in the satellite—enlightened self-interest versus fanaticism—and he would be damned before he would do anything to permanently bring it down.

But no one needed to know that just then. It was kind of a fine point to put on "Earthsiders, Go Home!" and "Aliens, Stop the Jumpgate!" For the time being, the ends justified the means. But for the time being only.

And wasn't this kind of thinking precisely how such things got started?

From the Captain's Log of Gambler's Star:

It's dangerous to write down my thoughts, but I need to keep my sanity. I'm used to making these entries, although I have been remiss of late in writing them.

I've been afraid that my logs would fall into the wrong hands.

I have no idea if Sparkle made it safely away. I thank God that she made the break without divulging her plans to me. If the !kth come to me, I can tell them nothing. And I can pretend that I still believe they will prove the boon to mankind I once thought they were.

I can't imagine the agony it must have caused her to leave the children behind. I must confess, I'm somewhat amazed that she managed it. That she could return to our space without them is a testament to her ability, to that practical nature of hers. It only underscores her special talents; she must realize how vital it is to stop the !kth.

How naive I was. I don't know why I did what I did. I can't explain it. I'm Hunter Castle. I would never have trusted a human partner the way I trusted these aliens. What the hell is wrong with me?

I have made a huge mistake. In my arrogance, I didn't see the warning signs. I certainly see them now, and I pray God that I have not engineered the death of my own family. Because, rather than allow the !kth to invade our space, I will blow up this ship and all aboard her, if it will stop them.

Hunter Castle
Aboard Ship, 2145.2

With Carmine and Stefano Scarlatti as backup, Nicky slipped into the employees' entrance of the Inferno. The door was conveniently left unlocked by one Half-Moon, who had been Carmine's squeeze until Carmine left for the front. He'd gotten back in, ah, touch with her, and now she was a convert to the cause.

She went over mainly because Carmine told her he was actually working undercover for the Family, and that when the time came, he was going to be in line for a Select of Six position for rendering such services on behalf of the Scarlattis.

Nicky could not imagine why anyone would believe such a thing, but if Half-Moon did, that was just fine with him. Further, Carmine creeped him out, so he didn't see why she was attracted to him anyway. But hey, they were just lucky that she was.

Because word on the street was, Angelo Borgioli was visiting today, and since he and the Scarlattis were currently on speaking terms, he had not brought that many bodyguards with him.

Nicky was there to kill his uncle.

They all three had on Scarlatti uniforms for working the floor: black pants and red shirts, holo name tags with stabbing pitchforks on them. Very old-world Mafia, which was surprising, since the Scarlattis were extremely cutting-edge in all other respects.

The three caballeros were packing all kinds of special antisurveillance stuff that the MLF had manufactured, which Iniya had then souped up in postproduction. Only, that part—the Iniya part—wasn't common knowledge, and these Scarlatti boys weren't in on the secret. Suffice to say it wouldn't matter what kind of detectors the Scarlattis had installed in the Inferno; they wouldn't sound the alarm no matter where Nicky and his *paisani* went.

No one else knew they were there. Nicky had promised the Scarlatti brothers all kinds of crap to help him out, including a couple of those nifty black grenades Iniya had churned out for Deuce. Also, preferential treatment if he, Nicky, ever became Godfather of the Borgioli Family. Which was very likely, given what they had gone there to do. A lot of Borgiolis were mortified that the Family was collaborating with the enemy.

They walked calmly through the employee sector, all of it very plain but not threadbare, the way it would be if it were the Borgiolis' Palazzo di Fortuna. There was a poster on the wall featuring a high-kickin' showgirl dressed like a sexy little devil. The poster read, SMILE. YOU WORK FOR THE E.C.N. GOVERNMENT. Someone had added a few choice words in Italian beneath, which, when Nicky and the Scarlattis read them, made them snicker under their breath.

At the main door, Nicky got his blaster and his credit card ready. They had arranged for a friendly Scarlatti security animal to be waiting to let them in, but with all the Earthsiders sticking their noses into everything, you never knew what the new protocol was.

The nice thing was, neither did anyone else. Moonsiders had heard about the legendary inefficiency of government bureaucracy, but few had ever before experienced it. Except for N.A.'s, and that was because they got lots of stuff for free, paid for by the money the government extorted from the Families in the form of "gambling taxes."

But the mismanagement was pretty incredible. Besides demanding forms and committees for every decision ever made, the Earthsiders truly had no understanding of gambling. They were shocked to discover that the odds for all the games always favored the house and set about correcting that inequity. Somehow, they were not making the vital link between profit and overhead. It stood to figure that some kind of money was being used to pay all the employees, keep the chandeliers twinkling, and the free drinks coming.

And it sure wasn't what the Inferno raked in at their all-you-can-eat buffets, which they practically gave away for free.

The overhead was in the odds, plain and simple. You tacked on a sort of "user fee" for every bet a player made, and that was the house advantage. There was nothing nefarious about it. The odds on each game were prominently posted on the card tables, or the slots, the Wheels of Fortune, roulette, baccarat—there were no secrets.

But the government didn't like any of it. So they started messing with it.

The casinos were bleeding money. They were like shot-up soldiers, staggering around after a battle.

The walking wounded, soon to be the walking dead.

They stood behind the door. Nicky took a breath. He gave the signal—three sharp raps—and the door opened.

It was their operative, a gorgeous, swanky chick who looked like she wanted to become a spokesmodel. Nicky didn't so much as blink as she let the door swing open. The trio slung easily into the casino like they were going to work, no one paying them any mind.

Their sole objective was to get across the floor to the little door behind the roped-off baccarat area. Nicky's heart started beating faster as they passed through the world's best holos of the fires of hell complete with swirling smoke and the occasional very sexy devil man or girl, coalescing out of the flames into a figure so real and so attractive you wanted just to reach right out and squeeze something.

However, not anything belonging to the devil man. Nicky was not like that, himself. Not that there was anything wrong with it. You had your men who cared for that sort of thing, and that was all right.

For them.

They were halfway across the floor when Carmine sucked in his breath. Little Gino was screaming at some poor cocktail waitress. She was backed up against a slot machine, her little silver tray held over her chest like a shield. Her eyes were so wide he was afraid they might pop out of her head.

Nicky was grateful to her for whatever she did; he might have a makeover, but his two companions did not.

So he whispered, "Keep walking, boys," and they did. They were cool customers; he had to give them that.

At the deserted baccarat area, they were three for three: the guy who owed Carmine a fortune in gambling debts stood with his hands folded, loosening the velvet rope that stretched across the entrance and letting them in. He replaced it and casually walked away.

So far, everything was so good. All that remained was the last door, and the inevitable small army of bodyguards on the other side. For that, all Nicky had was information. Nobody, but nobody, was willing to stand anywhere near that door when it opened.

"Okay, guys," Nicky breathed, as they reached it. He pulled one of the black bombs out of his pocket. "Turn on your shields."

They flummed on invisible but highly effective body shields that could repel anything the guards threw at them—or so Iniya claimed. Thing was, they didn't last too long, or they would have turned them on oh, about a week ago.

The code for the door was etched in Nicky's memory. It was a long string of letters and numbers which meant nothing to him. Before he punched them into the reader on the side of the door, he made good on his deal with the two Scarlattis and gave each of them one of the black grenades. If they survived, and he didn't, they could retrieve the rest at his base locker, voiced to open for either or both of them.

Then he punched in the combination, soundlessly mouthing each letter and number as he put them in. One wrong button, and the guards would be alerted by a silent alarm. There would be no way for Nicky to know if he'd made a mistake until the shooting began.

The door clicked.

It had unlocked.

"Shields on?" he queried the two. Because of their anti-surveillance equipment, the casino's scanners and sweepers had not detected the other weapons hidden in their pants and shirts, which they now pulled out—hypercharged blasters and Tycho 217s, which delivered 217 pulses a second.

And then Nicky realized it was a setup.

He put all his weapons away and raised his hands, and gestured for Carmine and Stefano to do the same. But they got the message too late.

They were both dead before they hit the floor.

Because they didn't actually hit the floor right away; shot in the back, their limp bodies were caught in midfall by their assailants as the door was thrown open and Nicky was dragged inside.

On the other side was Nicky's Uncle Angelo, white as a sheet, and clearly enraged.

"Don't say a word," he said to Nicky, taking his arm and herding him down the hall. "Not a word. Not a lie. Not the truth. Nothing."

Nicky raised his chin. "Ronnie."

"Damn it, kid."

At a nod to a Scarlatti animal, the enhanced guard hissed

open a door and Angelo barreled through, Nicky in tow. He
threw him to the floor.

"She was a *puttana*," Angelo said bluntly. "She went with
me as soon as you were out of the picture."

"Well, sure," he said, shrugging. "Good for her."

"But you loved her, *putz*."

"You killed her."

"No. Your precious Deuce killed her. Ask him."

Nicky blinked at him. "I don't believe you."

Angelo grunted.

They were in a sit-down room, dominated by a large table
littered with bottles of Chianti, Atherton Gold, and half-eaten
plates of pasta. Nicky missed good food; even more, he missed
good booze.

A stooped woman in black and red was shuffling around
the table, emptying ashtrays into a plastic bin. A cigarette dangled from her lips.

Angelo looked at her, and said, "Grandmama, please. May
I have some moments with my nephew?"

An ashtray in her hand, she stopped and looked at the two
of them. She cocked her head, and said, "Just don't shoot him.
I already washed the floor."

Then she set down the ashtray and the bin, took a drag on
her cig, and started shuffling toward the door. She shuffled
very slowly. The men fell silent, watching her.

And watching her.

And waiting.

She shuffled.

At last—long last—she hissed open the door and shuffled
on out. The door closed, more slowly than ever before, it
seemed.

As one, the two Borgiolis burst into laughter.

Then they looked at each other. Angelo opened his arms
and said, "Idiot. *Cretino*. Come here."

Nicky hesitated. His uncle's obligation was limited to death.
And he had, after all, come here to kill him.

Still, blood was blood, and Angelo could whack him from
across the room just as easily as he could stick a knife in his
back. So Nicky went.

When you grew up in a Family, you did not turn down an
embrace from your Godfather.

"Now, what was this all about?"

"You're in bed with Earthside," Nicky said. "It's a dishonor."

"You're telling me. Biggest mistake I ever made," he confided, lowering his voice. "You tell Deuce I said that. Tell him I've reconsidered, but of course I haven't told the goons that. I can work inside now."

Nicky nodded. "We're going Earthside," he blurted, then wished he hadn't. He should have kept his yap shut, made sure this was all on the up-and-up. One of the most important requirements for being a Godfather was being an excellent liar.

"Earthside? Really? What for?" Angelo asked casually.

"Reinforcements," Nicky lied. "There's a group down there wants to join the MLF in return for some action if we ever get the friggin' Earthsiders off the Moon."

Well, it was kind of true.

"That's good to know," Angelo said, clapping him on the back. "That's real good to know. You've done well, Nicky. I'm very proud of you." His face softened. "Your mother, God preserve her with the Virgin and the angels, would be proud, too."

Nicky's blood ran cold.

FIFTEEN

If the MLF had a strong suit, it was covert operations. Those guys could sneak around in spades. Deal them any card, they turned it into a winning hand.

In other words, it was a minor detail to sneak Deuce, Iniya, and Nicky onto a freighter bound for Earth. Had the MLF been in on Nicky's visit to the Inferno to kill his uncle, there would not be two dead Scarlattis in the Inferno's private morgue.

Nicky was awaiting word on if the Scarlattis planned to go into Personal Vendetta with him. Deuce figured not, since Carmine and Stefano had officially turned traitor and therefore were not protected by the Family anymore. It dawned on Nicky what chaos he and the other Family Members and Affiliates were causing by abandoning their Families and joining the MLF.

Shamefaced, he had confessed to Deuce everything that had happened in his badly planned assassination attempt. To say that Deuce was not pleased was an understatement. Nicky had never seen Deuce so angry, and it both frightened him and filled him with awe. Guy like Deuce, he was the kind you forgot could be very, very dangerous.

Even more dangerous than Uncle Angelo.

They were crammed in with the actual freight, the fact of which surprised Nicky. You lived in the Moon, you assumed nothing was actually made there; that the only industry was tourism. But here were large Kevlite containers of precious metals mined from the crust; and there, some intricate machine parts; and crystals grown at ZeroGee ApoGee, which was a high-tech company Deuce had forgotten even existed.

There were crates of Atherton Gold as well, and some cases of Bad Moon Brew. Most Earthsiders thought the Moon-produced beer was pretty bad, but there was an exotic factor to it.

There were also dead Earthsiders, who had died on Moonbase Vegas and whose widows wanted them shipped home for burial. Nicky, no stranger to ostentatious displays of wealth, was nevertheless shocked. All his acquaintances who had died had been cremated.

When they'd heard about the bodies, Deuce had raised his brows, and said, "Some world, huh, kid?"

Deuce's stomach was grinding against his bones. Or so it felt. He had no idea what was going wrong; free-fall drugs, makeover incompatible with his !kth DNA, or what. He was in terrible pain, and nothing he had taken so far was helping.

That was saying something. There were no finer and more specific painkillers anywhere than those the Chans could provide. Lee Chan had given him some truly amazing stuff, which Deuce had used before after a couple of shoot-outs. He kept wondering if the pain had been dulled, then how intense must it have been before he took the drugs?

All his life, everything worked fine. All drugs took effect. He had no known allergies to anything. Then his cloning, and *pffft*. His makeover doctor had confirmed that all his new guts were in perfect working order. The medico had found no lesions, injuries, or anything to explain any amount of pain.

Not that Deuce had exactly asked him for an explanation. When you're the head honcho, you don't mention weaknesses of any kind, including not feeling good. Guys conducted business as usual when they had one foot on the welcome mat in front of death's door. Any other way, you might as well paint a target on your chest, jump up and down pointing at yourself and yelling "Come and get me!"

The trip took so little time that Deuce had just settled in when they got the announcement that Earth gravity would be established in three minutes. Deuce took a deep breath and swallowed the culminator in the free-fall med series. He wasn't sure how it all worked, and he didn't want to know. The entire business made him nervous.

He, Nicky, and Iniya were silent. Deuce wondered how

Iniya had contacted the Eight; if her long-distance alien eyes had already seen the things he could only imagine; and what they meant to her. Her opinions and assessments, as in:

Primitive.

Conquerable.

As was also done on the Moon, the freighter would land on the surface outside the domes, and robot shuttles would load and unload the freight. It was time for the stowaways to get into their enviro-suits. A hell of a combination, that, space suits and new gravity.

They had three empty containers to hide in, bought and paid for with MLF money. Of course, you always had to expect a double cross. Given that the Eight were involved, Deuce was hopeful that they might actually live long enough for the sit-down. Depended on if the dice were shaved, he supposed.

He cracked all the knuckles on his left hand, for as much luck as possible, and also crossed himself. Silently, he nodded as Iniya and Nicky checked each other's helmets and gave each other the thumbs-up that they were secured. He figured that technically, Iniya didn't need a helmet, except that she was so good it was hard to tell she was a mechanical. Mr. Wong had been obvious. Most mechanicals were. And that party doll . . . *Mamma mia*, what had those two boys been thinking?

Iniya climbed into her container. Deuce closed the hatch, patted it, and waited for her answering rap. Next was Nicky. Last was him, Deuce, and he pulled the hatch shut from the inside and secured it in place.

Then he waited. As the minutes ticked by, he realized he had to go to the bathroom. He grimaced. It would have to be a very desperate situation before he would go in his suit, fancy-schmancy hookups or no.

Then there was a horrendous bumping and battering, and he hunkered down instinctively, trying to compact himself into a smaller target. The noise increased, and he reminded himself that even though the atmosphere outside the domes was poisoned, it was still atmosphere. Unlike his beloved Moon, where beyond the Kevlite bubbles there was no noise at all, because of the vacuum.

Suddenly, something grabbed the sides of his container and yanked it forward. Then it was bumping down what had to be a conveyer belt. The ride was less than smooth. He thought about all the bottles of Atherton Gold, and the delicate crystals, and hoped they were packed better than he was.

Deuce had no idea how long they jostled and bumped around. His bladder was about to burst. He hurt in general, plus bruises. Plus he really, really had to go.

Just when he thought he couldn't take it anymore, the hatch was ripped open and a gun pointed directly in his face.

Thank God, he thought. *Now I'll either get to pee, or I'll get killed.*

The gun gestured for him to climb out. Deuce looked up. The sky was a flat, grim brown that made him squint despite the tint in the Kevlite screen of his helmet. He stifled a scream. It was nothing he was used to, and he had an unreasoning terror that he was going to float right up and drift off into space. Everything wobbled and tilted; sweat poured down his forehead, and he got the shakes big-time. He took a few deep breaths and fought to steady himself.

The other guys were wearing breathing apparatuses (apparati?) and goggles. They looked at him, Nicky, and Iniya and gestured mockingly at their enviro-suits. Deuce didn't care; he was in extreme pain, and it was getting worse. Even though he had medicated himself for the gravity, the drag was incredible. He weighed six times more than he was accustomed to, and he could feel it through and through.

His helmet crackled. Nicky said, "Are you all right?"

"It's just the gravity," Deuce rasped.

There was a pause. "I don't feel it," Nicky told him. "Did you take your meds?"

"Yeah." Deuce was alarmed. "You don't feel it?" Maybe he had taken the wrong dosage. Maybe any minute, he was going to collapse and die.

"I don't feel it, either," Iniya cut in.

Someone new said, "No talking." Deuce realized they were stupid to assume the other side wouldn't have the frequency of their helmets.

The gun retuned to Deuce's face. Deuce shrugged and raised his hands.

"Sorry, *paisan*," he said easily. "Is there anywhere to go to the can?"

The man with the gun stared at him. Then he began to

laugh. He put the gun down and put out his hand.

"You must be the General."

The General. Deuce thought about that for a second. Then he said, "Yeah, I am." He shook the guy's hand. "And you are?"

"David Schulman. Michael's brother."

"I'm honored," Deuce said sincerely.

The man clapped him on the back. "As for toilet facilities, we have some back at camp. It's about an hour."

Damn.

He sighed and accepted the inevitable.

"No longer an issue," Deuce assured the man in a droll voice.

Schulman laughed harder. "Sorry, General McNamara."

"Yeah, yeah, yeah," Deuce replied. "Allow me to present my colleagues," he continued. "Alan Davison and Nina Borgioli."

"*Nicky* Borgioli and our esteemed Iniya," Schulman said pointedly, shaking hands with each in turn.

He gestured toward his buddies. "These are some of our people." They inclined their heads.

Just soldiers, Deuce translated. He nodded back.

They walked toward a couple of heavily armored vehicles. At David's invitation, Deuce climbed into the passenger's side of the largest one. He quickly realized that with all the bumping, he would not be able to wait.

He muttered, "Thank God for catheters," and Schulman started the motor.

"We'll get you some fresh clothes back at camp. Unless you have luggage?" He looked back at the freight containers.

"We figured we would depend on the kindness of strangers," Deuce drawled.

Schulman chuckled. "Nobody told me you were so funny."

"Just a barrel, that's me." Deuce gave him a look. "What *did* they tell you?"

"Not to piss you off," Schulman said. He turned his attention to the vehicle. To Deuce's complete and total astonishment, they rode along on the ground. After about half a minute, he looked out the window.

A hideous sense of vertigo washed over him. His stomach

churned, and he thought he was going to be sick. The ground was unbelievably bumpy, and the armored car lurched over each dip and hill with all the grace of a drunk.

Schulman glanced over at Deuce. He said, "Only government-issued vehicles are allowed to fly. Needless to say, our cars aren't government issue."

Deuce nodded as if to say, I knew that. He was fighting like crazy to keep his guts inside his body; it was that bad. He was awash in sweat.

The last time he'd thrown up in an enviro-suit had been after *Gambler's Star* blew. He remembered that day clearly, vividly. The carnage had been terrible. Hunter had caused it by testing some of the capabilities of the crashed alien ship—the !kth ship—he had built into the cargo hold.

Hunter, who was his father.

Deuce began vomiting hard. He couldn't stop. The car was spinning; he doubled over, hanging in his restraints, and saw blood gushing into the bottom of the helmet.

Schulman said, "Hang on. There's nowhere to take you except camp."

An hour away.

Sparkle woke.

She sucked in her breath.

She could see.

She was lying on a soft mattress of some sort. Overhead, rainbows were rushing over a low, curved overhang of some sort, perhaps a ceiling.

She sat up.

She appeared to be in a sleeping chamber. A swirled, shell-like object the size of her fist was perched on a slender filament beside the bed; it turned on and illuminated the room with soft pastel colors, a rushing aurora of glowing hues surrounding her.

She whispered, "Hello?"

There was no answer, and she realized she had not expected one. Somehow she had already known she was alone.

As she stood, another filament rose from the floor. A small scroll dangled from a gold cord attached to the end; she plucked it up and opened it. It read:

Greetings, Sparkle de Lune di McNamara,

I, Iniya of D'inn, directed the placing of you in this vessel. It is cloaked against the detection equipment of the !kth and of Gambler's Star.
   You must return to your space.
   Warn Deuce. He is Earthside.

The rainbows and auroras faded, then disappeared.

The curved walls, which were white, faded next.

She stood on an endless field of stars. The vessel surrounded her—if indeed it still surrounded her—and then it slowly veered to the right. Now it directly faced into a brilliant white light so intense that Sparkle had to shield her eyes.

Then, as the light hit her fingers and eyelids, she saw everything clearly.

She wasn't certain if she took her hand away and opened her eyes, or if she was seeing a vision, but it was the jumpgate.

It hung in space, a broken circle of what looked like chunks of multicolored glass, much like the rushes of light that had streamed around her. Fingers of blue energy snapped and flashed from different sections.

Too close, someone said in her head, a strange resonating voice she knew to be that of a female, and which she knew to be Iniya of D'inn.

The invisible ship backed as if of Sparkle's volition. It slowly arced through the brilliant starfield until it was facing a silver, glowing bubble.

It was also a ship, Sparkle knew.

She drew closer; closer still, until the bow of her ship intersected, then transected, the other ship's.

She saw inside.

It was a ship's bridge. Several pale, luminous creatures with strange, stiff faces sat in chairs or walked along consoles, alert and at the ready as they went about the business of navigation.

They were almost wraithlike, although still retaining humanoid shape. The splendor of their clothes was in sharp contrast to their indistinct, smooth-featured faces. They were insubstantial as ghosts, seemingly weighted to the silver floor by the thick fabrics of their ornate robes and heavy, thick sashes. Their sleeves were so massive one would imagine they would break their arms if they lifted them.

One of them stared straight at her. She was female, and statuesque, her face a white oval; her head adorned with large curls of silver hair streaked with jade. She wore a gown of deep, rich scarlet and, over that, a cloak of deep purple. Her hands were hidden inside the cloak.

"You look like an angel," Sparkle said, but only in her mind.

Perhaps in your space, I am one.

Sparkle woke up.

Someone was standing over her: Connie Lockheart and another woman Sparkle had never seen in her life.

"Get up," Connie said, none too friendly.

Sparkle was confused. She must have had a dream. She was in one of *Gambler's Star*'s shuttles.

She murmured, "I have to go to Earth."

"Who says?" the stranger demanded.

"Deuce is there," Sparkle informed her.

Connie set her jaw. Her face was stony, her eyes narrowed with anger. Sparkle flushed.

"I know your opinion of me," she said. "But I need to get to Deuce. I have information."

Connie shrugged. "Tell me what it is, and I'll be sure he gets it."

Sparkle hesitated. "I made contact with an alien named Iniya."

Deuce's birth mother paled. Then she snorted. "It's a trap."

"I've no idea." She decided to say nothing more; she was unsure how much she could trust Connie Lockheart. She glanced at the stranger.

"I'm Leslie Bonnanio, Mrs. McNamara," the woman informed her. "We're with the MLF."

Sparkle blinked. "*What?*"

"It's a long story," Connie cut in, glancing at the other woman.

The two took a couple of steps back, and Sparkle got up out of the sleeper capsule she'd rested in on the journey back.

"How long have I been away?" she asked.

Connie shrugged. "About a month."

She was astonished. It had seemed like days at most. "I have to talk to Deuce. I know he's Earthside."

The two women looked uncomfortable. Connie asked, "Who else knows?"

"Iniya. I don't know about anyone else." She hesitated. "I escaped."

Connie guffawed. "In a Castle Industries shuttle."

"It was cloaked. Iniya told me."

Leslie Bonnanio looked at Connie. "Who's Iniya? Escaped from where?"

Connie's face became smooth and unreadable. "You don't need to know."

"What a minute." The other woman was angry. "What's going on?"

"I'll fill you in later," Connie said. Tapping her comm badge, she kept her gaze on Sparkle as she said into the badge. "Security. On the double."

"No!" Sparkle cried.

Pushing both women out of the way with ease, she jumped up and raced for the controls of the shuttle.

She felt the blaster pulse before she heard the security officer shout, "Halt!"

As she went down, she begged, "Deuce. Get Deuce."

"Iniya," said a voice.

Deuce opened his eyes through a red-orange haze of pain. Something was covering him; a gleaming silver covering that reminded him of the silver rain aboard *Gambler's Star* that had grown back his arm.

"Iniya." It was a male voice.

His.

The sheet was pulled away, and Iniya stood in her robot body, staring down at Deuce. When she saw him looking at her, she said, "The !kth healing device on the *Star* contaminated you. You had far less !kth material in your physical makeup than your father. It didn't calibrate for that, and when it grew your arm back, it injected more !kth material into your cells than your body originally contained."

She added sternly, "You should have told me you were in pain. I might have been able to do something."

"Am I . . . dying?" he asked.

Saying nothing, she looked down at him, and he felt a thrill of panic. He worked it down. Nothing to be done about it now. Maybe later, there would be a miracle. He was Catholic; those kinds of things did happen.

"The !kth are designing the jumpgate to accommodate !kth DNA, and !kth DNA only," she explained. "They want to test it on various subjects. Prisoners, conscientious objectors." She gazed at him steadily. "Your children."

"What?" He tried to sit up, but he hurt too much.

She said it again.

"You've got to fix me. Repair me," he said.

She took a breath. "I don't know if I can, there, where my data terminal is with you. I can . . . here. Where I really am."

A man with dark hair and eyes, a thick beard and a moustache came into Deuce's view. His face was very angular. A female version, much softer, joined him in staring down at Deuce.

"Michael Schulman," the man said. "And this is my sister, Shoshana."

In great pain, Deuce nodded. "I'd get up, but . . ." He gestured weakly. "Let's talk while I'm still able."

The Schulmans exchanged glances. Michael said, "You've got pull with the Smiths."

"Some of them."

"Abraham Smith is here with us," Shoshana cut in. "He tells us the Family has a new kind of fuel. We need it for the project."

Deuce closed his eyes and laughed silently. "That was a bluff. They wanted everyone to be afraid of them, so they made that up."

Shoshana shrugged. "They pulled a flip-flop on you, Don General. It was real. They just let you think they were bluffing."

Deuce grunted with admiration. "Get outta town."

"It's true." She took a breath. "Can you get some MLF forces to steal it?"

"Where is it?"

"The Smith bunker," Michael told him. "At least, that's what our recon says. Abraham figures it's true."

"Mmm." Deuce thought a minute. "I'll need to talk to my guys."

"We can patch you in, no problem," Michael assured him.

"But we need to hurry, if I'm dying." Deuce coughed. He really hurt.

Iniya said, "I'll keep trying to find a solution."

Deuce closed his eyes.

He really, really hurt.

Then there was a *ping* against the floor, and hissing, and suddenly the room filled with tear gas.

Pulses shot into the room, narrowly missing Deuce. The heat of the blasts singed his hair. But he couldn't move. All he could do was cough violently and let his eyes water.

"Freeze! Earthside Security!" someone yelled through a speaker.

Someone clapped a wet rag over his eyes and nose. Then his stretcher was lifted up, and he was being carried off somewhere.

"Move, move, move!" someone else shouted.

The sounds around him spoke of a firefight; there was shouting and pulsing, exploding and blasting. He didn't think he had ever felt more useless in his life, and that pissed him off more than the realization that he had never felt more helpless in his life. You died, at least you took someone with you. That was the Family way.

This was a *stupidaggine*, going out like this.

There was a lot of bumping and jostling, which made him wince, but he didn't cry out, and then he was being slid onto some kind of hard surface like a body in a morgue. The wet rag was yanked from his face, and a stern-looking woman with a tan—wow—glared at him.

"Deuce McNamara, by order of the People of the Conglomerated Nations of Earth, I place you under arrest. I will now tell you your rights. You have the right to remain silent. If you speak, I will record every word you say, and it will be played back at your trial. If you attempt to flee, you will be shot."

She went on with the litany, which Deuce knew by heart. It was the same one the Lunar Security Forces used, only substituting lunar phrases for Earthside ones, such as in the bits about attempting an ocean-route escape, and so on. Every Family kid had to learn it during catechism, and you had to recite it when you got confirmed. At least in the Italian Families.

Traditions like that were good. Gave you a sense of rootedness.

She droned on, but Deuce stared without blinking at her tan. He'd seen them before, of course, in the tunnels and caverns of home. And he, of course, was currently much darker than she. But his darkness was artificial.

Next he had been slid into the back of a van. The doors were open, admitting sunlight. He was completely dazed. He even managed to forget about his pain for a few seconds.

Then he said, "When the sun browns you, does it hurt? Like a roast?"

"What?" She stared at him as if he were trying to put one over on her. Hypnotize her or something. "What are you talking about?"

"Forget about it," he told her. "Never mind."

Then she cracked a hard, funny smile. "Oh, yeah. A Moonie. How could I forget? Nice makeover."

He groaned as the pain reasserted itself. "Do I get to see a doctor?" he asked through clenched teeth. "I am majorly messed up."

"The D.A. will decide," she informed him, like he was such a stupid lowlife rebel that he didn't know the ropes.

"*Mi dispiace*," he said courteously. "Being a Moonie, I don't know your folkways and customs."

"Such as being caught in the company of subversives?"

"You might notice that I'm unable to move. I had little choice whose company I was in. Those nice people found me on the surface."

She snorted. "That's really lame."

If he could have shrugged, he would have.

"Can't win 'em all."

"But down here, you can lose them all," she replied. She wasn't smiling. It wasn't a joke.

Dying might be his best option.

SIXTEEN

They got Iniya, too.

Nicky and the Schulmans made it out. Deuce had to wonder about that. Anytime you got nabbed and someone else didn't, particularly your host, you assumed they'd sold you out.

So. The Schulmans. Not such nice people, perhaps.

And Nicky? Just lucky, or was all this crap with Angelo a bunch of *sciochezza* designed to get Nicky in the loop so he could betray Deuce?

Deuce sighed, fanning out the possibilities like a deck of cards on the baize. It was all too much to think about now.

However, being captured was actually paying off for him in the short run: The government police medicos had access to really terrific painkillers, which kept you fairly lucid while completely wiping out all the pain. Deuce felt like he could go a full hour with Sparkle at the kickboxing dojo.

"Where's my companion?" he asked his guard, a youngish man bent over a mini on a desk in the hall.

"She's a mechanical," the guard answered derisively. "We locked her in with the other household appliances."

"She's a very advanced model," Deuce said. "She will probably take offense."

The man shrugged and looked back down at his mini. "I'm trembling."

"Your appliances might be also."

The guard didn't bother to reply. Deuce lay quietly as pieces of the ceiling seemed to drift away like ice floes in a river.

Which they used to simulate during Earthside America's wintertime at the Smiths' Wild West.

"I'll take over, Osborne," a rotund, sort of Big-Al-style guy said to the surly little punk at the desk. "You go on your dinner break."

"Yessir." Osborne rose and started to put the mini in his pocket.

The other guy shot out an arm, grabbed the guy's wrist, and said, "I'll take that."

Osborne did not look so happy as he handed it over. Deuce perked up, watching the exchange. It was something to do.

The round man looked at the mini. He pressed a couple buttons. Then he muttered, "That's disgusting filth," and handed the mini back to Osborne, who slunk away, red-faced with shame.

"What was it, picture of a girl in a full-length snowsuit?" Deuce asked.

The rotund man huffed. "It's not open for discussion."

"You're League," Deuce said, meaning, of Decency.

The man smiled pleasantly. "Most of the high-ranking individuals in our government are, Mr. McNamara. And I'd like you to know, that if were up to me, I'd shoot you now and save the people a lot of money."

Deuce took that in, and all it implied. Sooner or later, they were going to shoot him expensively.

"I want counsel," he said.

"In your dreams, moron."

Deuce became alarmed. He knew the drill. The drill included lawyers.

"Does anyone know I'm here?"

"A lot of people," the man said pleasantly. "Some of whom you know quite well."

Angelo, Deuce figured. *Via the Schulmans? Nicky?*

"I'm supposed to get a fair trial."

The man snickered.

Deuce tried another tack.

"Lotta guys, they'll know what happened."

"Then you don't have anything to worry about," the man drawled.

He folded his hands over his bulbous stomach. Deuce was fascinated. In the Moon, very few people let themselves look fat. Also, the man had lots of wrinkles. It was the gravity. It pulled your skin down. Literally.

Deuce was very grateful for the free-fall drugs, which had adjusted his body for the pulling down and all like that.

His human body.

However, he doubted it had done a thing for the !kth part of his body. So maybe that helped account for the fact that his overall physical condition was steadily worsening.

"What's your name?" Deuce asked.

"You don't need to know."

"Do I get to talk to anybody better than you, or are you my final destination?" Deuce queried.

"You don't need to—"

"Okay, *prego*, I can only stand so much discourtesy."

A silence fell between them. Deuce dozed, woke up, dozed some more.

He wasn't certain if he dreamed saying, "How long am I in for?"

Or if he dreamed only the response: "Until we take over your space."

Aliens.

Deuce drifted and, well, spaced out. The fat guy was an alien. If he was !kth, Iniya was probably permanently disconnected. D'inn, maybe they were going to break Deuce out.

Or maybe he had dreamed the fat guy talking about his space.

Maybe he dreamed the operation: guys with masks talking in blurry voices, then someone putting something in his gut, and nodding in a serious kind of way.

His nurse was . . . chubby, so he figured she was an alien, too. Still, she bustled around in that unfeeling way human nurses did, more keen on getting the bedsheets wrinkle-free than making sure the patient was comfortable. So either she was human, or really good at faking it.

"What did they do to me?" he asked. His voice sounded very far away.

"They put a stabilizer inside you," she explained. "We understand some of you Moonsiders have undergone a genetic mutation that contraindicates your coming Earthside. Although you're my first actual case, the stabilizer is supposed to help in such situations. But this underscores why there are procedures in place for obtaining visas," she added pointedly.

Genetic mutation? He was intrigued. Who had so deftly planted such a notion, which had spread widely enough such that a government nurse believed it? Disinformation, or something she'd read on a cheesy tabloid zipper?

"How long will the stabilizer stabilize me?" he asked.

"Long enough for your trial. You'll probably die in prison, though. Medical services are rationed, and prisoners aren't high on the list." She almost looked compassionate. "Especially political prisoners."

"Oh. Am I a political prisoner?"

"You're the man who declared war on us," she said flatly.

"Well, pardon me, but I find it difficult to believe that I caused that war. For example, and I mean no disrespect—" He raised his hand, and he was delighted to discover that he could move. He flexed his dark fingers, wiggled them. His grin nearly broke his face.

"You were saying?" she prodded, unimpressed.

"Ah. No disrespect," he said, refocusing. "But for example, if you stood on a table and declared war on the Moon, nothing would happen to you."

She frowned. "It would so. I'd be thrown in jail."

"Oh, that's right." He nodded earnestly. "Free speech. You don't have it here so much."

"And you people do, where you shoot each other over a meaningless insult?"

"No, no," he said. "Not meaningless. When we insult somebody, it's more than a—I beg your pardon because I certainly don't mean to trivialize anyone's anger—snotty remark. But it's kind of complicated," he added, because he was beginning to tire.

"It's ridiculous. You people are like little children. You need supervision. It's a good thing we came in when we did."

"So our casinos can go bankrupt?" Deuce asked. Then he wished he'd just shut up, because she looked incredibly angry.

"My brother is up there," she said. "Risking his life to run one of your godforsaken dens of vice. It's killing him, wading through that filth every day. Only his dedication keeps him going."

"Ah. League." His lids were closing.

"League. I've begged him to resign, or at least to let the Lucky Star fail so it can be closed down. But my brother is a man of integrity."

Deuce sighed. He had landed in some kind of weird nightmare. There was no other way to explain this terrible state of affairs.

He said to her, "Have you ever been to the Moon?"

He might as well have asked her if she ate babies. Her face clouded up, and she actually quivered with rage.

"No decent person goes there willingly," she said.

"Wow. You're sure of that."

"I've been sure of a few other things, too," she informed him. "Good people don't want any part of what the Moon has to offer."

"Yeah, well, some people think I'm the Messiah," he retorted.

She guffawed.

Footfalls sounded in the hallway. The nurse looked expectantly in the direction of the door.

Three Earthside Security Force guys stomped into the room and showed her some credentials. She hupped-to. The League, the MLF. They all had this thing about standing at attention like you had a stick rammed up your—

"We're here to transport the prisoner," the tallest of the ESF guys announced.

"Thank goodness. I've had more of him than I can stand," the nurse muttered.

What'd I do? Deuce thought, wounded.

"You'll see him at Lincoln," the tall guy said.

She made a face. "I'm still fighting my transfer."

They cuffed him and made him stand. He was very weak. His guts didn't hurt, but he didn't know if that was because they were better or his pain receptors had been numbed past feeling. At any rate, it wasn't too hard for him to walk between two of the three guys. The third brought up the rear.

"There's a blaster pointed directly at your heart," the man said. "If you so much as sneeze, I'll blast it out of your body."

"That *would* make me sneeze," Deuce said, but his voice shook. It was now not a secret that he was scared.

"Just walk along," the man said.

The other two were silent. Deuce figured #3 for the big shot of the detail.

"Where we going?" He half turned, despite the potential harm to his organs. "Please don't tell me I don't need to know. I just want to know. Would like to know."

"Abraham Lincoln Political Prison," #3 said. "You're well enough to be treated in their infirmary."

"How long have I been in custody?"

"You don't know?" The man sounded surprised. "Three weeks."

Damn. He made peace with that notion as best he could, and said, "What about my companion?"

"Dismantled."

It was a blow he couldn't deny. But more importantly, he wondered if they had the data terminal, and if they knew what it was. If they had accessed it.

"Hey, don't look so glum," the other guy said. "You know what they say. Parts is parts."

Parts is parts. And so the connection to an alien race—or twenty-five races, or a hundred—might have been permanently severed. Except that Michael and Shoshana had communicated with her, too. So there was hope of accessing her, unless the two were liars or traitors.

Deuce was beginning to overtire just as they went outside to a waiting car. The sun made him flinch, and stare. He could hardly keep his eyes open, but he couldn't stop taking in the incredible, terrifying scenery. He decided that if he got to go out much, he was going to have to invest in sunglasses and sunscreen. Already, he could feel the sun scorching his skin and his retinas.

But he couldn't stop looking around. It was such a different world. The amount of open space was daunting. He could see why Moonsiders who visited Earth often pretty much went insane. It was like someone kicking you into free fall and saying, "Don't worry. There are places to grab on to. Somewhere."

Maybe the locals would attribute his swaying to his injuries. He had no idea. But as they made their way to the car, he was so disoriented he thought he would throw up.

Lurching, he reached the opened gull-wing door of the sleek, black Nebula—same make, same styling as in the

Moon—that was nice to know, that they didn't pawn last decade's models on the innocent hicks up in the night sky—and tried to effect a graceful climb-in, although by then he was covered with icy sweat and barely able to think straight.

O Mamma mia, talk about your wide-open spaces. How did these people keep from going completely insane? Maybe that accounted for the League of Decency. But not for the MLF.

They helped him in, maybe figuring his cuffs were to blame for his awkwardness. One sat on his right, one on his left, and #3 up front with the driver, who, if he wasn't a mechanical, had been pithed.

But then he sort of activated, adding fuel to Deuce's suspicion that he was a robot, and started requesting clearances and name-dropping with the codes and all like that. The sheer amount of gobbledygook impressed Deuce; you wanted to translate this stuff, you'd have to have a codebook the size of the Family Bylaws for running Moonbase Vegas.

All of which, he supposed, had been thrown in the garbage since the Earthsiders had horned in.

Clearance was eventually achieved, and the aichy went straight up. Deuce tried not to look too eager to get his first decent view of Earthside. Still, his gaze was glued to the windows as they continued their ascent.

They were inside a dome, as he would have expected—and hoped—but it was enormous compared to Moon standards. Miles and miles across. Beneath it, buildings rose hundreds, if not thousands, of feet. He saw a few trees and bushes, which to him was the same as a million trees and bushes, in luxurious abundance; a couple of pools or ponds. Maybe those were the lakes he had heard so much about, or seas. The seas of the Moon were dry plains—Fertility, Tranquillity, Storms, and all the others—but these seas contained actual water.

It boggled his mind.

Then he saw something so shockingly amazing that he almost shouted for joy: birds. About five of them, flying in a little bird group-formation. Deuce had never seen birds. Not even one, much less a group of them. You couldn't have them in the Moon. There wasn't enough gravity for them to eat their feed; they would starve to death.

But in the filtered, heavy-gravity sky, these birds flapped their blessed little wings and flew. The tears welled in Deuce's eyes and he had to wipe them with his cuffed hands. He was so moved he couldn't hide it.

"Mr. McNamara, are you in pain?" one of the ESF goons queried.

He shook his head. "Allergies. In the Moon, we don't have hay fever and like that."

"Of course not." The man was trying to sound courteous, but he was patronizing. Deuce didn't care.

There were birds.

And clouds.

The car swooped up toward and into clouds. They were wispy, like whipped cream or cotton candy, both of which Deuce had not only seen but frequently consumed. He was practically beside himself, and he thought about all the times he and the others had laughed at the tourists for gawking at what to Moonsiders was so very commonplace: GIRLS! GIRLS! GIRLS! doing various exotic things in zero gravity; hundreds of guys made over to look like Elvis for the look-alike contest at the Lucky Star; the tunnels and warrens that made up everyday life.

The lack of sun, the lack of atmosphere, lack, lack, lack, which was, to Deuce's way of thinking, the only civilized way to live. These Earthsiders, with their excesses, were just plain nuts. You had to have a death wish to live here. Or else be really, really certain God wanted to admit you to heaven.

Decency Leaguers were certain God was just itching to claim them as His very own major players; Deuce wondered about the rank and file. Shills for the Lord?

"First time Earthside, Mr. McNamara?" his left-side goon companion asked.

"Whatever." Deuce shrugged. Both animals chortled. It was so different here; in the Moon, you did not chortle in front of a Godfather, even a captive, unless he chortled first and gave you permission.

But there were tall buildings, and tiny flecks of grass, which he assumed was grass or something like it. And somewhere down there, more people than lived on twelve Moonbase Vegases, if he had retained anything from his Earth Studies classes.

I want this kind of action, he thought, *I want life to be big like this.*

Then, *What am I thinking? Aliens from outer space is a lot huger than this. It just gets a little abstract now and then.*

Oh, Iniya . . .

"What am I charged with, anyway?" he asked. "I drifted off during that part. No, let me guess. Conspiracy." It was the lawman's charge of choice. It covered a lot of ground and it didn't really mean anything. You could hold people for conspiracy a lot easier than, say, shoplifting or vandalism.

"That's one of the charges." *One of the lesser ones,* sounded like the guy wanted to add.

Fabulous.

"I need a lawyer."

"One will be assigned to you."

"No, thanks. I got my own attorneys. Earthside and Moonside Bar and all like that."

"One will be assigned to you," Leftie repeated.

Deuce knew then that all she needed to write was the date of execution. Perhaps before he had been living in the land of denial; it seemed pretty obvious now. Just about everyone else had basically promised him he wasn't going home again.

Well, okay, short life, but it had been an exciting one. You played high stakes, you had to be willing to lose it all. He'd been willing.

Time to fold.

"Okay," he said.

He kept staring down at the Earthscape. First view, last view.

Oh, well.

Yuet Chan sat with Connie in Connie's quarters. Yuet had brewed jasmine tea and the two women sat contemplatively, sipping in silence. Not far from where they sat, Sparkle lay close to death.

Everyone was worried about Deuce, Gabriel most of all. Her agony was painful to watch, and Yuet felt even more protective of Sparkle. Her dear friend had not acquitted herself very well in the wife department. Gabriel was much more his type. Even she, loyal as she was to Sparkle, could see that.

The Schulmans assured Gabriel that they were looking for an opportunity to break Deuce out, but thus far, none had presented itself.

Or so the Schulmans claimed. Gabriel was investigating. Yuet also had her own people looking into the situation privately. The leader of the MLF was in the Abraham Lincoln Political Prison. As a rule, political persons who were sent there died there.

There were more political prisoners Earthside than criminals.

Of Iniya's remote interface, there was no word except that she had been captured along with Deuce. What Deuce had not known was that, with Bernardo Chang's help, the Eight had duplicated a facsimile of the remote data terminal, but it had never operated one hundred percent. They had been waiting for the prize: the terminal Deuce had in his possession. Then Iniya had insisted upon working with Deuce, and that had probably saved his life.

Yuet said now to Connie, "Let's go look at the prisoner."

"Why?" Connie asked, her voice sharp and hostile.

"I want to see if she has anything more on the situation with the jumpgate," Yuet said. "She's getting weaker; her mind's fuzzy. She might tell us things she meant to keep to herself. Maybe she'll make a deathbed confession."

Connie look pleased at the prospect.

Yuet let Connie lead the way. The two sauntered along like Family wives at a get-together, although it took everything in Yuet not to run to the infirmary. However, she had been a Godmother—twice—and would be again—and one did not rise to the top by giving in to impulse.

So she acted just as nonchalant as Connie, as uncaring and callous, though her heart was pounding.

They were almost to the door when a soldier came out, white-faced, looking startled to see them.

"Ma'am," he said to Connie, saluting her, "I was just coming to find you."

"Why?"

"The prisoner ... Mrs. McNamara ... she's talking all strange."

Connie's eyes gleamed. Her expression spoke volumes: She was hoping that Sparkle was dying.

Yuet took a silent deep breath and prayed to her ancestors like a good Buddhist.

The soldier fell into line beside them and began to walk

them back. Connie said, "That will be all, soldier."

He looked disappointed, but he gave her a quick salute, and said, "Yes, ma'am." He peeled off and left them to go on without him.

Yuet took her time, once more allowing Connie to go in first. Once more she held her breath and kept herself outwardly calm, as there was at first silence, and then, soft whispering.

After a few seconds, Connie said, "Yuet, you'd better come in."

Sparkle was lying inert, but her eyes were wide-open. She was staring straight at Connie with an intense gaze. Her lips were moving, but she was speaking so softly that Yuet had to move closer.

"Iniya. I am Iniya," she said. Her inflection was strange and stilted. "Sparkle de Lune has an approachable mind. I am Iniya. Sparkle is dying. Don't let her die. She's the only link. Deuce's link is destroyed. The Eight's link is destroyed. Sparkle is my only link."

Yuet stared. The hair rose on the back of her neck.

"Where is Sparkle?" she asked. Connie glanced at Yuet as if that question had not occurred to her.

There was a pause.

"I don't know," Iniya said.

Yuet sucked in her breath.

"This is my first link with an approachable mind," Iniya continued.

"You speak our language very well," Connie said warmly. "Is Sparkle de Lune deceased?"

There was another pause.

"I don't know," Iniya said frankly. "You must get me to Deuce McNamara. I have vital information."

Connie frowned at her. "Is this a trick, Sparkle?"

Iniya gasped. She said, "This body is dying. We should establish a linkup from another source. However, to do so will require time I might not have. Using Sparkle as my remote data terminal is also risky."

"What if her body gets better?" Yuet cut in.

"It would be the preferable means of communication," Iniya said. She sighed heavily. "This is very difficult for me. I'm going to cut off contact. I'll return in one full lunar day."

"We'll get to work healing her body," Yuet promised. "Hopefully, we can keep this link alive."

"Please explore ways to get me Earthside," Iniya added. "It is vital I assist Deuce."

"He's been captured."

"Understood. We must free him. As soon as possible."

"Understood," Connie said, overriding Yuet as she began to answer. "We'll look forward to speaking with you tomorrow."

Sparkle's eyes closed. Her body slumped. She looked pale as death. Yuet wasn't certain that her chest was moving.

"Well." Connie looked at her. "I guess that settles that." She tapped her comm badge. "I need some medical staff to the infirmary on the double."

She disconnected. "Do you think it's a trick?"

"I don't think so," Yuet told her. She would have told Connie that no matter what she really thought. It was useful that it happened to be the truth.

From the Captain's Log of Gambler's Star:

The babies and Stella are well, thank God, but they are not thriving. When I hold them, they simply stare at me. Perhaps they understand that I'm sick with worry for their mother.

Chang and Shiflett are also missing, and I presume they're dead. The !kth have questioned me several times as to the whereabouts of my "mate," and I have told them I know nothing. Which is true.

I think they have scanned my mind at night, and found that I'm not lying. If so, they probably also know I have stopped trusting them.

I was approached yesterday by a mechanical who informed me via old Earthside sign language that he is an operative for the D'inn. Apparently, Iniya's father has been working for the !kth. I was dumbfounded. I never saw that coming. What inducement could they possibly have given the Leader of Ships? He's one of the most exalted D'inn on their world. Yet he has turned traitor. Incredible.

Perhaps he, like me, was misguided in his assessment of the benefits the !kth could bestow. In my case, for my species, and in his . . . I'm not certain. If so, he and I are guilty of terrible judgment. In other wars, men have been killed for less.

I wonder if Iniya's father is dead yet.
I know he will be soon.
It seems likely that I will share a similar fate.

Hunter Castle
Aboard Ship, 2145.2

SEVENTEEN

Standing in the darkness, Connie heard them leaving. Footfalls whispered over the ground.

Two shadows flitted toward the guard tower, where Downtown Dallas carefully looked the other way.

Connie had agreed to accept whatever consequences there were if the escape got traced back to her. So had Dallas. Connie didn't think it would; they had been very cautious. Still, if it came to that, she'd take her lumps.

People were talking about the strange things General McNamara's liaised wife had been saying while unconscious. They said it was further proof that Deuce was the Messiah. They were beginning to talk about starting a holy war.

After a few more moments, Connie decided Yuet and Sparkle were safe. It would be best to try to get some sleep.

But sleep did not come.

Her heavy dark cloak wrapped around her, Yuet said to Sparkle—or to Iniya, she was not certain how to go about this—"Night is best for secrets. It's always been best." She gestured to the window in the center of the top floor of the Lucky Star, where a single, dim light was illuminated. "He's waiting."

Beneath her hood, Iniya looked up at the window. The bruises had been polished off Sparkle's face, and she was pain-free. But it was awkward using a living body as her vehicle. She far preferred a machine.

The noise and light were overwhelming. The streets were overrun with laughing human beings, human music, and an incredible amount of noise. Yuet kissed her softly. Iniya was startled. It was a pleasant sensation, not altogether unwanted, but not like the melting of her kind. When humans pleasured one another, they remained solid throughout. It was very strange, and she wasn't certain she would ever get used to it.

Wrapping her own cloak around herself—it whirled in slow motion in the light gravity of the Moon—she moved with Yuet as the two melted into the shadows.

Overhead, ships spied on the populace. None of the humans tourists appeared to take the slightest notice.

"They don't mind the constant observation?" she asked Yuet.

Yuet shrugged. "Polls indicate they're reassured by an increase in law and order. And I quote."

"Was it so lawless?"

"We didn't think so."

She gestured to the small side door in the Caputo casino, cleverly concealed to look like part of the wall.

"Our contact is waiting."

Iniya nodded. The body of Sparkle was tired and not completely healed, which made it more difficult to maneuver. As with her human counterpart, she was extremely curious about where Sparkle's psyche had gone. She didn't know if it would come back.

"Do you mind the constant observation?" Iniya asked Yuet.

"Absolutely. But of course, most of what we go through is invisible to the Earthsider tourists. The extra layers of surveillance; the amazing amount of paperwork—not to mention the loyalty oath."

She frowned. "Not to mention the large numbers of lost jobs, ruined businessmen, and the entire crumbling Family structure. Or the ruined economy, and the need, for the first time in our history, for welfare."

Iniya took that in. "Soon they will tire of it. Or their people will demand that they leave. Unless they achieve a return in some other way."

"I like the way you think," Yuet said. She grinned. "It's the way I think."

The two stood in front of the door. Iniya pressed a small button on her wrist; it was a signal to their operative inside. The door hissed open.

Yuet went in first. Then she gestured for Iniya to follow her.

In silence, Yuet handed over two of the hard, round grenades Iniya had manufactured for them before she'd run out of materials. They were already on their way to becoming a form of legal tender among the Families.

They went through a dark tunnel and then into what appeared to be the human version of a float. Iniya closed her eyes against a thrill of fear as the doors hissed shut and the machine soared upward.

They stopped. The doors hissed open.

The man was standing waiting for them just outside the float.

He smiled at them.

"Ladies."

Iniya felt Yuet tense. She fought down the impulse to use hand gestures to indicate her own unease, but these people did not use sign language very often. It had been exhausting to employ her facial features for that purpose. Not a single creature on this Moon wore a mask.

"Mr. Dwyer," Yuet replied. She gestured to Iniya. "May I present my associate."

"Mrs. McNamara, I'm charmed." He took Iniya's hand and lifted it to his lips. Iniya wasn't certain what it signified, so she kept her face calm and pleasant. That appeared to be the appropriate response.

The man said, "Did you bring the agreed-upon payment?"

Yuet hesitated. Then she reached into the folds of her cloak and pulled out a clear sack. It was filled with cylinders of various colors.

The man took the sack and examined it. He narrowed his eyes at Yuet. "This better be real."

She shrugged. "Test it."

"I intend to."

He gestured for them to follow him into a room. Iniya could feel the tension in his mind. Waves of mistrust radiated from him like heat.

"Would you care for a drink?" the man asked Yuet.

She smirked. "Alcohol?"

He exhaled. "Suit yourself."

Iniya looked questioningly at Yuet, who held her hand out

flat. Iniya gave her head a slight shake, to show that she didn't understand, but Yuet simply repeated the gesture.

The man opened the sack, took out one of the cylinders, and poured a small amount of a green-colored powder into another cylinder, this one half-filled with a clear liquid. Immediately, the liquid turned a salmon color.

The man's brows shot up.

"I told you it was pure." Yuet waved her hand at the sack. "You have enough Chan base there to start your own drug empire."

The man's tension mounted. Iniya finally understood. He was terribly conflicted about what he was doing. She only hoped her own father was suffering such turmoil. One could only assume he was with the !kth now, spilling every secret the D'inn had.

The man said, "All right. I'll take you to the freighter."

They were going Earthside.

Iniya rubbed her wrist, D'inn sign language expressing urgency and anxiety.

Nicky sat with Shoshana and Michael Schulman at dinner. Shoshana, with her wild, curly black hair and her cute little bod couldn't keep her huge brown eyes off him, and Nicky figured it was only a matter of time before Michael realized that his little sister had just rolled out of Nicky's bed. He wasn't sure what the customs were around there, but he was fairly certain big brothers were the same everywhere in the universe.

Now, as Nicky took another bite of the most bland and unappetizing food he had ever eaten, he nearly choked when Shoshana said, "I've been thinking about becoming a Connie Lockheart." She smiled adoringly at Nicky.

"What's that?" Michael asked.

"You have babies for rich and powerful men," she said, never taking her eyes from Nick's face.

"*What?*" Michael thundered.

Nicky carefully set down his fork. "It's an old program, and very few people do it anymore.

Shoshana said in a pouty-girl voice, "Deuce did it."

"No," Nicky told Michael quickly. "Hunter Castle did it. He

had three children that way, the twins and an older girl named Stella."

"To preserve his line," Shoshana cooed.

"Thank God we don't have to do that in Families," Nicky blurted, before he remembered that he wasn't in a Family anymore. "Let me put that another way. There are so many Borgiolis in the Moon that we sure don't have to worry about things such as that."

"That's not what I heard," Shoshana said, tossing her wavy, gorgeous hair this way and that.

"From whom?" Michael stared at her.

She squirmed. "Well, some of the girls in the Eight. They're doing it so their Family names won't die out."

"That's a whole different thing," Nicky said. He pushed his chair out. "This was delicious."

Shoshana frowned. "You haven't eaten a thing."

"I'm too worried about Deuce."

"Speaking of whom," Michael interrupted. "I have news. We've gotten in."

Infiltrated, Nicky translated. His heart soared.

"You made us sit all the way through dinner before you told us that?" Shoshana asked indignantly. "Nicky half-starving and you kept that to yourself?"

Michael looked at his sister. "This may be the last meal we share together."

"You say that all the time," Shoshana accused. "You're such a doom-and-gloom guy."

"When are we breaking him out?" Nicky asked.

"Tonight." Michael looked grim. "It's a bit of a long shot. But we need that terminal. Ours just doesn't cut it."

Nicky didn't take offense. If Michael had wanted to break Deuce out just to be nice, Nicky would have suspected a trap.

"Oh." Shoshana put her hands around Nicky's forearm.

The gesture was not lost on her brother. Michael cleared his throat, but she acted like she didn't hear it.

"Shoshana," he gritted, "don't you have a gun to clean?"

"It hasn't been fired recently," she purred.

Nicky almost rolled his eyes, but he maintained a stone face. But the Italian male in him kept wondering, *Wow, was I really that good?*

"Shoshana," Michael said sternly.

A look passed between brother and sister. She sighed, released Nicky's forearm, and pushed away from the table. With a huff, she left the room.

The Schulmans lived alone, which was unusual in their underground movement. Usually, at least half a dozen people lived together in a nondescript house or apartment building in a nondescript neighborhood. The goal was to be as unnoticeable as possible.

The various Families of the Eight owned vast parcels of land throughout the area, which Nicky had learned was the former state of Southern California. Southern California had been absorbed into Conglomerated Western America. All the Families went by fake names; they had a "public" name and a "true" name. The Schulmans made their way in the world as the Cohens.

Nicky had yet to meet the others. He'd been kept isolated from them, which he understood but did not particularly like. If they couldn't free Deuce, Nicky would probably be sent back to the Moon alone. Most Moonsiders who had wanted to live on Earth found that sooner or later, the gravity got to them. So the fewer names and faces he could put together, the better.

Nicky wouldn't mind going back to the Moon. The Earth was grim. People dressed in drab colors, and they kept their heads down, hoping not to be noticed. There weren't a lot of smiles, and everyone was afraid to do anything.

There was almost no action. Few restaurants, no clubs, and "community gathering halls," where people watched the viso scan, drank juice and tea, and attended incredibly boring lectures about things like container gardening, morals, and values.

Everybody was frugal, poor, and earnest. They worked hard but they didn't play hard. The buildings they lived and worked in were featureless blocks of gray stonework surrounding courtyards where mandatory exercise sessions were held once a day.

All in all, Earthside was not what he wanted in a place to live. No wonder they loved coming to the Moon.

Michael pulled out a cigarette, lit it, and inhaled with true appreciation. He had jimmied his pollution calibrator, such that it never charged him pollution levies for cigarettes or small kitchen fires.

"The situation is not the best," Michael said, offering a metal box of cigarettes to Nicky, who declined. "We have a woman on the inside. Her brother runs the Lucky Star, and he's as dirty as they come. He's bringing Yuet and Sparkle down here."

"Sparkle?" Nicky was stunned. "She's back?"

Michael nodded.

"So Hunter's back."

Michael shook his head.

"We think she escaped with the help of Colvin Pines. He works for the MLF."

Nicky was dumbfounded. "How does Yuet fit into this?"

"She and Sparkle go back a long way," Michael explained. "They're very close. I understand it was Yuet who broke her out of the camp."

Michael took that in. "And our break-in is tonight because . . . ?"

Michael looked surprised. "That's the soonest they could get here. We need Yuet. She's on extremely good terms with the prison guards, on account of her having been there. Our guys on the inside were bribed, pure and simple, but we can't discount Yuet's charms." He smiled wistfully.

He's in love with her, Nicky thought. That was good. If Michael was in love, he might not kill Nicky on account of Shoshana falling in love with him. That part was not his fault.

As for the other part . . . well, that had been just plain stupid. But hey, he was a young Italian. What did people expect?

Better, he told himself.

From the Captain's Log of Gambler's Star:

I have been told that Iniya's father, Foriniyar, is aboard, but I haven't seen him. I have only seen a D'inn once, on a screen. It was after I had aligned myself with the !kth. The D'inn was dead, fading before my eyes, like a weak holo-projection. It was eerie.

They are beautiful, the D'inn, rather insubstantial and vaporous. I don't understand their physiology, nor how they can exist in the same space as the !kth, who seem much more fully "present." Solid, and substantial. It's as if they contain more mass, to make up for the wraithlike D'inn.

They've been at war forever; no one can explain the intense animosity between them, only that they hate each other. Perhaps that's the best definition of war: extreme mutual hatred.

However, almost coincident with the arrival of Foriniyar, Colvin Pines revealed himself to me as an operative of the MLF. At first I was livid, feeling that he had betrayed my trust at the most basic level, but we have become allies in our quest to end my association with the !kth.

Work on the jumpgate continues very slowly. I am doing everything I can to ensure that those in my employ get very little done each day. We are implementing some state-of-the-art cloning processes at the cellular level to enable the jumpgate to act almost like one of the transporter machines in the old science-fiction gas movies. Back in our space, I'd be applying for at least a dozen patents. We are currently selecting for the presence of !kth DNA, thus preventing D'inn from using the gate.

Sparkle was convinced they wanted to harm the children. All I can imagine is that they want to use them as test subjects to see if hybrids can use the gate as well. It seems a foolish waste of hybridized beings. They know I'm part !kth, but also that I'm sterile. Deuce is another story.

Which makes me wonder if Sparkle struck some kind of deal with them—if she brought back Deuce, would they let her own children go free? His cells can be used to create more !kth children.

I wouldn't put it past her.

It's what I would do if my child was in danger.

God help you, Deuce.

Hunter Castle
Aboard Ship, 2145.3

"McNamara," the voice said, "wake up."

Deuce was dreaming about the nun who had taught his Fraud and Graft class back in high school (each Family educated their own children, and the N.A.'s went to public school). So he was momentarily confused about whether the person speaking to him was Sister Lucia or the night guard at

Abe Lincoln. Funny how your realities all started blurring together.

"Damn it, wake up."

"Such language, Sister," Deuce murmured. Then his eyes fluttered open, and he realized it was the night guard after all, flashing a light on his face.

He moved out of the light and looked past the guard. Standing behind the man were Yuet Chan and Nicky B.

"We're breaking you out," Yuet said.

The guard coded the door and it *ka-cachunnged* open. Deuce was on his feet before you could say whatever you wanted to say at a time like this, and it was then that he saw that Nicky had a superpumper pressed against the back of the guard's skull.

After Deuce stepped out of the cell, Nicky urged the guard in. The man said dully, "I'll be fired. My kids will starve. They may execute me."

Deuce said, "Let's take him with." To the guard, "You want to join the underground? We'll send people to get your family. They'll join you at a safe house."

The man brightened. "Thank you. I'd be so grateful."

"It's nothing." Deuce gestured for him to come back out of the cell.

"Godfather," Nicky said, exasperated.

"Hey. Mind your business," Deuce shot back, all Family.

Nicky had the good manners to look abashed. "I'm sorry, Godfather," he said.

"That's better."

The man held out his hand. "My name's Frank Page." He laughed softly. "Not very Italian, is it?"

"Don't matter. I'm Deuce McNamara. How do you explain that?" Deuce asked. "Okay, so is it hard to get out of here?"

Nicky nodded. "We've got a bunch of guards bribed, but there are an awful lot of places for us to mess up."

Deuce took that in. He said, "Weapons?"

Nicky passed him the superpumper and took another one from Yuet. Deuce was about to protest when Yuet picked a third from the floor.

"You armed?" Deuce asked the guard.

The man shook his head. "Your friends disarmed me."

Deuce said to the others, "Give him back his stuff."

There was a moment's hesitation.

But a moment's only, as a voice cried out of the darkness, "Freeze or you're all dead."

The guard murmured, "Don't do it. We're trained to kill from this point on."

Nicky whirled around and shot in the direction of the voice. There was a cry of pain, and then fire was returned.

Deuce jumped in front of his people, screaming, "Move, move!" as he swept an arc. He backed up, running into Nicky, and bellowed, "*Su, sbrigati!*"

"*Sì, Padrino, sì*," Nicky said urgently. "Go, go, go!" he shouted to the others.

The pulses were coming fast and furious. Deuce started calculating the odds that this was the only cadre of guards after them. More than likely, there were others posted in the hallways and at the exits. A clean escape did not look too likely.

Then Nicky shouted in his ear, "We got people stationed all over the place, Godfather. I don't know how those guys got past our guys. But we've got help along the way."

"Okay. Good."

It was true. As they backed down the corridors, more of the Eight's people popped out of their hiding places and joined in the battle. Dead guards were strewn everywhere, and the floors were slick with blood. Prisoners were shouting and cheering, begging to be sprung. Alarms blared; sirens screamed. A voice kept saying, "Freeze at once. You may still survive this. Freeze at once."

At one point, Yuet slipped and fell, and their new comrade, the guard, risked his life to help her to her feet. Deuce swore he would never forget that. He was going to make the rest of that guy's life nice and easy.

If he lived through this.

They kept blasting, moving swiftly toward the side exit, which was sure to be heavily fortified, mined, and booby-trapped. Deuce sure hoped they'd figured out all the codes and sequences, and that no surprises had been added since the last time Michael Schulman had had this place checked out.

Speaking of whom, there he was at the juncture between two wings of the prison. Big-cheese Michael himself was faced down one way, and with her back to him, shooting in the opposite direction was . . . Sparkle?

Deuce stumbled. But the stabilizer inside him somehow helped him keep his balance, sort of like a gyro.

It was Sparkle. She was shooting like a madwoman, and hitting guys, too. A steady stream were running toward her like at a shooting gallery, which they had in the Moon, and she was picking them off with ease.

Deuce had a moment, watching her, and then he darted up to the two of them, clasped their shoulders, and said, "Let me through."

He took up residence on Sparkle's left, and none too soon, as guards raced around the corner at the opposite end and flew toward him, their massive firepower seeking him out.

He ducked more times than he stood up straight; and just as he figured he was going to get too tired and die, yet more Eight guys appeared behind Deuce's corridor of opponents and started picking them off.

Deuce hit Sparkle's and Michael's shoulders, yelling, "Go, go!"

They wove down a course of hallways which had to be a maze, and which Michael appeared to have memorized. Anyone who got in their way, died—often because someone had sneaked up behind them to take them out.

It was a beautifully planned operation, and it gave Deuce a lot of heart. The Eight were definitely professionals. It was great to know he was working with a Class A group.

He kept his eye on the guard, because if this were a gas movie, the guy would get killed just before they made their final getaway. He'd be the expendable one. Deuce believed in fate, and he believed those clichés in movies got to be clichés for a reason.

The old guy made it out.

Yuet didn't.

The pulse that got her threw her high into the air just as Michael and Sparkle blew the back door with a hyperexplosive. For a moment, Deuce thought she'd been caught in the force of the explosion.

It was only after he joined Sparkle at her side that he saw the enormous hole in Yuet's chest, and the smoke that was pouring from the gaping wound.

Yuet raised her hand to Sparkle's face, and said, "Tell her good-bye for me. Tell her I loved her."

"I will," Sparkle said.

Yuet turned to Deuce. "You can trust them," she said.

It was hard to say exactly when Yuet stopped living, and when she died. In the dim glow of the guard's flashlight, her face was white and her eyes were glassy, but her chest moved—incredibly—for some long seconds before she lay completely still. Eerily, her mouth opened, closed, then opened again, despite the fact that the rest of her looked totally, completely dead.

"Go with God," Deuce murmured. He made the sign of the cross over her.

Beside him, Sparkle also gestured, although Deuce couldn't decipher what she was doing.

Then they raced out of the prison, where a firefight was in progress. It was complete chaos. Deuce was astonished to see how many troops the Eight possessed, and what seasoned fighters they were. Plus they died with a lot of zest.

Not to sound callous.

His little band rallied around Michael, who shouted out orders like a Dallas Cowboys cheerleader, and Deuce had a momentary realization that he could watch a real, live football game before he went home.

Then he was running toward an armored vehicle, his arm around Sparkle, hoisting her in to some big, muscly guy who took one look at him, and said, "Who the hell are you?"

"I'm Deuce McNamara," he said.

Sparkle looked startled. Then Deuce realized she didn't know about the makeover. He was pleased that she'd been fooled.

And he couldn't help his relief at seeing that she was alive.

"How did you get here? Are the kids safe? Is my fath—is Hunter with you?"

The vehicle slammed into high gear and soared away from the battle, guns blazing. It rocked and shuddered as it was pummeled, but it took that licking and kept on ticking.

Sparkle said, "Deuce, I am Iniya."

"Say what?" He stared at her.

"I am inhabiting Sparkle's body," she said. "I don't know where she is. How this is possible."

"You don't know where she is?" he asked hoarsely.

She shook her head. "She was severely injured. My interface with you was destroyed, and the device which the Eight built eventually stopped working. Somehow, I was able to enter her mind."

"Oh, my God." He closed his eyes and pinched the bridge of his nose. "What about the *bambini*? The little kids?"

"I believe they're still in !kth space, with their grandfather."

"No, Hunter's their father," he said.

She looked at him. "Deuce, you are their father."

He couldn't say a word. He simply stared at her.

"You're their father," she repeated.

His heart nearly burst out of his chest. "Mine?"

"Hunter Castle tricked you. They are yours, not his. He's their grandfather."

"*And she left them there?*" he shouted. "She abandoned her own—my—children?"

"I'm not certain of that, but if they are still alive, they're in !kth hands."

"Oh, my God," He covered his face with his hands. He was completely overwhelmed. "*O, Dio.*"

"We'll finish the ship," Michael Schulman said. Deuce had forgotten where he was and who he was with. "We'll finish it as fast as we can, and we'll get your children back."

Deuce nodded grimly.

"Or die trying," he said flatly.

EIGHTEEN

The knowledge that he was the father of three children kept Deuce going. But he was stretched very close to the edge of his ability to cope.

There was much to do. The ship was almost a reality, and he was intrigued by how much like his father's vessel it looked, albeit on a smaller scale. A much, much smaller one, in fact: If it could hold three dozen people, he'd be surprised. That wasn't the stuff of which armies were made, if they needed armies to fight the !kth. Maybe they could hurl a few super D'inn grenades and like that. Do to the !kth what Iniya had done to that one Earthside ship when the war broke out.

But this new vessel was amazing, very revolutionary even, in its exterior design. It was black matte and shaped like a single bird's wing. There was a dish at the rear, almost like the turned-up feathers of a bird. It reminded Deuce of a little blackbird preparing to leave the nest.

He christened it *Gambler's Son*.

At the moment, Deuce and his pals were living in the Borrego Desert at the heavily camouflaged construction site. The desert was astonishing to him. He was invigorated by the heat and even the dryness. If he ever lived Earthside, he would live in a desert.

Beneath the shade of the flap of Deuce's tent, Iniya was sitting across from him in his wife's body. She was wearing shorts and her feet were curled underneath her. She took a drink of beer, covered her mouth, and burped delicately. It was actually very charming.

Then she said, "I have something to tell you."

He closed his eyes. "Let me guess. Sparkle's pregnant with Elvis's children."

She shook her head. "I find that I am unable to return my consciousness from this body into my own."

He stared at her.

"I am, in essence, trapped inside her physical form. And," she added, "I still don't know where the consciousness of your wife is."

After a long time, Deuce said. "*O, Dio.*" He tried to think straight, but he couldn't. "Did the !kth do this somehow?"

Iniya shook her head. "I don't know. I don't know how it happened. We had a bonding; we saw each other, and we communicated. Perhaps we exchanged something at that point."

He took that in. The strange thing was, he didn't know how he felt about it. Sparkle might be gone. Dead.

He would mourn, and grieve, but she had been undeniably cruel to him throughout their marriage. She had treated him shabbily and lied to him. The average marriage in the Moon lasted less than 3.2 years, and he'd always wondered how long theirs would last.

Nevertheless, she was a person. A human being. And the mother of his children, in a very cockeyed, roundabout way. He had history with her. And this alien woman was claiming that she had, in essence, taken possession of her body.

Then he thought about her. Iniya. Probably she hadn't signed up for any of this.

He leaned forward and said, "You okay?"

She sighed. "No."

What a bum rap. First she got stuck in the body of a former showgirl/kickboxing champ; and now she was helping humans launch themselves in her space without any guarantees that it would do her any good.

"I'm sorry."

He touched her arm. To his surprise, her muscles jumped, and she softly caught her breath. She kept her gaze focused on her beer, and then her hands started making interesting gestures, almost like hula dancing. She had explained their bit on D'inn, with the masks and the hand gestures. He'd been afraid to ask why the masks; were they hideously ugly?

But she was still wearing a mask; she was wearing Sparkle's face. Perhaps that helped her feel safe.

"Iniya," he murmured.

She took his hand and held it. Squeezed it. Then she burst into tears.

He pulled her against his chest and held her. She sobbed. Sparkle had shed maybe a total of three individual tears their entire time together, so it was very strange to see her face twisted in such agony.

He rocked Iniya. He murmured to her in Italian and stroked her hair.

After a time, he kissed her.

She kissed him back.

He touched her cheek, her neck, a handwidth of flesh below her collarbone. Her heart was thundering.

"*Mi scusi*," he said, starting to pull away.

"No." She urged his hand lower. "Please."

"If you're sure," he said, almost automatically.

Her whispery laugh was hollow. "Of course I'm not sure."

He picked her up in his arms and carried her to his tent.

In the darkness, the stillness, Shoshana and Nicky lay on their backs and stared up at the stars. Nicky listened to her gentle breathing and thought, *What an amazing time to be alive.*

He wondered if she would consider marrying him.

He was about to turn and ask her when she blurted out, "Nicky, I'm pregnant."

He laughed, and she looked like she was about to die.

"No, no," he said, cupping her face. "I'm laughing because I was just about to ask you if you want to get married."

For an answer, Shoshana launched herself into his arms and covered his face with kisses.

"Easy, *cara mamma*," he admonished. "I don't want to hurt the baby."

Her laughter was filled with joy.

From the Captain's Log of Gambler's Star:

I can't leave. I have tried a hundred different ways to simply get the hell out of here, and it's clear the !kth have got me

*cornered. "Engine failure," then this, then that. The capper
came when one of the twins became quite ill.*

*We're prisoners. They've absorbed just about every bit of
advanced technology I possess that they didn't, and everything
they could get their talons on regarding the Earth and the
Moon.*

*I feel like I've handed them my species on a plate. Did I
once claim I was not a Judas?*

*My D'inn operative and I are working on a sting operation.
We have managed to corrupt Foriniyar's contact with the
homeworld, and he has unknowingly passed technology to the
!kth that will allow humans as well as !kth to pass through
the jumpgate. Naturally, we haven't been able to test if it
works, and we don't know if the !kth are on to us.*

*But this would make it possible for us to attack them in
their own space, if we ever have the opportunity.*

*My operative tells me the !kth are nearly finished with the
jumpgate. Also, that I am considered too valuable to kill. However, my grandchildren are scheduled to be used for experi-
mentation with the gate.*

Dear God, where's my son?

Hunter Castle
Aboard Ship, 2145.7

The Eight had a lot of pull.

Somehow, Michael Schulman managed to arrange a meeting with no less important a person than the President of the
Conglomerated Nations, who, Deuce was sure, would not believe a single word about aliens and spaceships and like that.
The only thing he figured he could count on was that the man
had promised he would not ambush Deuce. The esteemed
Godfather of the Moon had official safe passage, blah-blah-
blah and la-di-da.

So now they were sitting on an island somewhere, he and
President Smith, having both been flown in by their respective
sides, and Deuce was thinking that maybe if he ever moved
Earthside, he would live on this very island. It was warm and
covered with flowers, and the sea, which was actual water,
came up all the way around it.

Deuce had not known so much what "nebbish" meant,

which was how Michael described President Smith.

Then Deuce met him. Short guy, soft-spoken, a bottomless crater of nervous tics. He laughed nervously at the end of most of his sentences. After about five minutes with him, Deuce wanted to belt him, if only to stop that grating laugh.

Deuce had charts and graphs and all like that to explain things, plus Iniya in tow if he needed her. But President Smith surprised him. He halted him midstream, and said, "We know all this."

Deuce blinked. *"Mi scusi?"*

"Mr. McNamara, do you really think the Eight could build a spaceship in the desert, and we wouldn't notice?"

"Oh." He frowned. "Then why did you try to stop my prison escape?"

President Smith laughed his nervous laugh. "We can't look inept, Mr. McNamara." He laughed again. Always with the laugh. "In addition, Mr. Castle left a number of quicktimes and suchlike, which have begun activating. They provide ample proof of the existence of extraterrestrial life. Hostile extraterrestrial life, might I add." Laugh.

"He did that?"

President Smith nodded. "Apparently, he never expected to be gone this long. The quicktimes were a contingency measure, in case of his death or inability to speak directly to us."

"Hunter was in on this with you?"

"No." Laugh. "He truly believed in what he was doing. But we've loaded his organization with our own people, of course. And we've accepted for quite some time that we cannot simply permit aliens free access to our space, no matter their ultimate intentions."

Deuce processed that. They knew about the D'inn, too.

"Here's what we propose," the President continued. "We'll help you finish the ship. We'll put your people on it, but our people will be on it, too. In other ships, we'll pretend to chase you toward the jumpgate. Then we'll destroy it."

Deuce shrugged. "They'll just build another one."

The President raised his finger. "We'll negotiate a treaty with the D'inn. There are other species out there, as well. No one likes the !kth, Mr. McNamara. All the others would love to see them fall."

Deuce was amazed. He leaned forward, and said, "This

planet, it's so depressing. Can't you do a little something about that?"

President Smith laughed. "Rome wasn't built in a day, Mr. McNamara."

"But nowadays, it could have been," Deuce replied.

The man laughed again.

Not nervously.

With the minipad in his fist, Angelo paced.

Dear Uncle Angelo,

I am overjoyed to announce my official liaison with Shoshana Schulman, of the Eight. She is carrying my baby. In the spirit of my happiness, I wish to find a road to peace with you, me, and my Uncle Deuce.

With all respect,
Niccolo Borgioli

"*Idiota. Cretino,*" Angelo raged. He threw the minipad across the room.

A Borgioli with one of the Eight? What a shame. What a dishonor. Taking two insignificant N.A. girls hostage paled in comparison.

This was Deuce's doing. This was designed to push him, Angelo, beyond endurance.

Fine. It had worked.

He commed the DOF lackeys.

"I'm calling in a marker," he said.

The D'inn operative, a simple mechanical who was ordinary-looking in the extreme, quietly said to Hunter, "I have found the bodies of Shiflett and Chang. They have been dead for some time."

Hunter nodded. "What about Sparkle?"

"Still nothing. I must confess, I'm baffled. It's as if she simply vanished. She must have had help, and yet, I cannot locate it."

Sighing, Hunter thanked him. He patted his one-suit to reassure himself that his blaster was still there. At his discreet suggestion, the crew had opened up the weapons locker and everyone carried a sidearm.

Perhaps the tension level would decrease if the humans could actually meet a !kth or a D'inn. Not even Hunter himself had ever been in the presence of either of the alien species. Therefore, while being known, they remained unknown, and menacing in their mysteriousness.

He kept wondering what would happen when the !kth made it through the jumpgate. They would necessarily be altered in some way, in order to survive in the different environment. But the fact of Hunter and Deuce—hybridized beings—established that at one time, at least, the !kth could survive in Earth's atmosphere. Or perhaps they had always worn enviro-suits, or built special places to live. What of the women whom they had impregnated?

There were a lot of questions, and the explorer in Hunter couldn't stop asking them, despite the fact that they weren't top priority. Far more important was anything that would help them assert dominance over the !kth. The D'inn, as well. There was absolutely no reason to trust them, either.

Hunter spent a great deal of time with his grandchildren. They lived unaware of the tension surrounding them. Stella, at two and a half, had an amazing vocabulary. She spoke in long, elaborate sentences and loved nothing better than to take things apart to see how they worked.

She was gentle. Her nimbus of white hair would fan over Hunter's knee as she leaned her head on his leg and patted the back of his hand, saying, "It's okay, Dadda Grampa, it's okay."

He felt as though he had awakened from a terrible dream, or a hypnotic spell. How had he ever persuaded himself that clandestinely meeting with the !kth was good for him or anyone else? It boggled his mind. It was completely out of character for him.

And he was paying for it.

Everyone was.

With the secret aid of the Earthside government, *Gambler's Son* was finally completed. President Smith conducted a private christening ceremony, agreeing to the name Deuce had chosen. Then he presented the ship to Michael Schulman and Deuce jointly, as a pledge of support from the Conglomerated Nations.

It was decided that Nicky, Deuce, Iniya, Michael, and Yuki Sakamoto, of the famed Japanese *yakusa* Family, would go aboard. The pregnant Signora Shoshana Schulman di Borgioli would stay home. The other twenty-four chairs would be taken up by Earthside soldiers and navigational support; also a very shapely scientist named J.J. Ptacek-Hoffman and some other egghead types.

The time of departure was set. The "chase" ships were alerted and put on standby.

Meanwhile, back in the Moon, Angelo had received word that there was movement in Deuce McNamara's base camp on Earth. They were preparing to launch *Gambler's Son.*

"So, you're prepared?" he asked the man sitting at attention in Angelo's sit-down room, a glass of ginger ale perched primly on the armrest of his chair.

"Yes, sir, I am."

Angelo smiled. The man's name was Joseph, brother to one Brigham, who had run the MLF for a time. Deuce had killed him. No matter that Brigham had issued orders to whack Deuce.

Deuce had met Joseph, when he and his new bride, Gabriel, had arrived at the the MLF base camp after their wedding. He had commented on his resemblance to Brigham, discovering from Joseph that he was Brigham's twin.

"He looked nervous," Joseph had reported.

But he had never done anything about Joseph. But if Angelo had anything to say about it, Joseph was about to do plenty about Deuce.

The D'inn operative told Hunter Castle, "Deuce McNamara has launched. Your daughter-in-law is with him."

"Oh, thank God," Hunter breathed.

"They are planning to simulate a chase. They will arrive at the jumpgate. We are reasonably sure the !kth will burst through the jumpgate for a surprise attack."

Hunter nodded. "And the combined forces of my ship, my

son's ship, the Earth forces, and the D'inn will bring the !kth down."

"Yes," the operative said excitedly. "And we'll collapse the jumpgate."

At that moment, a holo appeared. It was Cor-!kth. The D'inn operative assumed a neutral expression, and Hunter stepped up to address the projection.

"Cor-!kth," he began.

The alien raised his hand. "We wish to test the jumpgate," he announced. "We wish you to send through your daughter, Stella."

The operative stiffened but made no other movement.

Hunter shook his head.

"Sorry, Cor-!kth. You're not practicing on my babies."

The alien was shocked. "You dare refuse?"

"Yes, I do."

"But I thought it was understood," the alien said silkily, recovering himself. "The progress of mankind would entail certain sacrifices."

"That's probably true," Hunter replied. "I'm sure we'll find other hybridized !kth-humans. But not my babies, and not me."

The alien looked long and hard at Hunter, and this was what Hunter saw:

A monster, pure and simple. The Devil of Christianity, with four horns protruding from a lumpy, misshapen head of brilliant crimson, slits from which red eyes glowed, a snout, and a mouthful of fangs. Vaguely humanoid, with talons instead of hands, and cloven hooves for feet.

What in God's name have I been doing? Hunter thought, panicking. And the answer was: Nothing in God's name.

Iniya caught her breath at liftoff. She wasn't used to Earthside gravity, much less the increased G forces as they shot through the atmosphere. She understood that the body she wore had been treated for this occurrence, but it was still unnerving.

She closed her eyes, and felt Deuce's hand around her own. She gestured the sign for contentment, but there was no response. Perhaps his own eyes were closed as well.

*   *   *

But what was happening with Deuce was that the stabilizer, or whatever was inside him, had stopped working. He was in terrible agony.

Oh, my God, I'm dying, he thought frantically. *I can't die now.*

His body was going. His mind was going. Everything was contracting into a pinprick.

He was dreaming: that he was with Sparkle, in a very different kind of world, in a very different kind of life: horses galloping on the beach, through the waves; horses, and he and Sparkle rode them, with children clinging around their waists. Everyone was laughing.

Moon over Miami played through his head as he dreamed.

He heard someone calling his name over and over: *Deuce? Deuce? Deuce?*

He was sorry, so very sorry.

He was going to have to fold.

It was the pain, you see.

The gut-wrenching pain.

And everything happened so fast:

Gambler's Son bulleted away from Earth, and began the sequence to send it into interstellar, lightspeed travel; while Joseph, brother of Brigham, moved into an intercept course before *Gambler's Son* could do so.

Then a fresh directive came in over the hotline.

As he read it, Joseph nearly fainted.

Deuce was not doing well. His forehead was covered with sweat. Iniya was holding his head, but he saw Sparkle; he dreamed of Sparkle. And he spared a good-bye for Gabriel, who was carrying his baby.

I just didn't think I'd die so damn young, he thought angrily.

The truth was, he was young enough that he'd thought he'd live forever.

Well, there was that old saying about wishes and horses . . . And he and Sparkle were riding their horses, through the waves, and she was gentle, and she smiled. . . .

The battle began.

As the Earthside forces harried *Gambler's Son* toward the

jumpgate, D'inn ships massed in formation and prepared for the anticipated attack of the !kth.

Pulse torpedoes rocked the *Son*. Deuce actually had a good vantage point; he realized he had been taken to sick bay, and as the skeleton medical staff, consisting of one Earthside paramedic and Iniya, pored over him, he grabbed Iniya's arm.

"I'm part !kth," he said to her. "You won't know how to fix me."

She smiled at him. "We know a lot about !kth physiology," she told him. "We invented it."

Angelo watched on the screen as *Gambler's Son* barreled toward the jumpgate.

"Increase speed," he ordered the helm.

"Increase speed, aye."

At the last, he had not been able to resist joining in Joseph's mission to take down Deuce. Deuce, and Deuce only, was his target. Joseph's orders—direct from the Department of Fairness, which, as everyone had suspected, was working with the League of Decency, which in turned owned the MLF—were to ignore everything except for the opportunity to terminate Deuce McNamara.

Knowing that, how could Angelo stay away?

So they watched from afar, as explosions illuminated the jet-vastness of space. The amorphous D'inn ships, crowding around the jumpgate. The *Son*, speeding toward it, trailed by false enemies . . . or were they false friends?

And then, at last, the jumpgate sizzled and thundered with energy, whirled and pulsing and crackling silently, out in space, as the hordes of !kth ships burst through and began shooting at everything that moved. Hostile fire, friendly fire, it made no difference, as long as it was fire.

An errant thought flitted through Iniya's mind: *What am I doing here? I'm not of this. My father . . . he was never found. Did I dream him?*

Sparkle woke slowly, her mind running through an ancient Earth hymn she now remembered her mother singing to her: *I once was blind, but now I see.*

Tears coursed down her face. Her heart broke.
So that it could mend.

Hunter stood over his dying son. Deuce's three children
were at his side.

Hunter gripped his hand and said, "Hold on, boy."

"Don't you see, Daddy?" Deuce managed, between spasms
of pain. "The D'inn, the !kth. Racial memories. Heaven. Hell.
The D'inn are angels. The !kth are devils."

"Deuce, don't talk," Hunter said gently.

"But don't you see?" Deuce groaned. "We've never met a
real D'inn. We've never touched a !kth. They're simulations.
Someone's running a huge con. It's a game. I dreamed it.
They're taking bets on us. In Heaven."

"Sir," said Colvin Pines to Hunter. "We're being hailed by
a ship. Angelo Borgioli is on it. He requests permission to
come aboard."

"Yes," Deuce gasped. "Angelo."

And with Angelo was Joseph, the brother of Brigham, who,
when he saw Deuce, leaned over and said, very gently, "Tell
me, Don General, are you afraid to die?"

The ship was being rocked from the beating it was taking.
Reports indicated that the !kth and D'inn were ignoring the
Star and the *Son* in favor of each other.

"Not exactly," Deuce admitted. "Dying, now. No. What
may come after, that's scarier . . ." He shrugged. "I think it's
time to call a priest."

In a loud voice, Joseph said, "Stop simulation."

The rocking ceased.

There were a few moments of silence, and then someone
said shakily, "Sir? The D'inn and the !kth . . . they just disappeared."

Deuce frowned through his pain. His father was equally
bewildered.

Angelo crossed himself and murmured, "*Grazie*, Maria."

Deuce raised a shaky hand. "Ask about the jumpgate," he
asked his father.

Hunter pressed his comm badge. "What about the jumpgate?"

"Still there, sir."

Hunter looked at Deuce.

"It's a portal," Joseph said, in a proud, awed voice. "To the real world."

"Are you a *pazzo* gravoid *cretino*?" Angelo blustered. "What the hell are you talking about?"

Joseph looked at the men. "Did you know that in the beginnings of the Mormon church, Brigham Young had a revelation in which he saw people dancing on the Moon?"

No one spoke. Who could say anything to that?

"Did you know that our beliefs hold that one day, we will all be gods, and rule planets and galaxies?"

Again, silence.

"And did you know that President Smith of Earth is a Mormon?"

Deuce said, "Please, could you hurry? I'm dying, and it's not of curiosity. But while I'm still breathing, I would love to know what the hell is going on."

Joseph made a wide gesture. "You're ready for bigger and better games, Deuce. All of this . . . it was real, in a way. It was a revelation. For you."

He leaned it toward Deuce. His eyes were glistening with tears. "If you go through that portal, you'll play for the real stakes."

"My soul." Now he was spitting up blood.

"Something even bigger."

"So why does it have to freakin' hurt so much?"

"Most growth does."

And the person who was speaking to him was no longer Joseph, but Iniya, in her true form, gossamer and glowing . . . *O, Dio,* glowing like an angel.

"And now, the players are waiting to see your hand, Godfather," she said gently.

Deuce closed his eyes.

"I'm too damn tired," he replied.

He died.

He was certain of it.

And Angelo said softly, "Does this mean that Ronnie's still alive? And . . ." he crossed himself. "My sister?"

EPILOGUE

From the Captain's Log of Gambler's Star:

This is not at all what we expected. None of us. All of this, a simulation to get us to build this portal, and bring my son to it? People dead, and races that never existed, or sort of existed, for am I not proof of that? . . . But no Iniya, no Foriniyar . . . and we are to be left behind, while Deuce moves on?

And yet, as I look out the window of my ship, and see my son's tiny shuttle headed for the jumpgate, I have a conviction that this is real, and it is right.

I limp home with my grandchildren and Sparkle, who has been restored to us. Gabriel awaits us, big with Deuce's fourth child. Nicky and Shoshana can look forward to years of happiness together.

But it appears that my boy was born for bigger things. Of all the people to show that to him, it was the Mormons. This all seems so incredible.

So did his life: He began life as a mysterious child with no connections, rose to prominence in a Family, and became the Godfather of the Moon.

Dare I hope he'll take over Heaven?

It doesn't seem far-fetched at all.

Go with God, Deuce.

Make Him proud of you.

Though I suspect He is already.

Hunter Castle
Aboard Ship, 2145.7

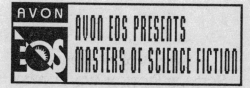

AVON EOS PRESENTS
MASTERS OF FANTASY AND ADVENTURE

LORD DEMON
by Roger Zelazny and Jane Lindskold
77023-7/$6.99 US/$9.99 CAN

CARTHAGE ASCENDANT
The Book of Ash, #2
by Mary Gentle
79912-X/$6.99 US/$9.99 CAN

THE HALLOWED ISLE
The Book of the Sword and The Book of the Spear
by Diana L. Paxson
81367-X/$6.50 US/$8.99 CAN

THE WILD HUNT: CHILD OF FIRE
by Jocelin Foxe
80550-2/$5.99 US/$7.99 CAN

LEGENDS WALKING
A Novel of the Athanor
by Jane Lindskold
78850-0/$6.99 US/$9.99 CAN

OCTOBERLAND
Book Three of the Dominions of Irth
by Adam Lee
80628-2/$6.50 US/$8.99 CAN

THE GARDEN OF THE STONE
by Victoria Strauss
79752-6/$6.99 US/$9.99 CAN